"If you would rathe[r] ... rather ACT th[an] ... then consult Doctor Mordant . . . call the Dreamhouse #1 . . ."

So read the advertisement, and so began Albert Jones' escape from the stilted, all too safe reality he lived, into a world with all the adventure and swash-buckling heroics he wanted. For what he wanted, he dreamed . . . and at the Dreamhouse, what he dreamed became what was.

There were only two minor catches to intrude into his perfect dreamworld, to remind him that he pos-sessed another consciousness: *Beware Compassion* and *Do Not Meet One Other. . . .*

Turn this book over for
second complete novel

WORLD
OF THE
SLEEPER

by

TONY RUSSELL WAYMAN

ACE BOOKS, INC.
1120 Avenue of the Americas
New York, N.Y. 10036

Part One: The Dreamer Sleeps

ONE:

THE BEAM of light originated at the Sun and extended in a more or less straight line through time and space, bent here and there by refraction of and reflection from other minute specks of dust and other intangible belts, pulses, waves and currents arbitrarily encountered on its way . . . extended then for roughly 92,900,000 miles, give or take a few man-clamored-for units of measure, to meet its penultimate semi-obstacle in the form of a window-blind undulating gently in an afternoon wind.

Its final destination in a measurable way after this uncaring travel was, of all things on earth, a thin layer of fleshy tissue forming the closed eyelid of a sleeper, born a man, fathered by a Jones, and unfortunately labeled soon after the event as "Albert." Semi-superstitiously given this name in memory of a then but recently-late philosopher of the same cognomen, with a hidden belief in the mind of father Jones that the name maketh the man, the man in question had thereafter been given the distasteful task of becoming either a Victorianated Albert, a man-of-the-masses Bert, or a straight-man Hemingwayesque Al.

The lid opened to the light, which now hit the exposed brown iris, and promptly closed again in reaction against this too-strong stimulus. The housing head, rumpling more the long hair worn in the manly fashion of the day, turned slightly on the cloth-swaddled air pillow and remained in the new position for several seconds before turning again into the beam of light, which now found itself halted, if not permanently so, by a high-bridged, somewhat pallid nose which gave a humorously melancholic air to the face which surrounded it. This face now animated itself in response to messages from within and the lips of the almost too-wide mouth parted in a yawn which seemed about to dislocate the jaw buried somewhere under the brown Vandyke beard: a Vandyke however which was personalized by the continuation of its upward reaches into the moustache, and the absence of it from the lower lip.

Other signals combined to open both the eyes and to wrinkle the normally clear brows. A finger reached from below the sheets to scratch musingly at one ear as the yawn subsided into a refined belch and then ended, leaving the lips settled into a sidewise and elongated "S," cynically turned up at the left, and bent discouragedly down at the right. The finger's arm dragged itself further from its sheets and reposed itself behind the head, revealing itself to be slim and muscled in but a minor way, sufficient for utilitarian purposes, but ill-equipped for more than, say, supporting a twenty pound stack of books for more than five minutes, even with linked fingers.

The eyes disclosed beneath quarter-lowered lids began to move.

They focused first upon the bed-overhead, which sloped upward from the wall to the ceiling at a 45-degree angle, and to which was plasti-taped, immediately above the eyes, an illustrated verse in Chinese, in the old pre-Neo-Chinese style. As though prompted by the thought behind this observation, the eyes next moved downward and over, to the center of the ceiling proper nicely aligned with the middle of the top of the wooden window-frame, where a violent barrage of primary reds and yellows in an abstract of the new Chinese style burst into color even in the shadow of the lowered blinds. A further apparent mental link moved

6

the eyes to a scrutiny of a pair of black-filigreed yellow silkiton chemi-shorts which hung flamboyantly yet not indecorously from the old-fashioned chrome light fixture.

Chemi-shorts! thought the mind of Al Jones. *What a perfect example of semantics being quicker than the mind. Chemi, because from chemical fibers, yet pronounced as in* chemise, *or* chemin de fer, *and so doubly French, exotic and sexy. Doubly? Triply? Triply! An acid commentary!* So mused the mind's surface, sinking slowly beneath the slumber line and at the same time seeping up so that the top show-face merged with the third "me"-face to form the conscious mask Al felt he was. Picking up the dropped clues, he mused on Mei-Lin, the Peking Exchange student who'd last occupied his bed and bored contemplation, and thought back through the so delightfully occupied shorts and the ecstatic boldly emblazoned gift of ceiling decoration to his own more subtle selection of the verse.

Pre-Neo? Old-fashioned? Nostalgic? What word suited his type of personality? *How can I be nostalgic for a time and place I never knew? Why do there seem to me to be more solid things rooted in the past than in the present? Since the past is smoke from a dampened fire? Since that time existed before my own pulses began? Since that place is a constantly eroding piece of landscape and artifact? Nothing exists except change. So why do I dig a past-existent pattern of things and abstractions, a hip archaeologist? Why am I a vicarious time-voyager? Why any of us?*

Yes, why any of us, in this day and age?

The thought took his eyes to the astrodayt on his desk, across the room. March 3, 1992, and (squinting) Tuesday at 2:30 P.M. West North American time and 22:30 World Standard Time. (*Wonder why they still include the archaic WNA calculation, and even put it above WST?* another part of his mind wondered.) This day and age. This time and place. What are we really researching for in the un-nostalgic past?

By inference his eyes were next drawn to the veritaped invitation lying next to the astrodayt. As his mind leaped to a rehearing of the tape, his overt memory drew up an edited revision of the sequel to his acceptance.

DR. NO: c/o ALBERT JONES: BERKSANFRAN: (94701:S54/1811/A4) WITH LOVE FROM RUSSIAN HILL CHAPTER BONDSMEN MEET TONIGHT: WEAR WHITE WALTHER: PASSWORD QUOTE SILENCERS ARE GOLDFINGERED UNQUOTE: COUNTERSIGN QUOTE SPIES ARE VARIETY OF LIFE UNQUOTE: DRESS WHITE TIE AND/OR BUNNY TAILS: 3/3/92 WST 04:00: THE MORGANS: NO RSVP: BE THERE OR LOSE OO STATUS.

M/GSF

(*Bondsmen,* he thought. *Yes indeedy, there was a world of unconscious irony there!*)

TWO:

Morgans' was the same as always, and seemingly, as of ever. The two 100-watt-bulbed portraits of the two pirates hung luminously in the store front, the florid countenance of J. P. setting off the wine-red doublet of Henry, against their dark-suited background. The same twin-paired sets of hard eyes still followed the observer one-up-manly through the spastic-plastic that expensively rippled their countenances into a risible, all-too visible sneer. The black-glassed door still carried a sinister, hump-shouldered swing as it opened silently after the exchange of sign and countersign.

On the threshold Al took a last glance back over the skyline of Greater San Francisco, to where a thumb of fog was blurring the outlines of the communopolis. The cold hurried him inward, past the invisible steward with the million dollar croaked voice, and he strove to see past the evanescent roils of kickapoo smoke beneath the clarifying light of fuzz-required 120-watts. Hastily he slipped on his infras and, clear of obfuscation, saw at the end of the room his particular ingroup, Thomas and the band.

Though at least half of those there were wearing their infras he managed to make his way to the far end without more than a hypocritical "Hi there" to two parties that rowdily hailed him on passage. He had to stumble over an outstretched leg at the last table, however, where yet another invariable Goldfinger Girl stretched, clad in nothing but a pigment of her own imagination, but an over-elaborate gesture of "Now I don't see you; later I will" sufficed to let him past the gilt barrier.

"Washington lobbyist?" queried Thomas, as Al arrived.

"What?"

"Investing in Government blondes; she's a Fed. Happily only a Natfed, not an Infed. Gaining experience as much as anything else. No harm done, or expected. What you might call a Goldfink."

"Pans for a low assay?"

"That calls for a first drink on me. What's your denature?"

"Usual, of course. Don't tell me I'm untreasured among your memories, Thomas!"

"Of course, the unexpected usual. Sirrah!" he hailed, turning toward the bar on which he poised, like an eagle on a fence. "Sirrah! A stirrup cup for my friend! A malt, no less."

Benignly and somewhat highly, he tousled Al's hair. Tossing the head back to fully reveal the minute bow tie which hitherto his down-jutting coffined chin had hidden almost completely from view, he quoted from memory: "Bring on the malt liquidity, you sons of spent iniquity; for beer, as well as being gassy, is absolutely so déclassé." His neighboring chortle startled the already unstable atmosphere for a moment, but all unworrying he scooped up the half-pint china mug that was scudding along the greased bar-top, and handed it to Al; the hand which up to now had been embracing his friend's shoulders now miraculously appearing with a small glass of his customary medium vodka dry martini, with a slice of lemon peel, (shaken and not stirred) all but lost in its vastness.

"Chin, chin, old fellah," mocked Thomas; and, "Cheers, m'dear," replied Al in the time-honored response.

9

A flat-chested female who seemed bent on proving her deficiency sidled up to Thomas at that moment and stretched herself on tiptoe to whisper in his ear. Al diplomatically let his attention wander elsewhere, surveying the frenetic assemblage, but Thomas had never been one to hold to an ill-kept secret.

"Elvira's an artists' model. Sleeps around more than stamina would seem to indicate," he leered, with heavy innuendo.

And Elvira stalked preysworthily off to the nearest table, where the Goldfinger Girl was having her gilt edges closely examined by a Bondsman.

Wise to the weary game, Al inquired, in that certain tone of voice that telegraphs a western union of word, whimsy and wit: "She acts like a call-girl. *But.*"

In a voice like the second gravedigger, Thomas asked, "But what?"

"Well, she'd be a nice girl to call for a visit, but I wouldn't want to live with her." And nonchalantly he finished his half of stout malt.

A full minute went by, with no audible or visible reaction, and when he took his nose out of his mug it was to discover that a full pint was lined up on the bar athwart him, and that Thomas was blandly regarding the room, his own infras firmly ensconced on his predatory nose. An aura of blanketed silence seemed to enclose their immediate area, but Al was conscious of the pervading beat from some hidden audiophone, pulsing out the rhythm of the Twist. *Nothing later than '64*, he thought. *Where in the past is the line drawn between* passé *and palatable nostalgia? Why not tom-toms? Or clavicords? Or the mouth-bows of our own heritage?* In an empty space between tables a buxom bikini-bottomed blonde began to gyrate and genuflect, making her orisons to the lost goddess of lust which she strove to exemplify. Surrounding cultists either laughed and clapped in time or suavely stepped into her dance at a slower beat.

Al was about to turn away when a black-bodied youth stepped into the area and stripped his shirt from him. The girl at first only noticed him as he responded to her

10

movements, but then she in turn responded to the moment, the music, and the mood, and for a full minute they acted out a miniature ballet of desire and conquest, which ended as he seized her hand and drew her, laughing and panting, to the bar.

At a gulp he finished half of the new drink, bothered somehow by something he had glimpsed and could but half interpret. *Safe sex by the withdrawal method. Why do they . . . how can they stop at such a point, without damaging their psyches? Do they imagine, really, that they've just only finished a hard set of tennis? Love all? God, what's the matter with me; am I beginning to feel that even open, naked lust should be romantic, and not just something healthy to indulge in?* He shook himself and finished his drink. Thomas tapped him on the shoulder.

"Meeting comes to order in a moment; see me after the show. I think we should talk together."

Al nodded and continued to lean against the bar. Someone had switched on the Sensoplex and music rhythms from the tapes were merging and contrasting as their random autoconsol directed. Walls, plain and decorated, the ceiling, the thick mat of room-height smoke, heads, bodies, drapes and banners, scintillascopes and sculptaloids all reflected and refracted lights, colors, patterns, designs, still and moving pictures and kaleidoscopic light sources thrown and projected from various points throughout the room. He felt himself get higher as the sequences changed through Poe-esque bizarre phantasms, through Arabian Nights' simplistic and exotic conjurations, through several of the hells of Dante, with lifts from Dore and Bosch, to pastorals of the graceful Greeks and back through a representation of a Bacchanalia, all without the "performers" doing other than what they had originally been doing—laughing, talking, fetching drinks, smoking, dancing, or whatever.

Three eccentric strobes were plunged into the circuit, and the consol decided to throw solid colors and shades rather than patterns. The box of room became intensely three-dimensional, with great eye-wrenching thrusts of objects and people toward the viewer.

A gypsy-costumed girl from the Chapter's own staff had somehow sorted her personal rhythm from among the elements flowing around, and began a wild, hair-lashing, finger-clicking, heel-stamping dance atop a central table, and in the strobes she seemed to be sometimes two, sometimes six separate images of herself. Her scintillating silks caught like flames as golds, reds, oranges and purples whirled around the room, then vanished into a symphony of sea-shades as blues, aquas, and greens merged with the purples and flooded out and displaced the fiery tints.

Mesmerized by her own selected tone a platinumed blonde drifted into an aisle and zipped down her one-piece gown, leaving it in shimmering coals of color around her ankles, while she swayed ever so slightly, and imperceptibly turned her body around on the balls of her toes, hands above her head continuing the slow undulations of her body. With her face turned upward, her eyes closed and lips parted, her nude body at times lost itself among the rushing display of lights. Watching her unwilled body wind itself into the topmost towers and turrets of her mind, Al was reminded once again of the similarity between this scene and that which disclosed itself in an internally-lighted home aquarium, with all other lights blacked out. As effortlessly as gaudy, beautiful or fantastic fish, people swam in and out of their own peculiar heavens.

Suddenly the mood was switched and electronic music whipped and sighed through the air, the only man-provoked tones being the lush, languorous, sensuous vibes which engoldened the room. The dominant color became lavender, with occasional deep swatches of dark green, and computer-drawn designs tattooed themselves fleetingly on the swaying girl's skin; the dips and swells of her body first collecting pools of shadow then overflowing them so that they ran down and across her body, crisscrossed with Inca-like tracings, and Japanese calligraphic brush-strokes. Transparencies of newsprint

12

mottled her body, and suddenly made her a flat, child's silhouette, cut from a print-magazine.

Her ensorcelled hair glowed with pale flame of coal-gas for a fraction of time, then grew into grass as her body was flooded and washed over with a green tint. Surrounding her was a moving mirage of characters, animals from no Earthly zoo, as other projectors began to trigger blowshots of microcosmic creatures, stained with pinks and pale yellows. With the strobes it seemed to Al that he could at times see through both furnishings and people.

Transparencies thrown onto a world screen: overlapping, impinging our presences and personalities on others, onto the real existing world of eroding objects, making no impressions, flashed on and off by a genetic trigger.

He signaled for another drink and drank slowly, his back to the room and its occupants, to the molten sculptures, the unfrozen paintings, and with his ears mentally blocked against the poetry in abstract, the solidified music, the unverbalized words. Against the back of the bar the singing light sources played over the multitudes of plain and fancy bottles, and he closed his eyes to the coruscating, forever uncapturable colors, dipped from a palpitating palette.

He wondered where Thomas had disappeared to, then, as the sound tapes began to grow quieter, and surmised he had gone to relax the consol.

Without the music, and with the participating audience sunk into a meditative silence, the effect of the still busy Vistors was to make the clashings and blendings of light appear as solid as a sun-impinged cloud at sunset, while the real substance of the scene appeared insubstantial and ethereal. Gradually, as the strobes flickered off and the lights one by one lost their intensity and glowed out to darkness, the necessary darkness allowing the viewer to regain his normality, Al wondered what would happen if, when the ordinary lighting system was switched on, the four walls and all contents had vanished, and only the illusory wraiths of sense-stimulators remained.

13

And if I accepted that happening, then would those wraiths become reality for me? Is the unsane, unseen world in a madman's mind any less real because it has only one viewer? He shook his own head to clear it of these demons of doubt but the impious thoughts persisted.

THREE:

They remained through the early part of the Chapter's official meeting, these fogging thoughts. As the ten Bondsmen and Handmaidens, the former attired in character costume and the latter in 'tards and bunny-tails, sat before M's desk on the room-width clients' couch, Al found his mind drifting off and away from the matters at hand and things discussed. As Barbra, the long-silver-haired Negro girl in skintight, body-fitting cream 'tards stood at attention before Thomas, the brilliant circle of light from the ceiling glittering the lines of jet-black trim that lined her costume while she delivered the financial report, Al found his attention wandering till his gaze fixed on the three-dimensional waximile of James Bond, as portrayed by Sean Connery, still the Honorary President of the International Society of Bondsmen.

What makes us sit here, like a bunch of Ju-His on our first Mary Jane Outing? We're told that we have now fully realized the complete reality of ourselves and the world in which we live. We take our Trips for variety, but more of us every year increase our dosage. Thank God at least it's legal and controlled, and it is neither allowed nor possible to become psychologically addicted. But even those of us who use Trippers either infrequently or not at all join something like this, which is so many steps away from reality—based on the old movie portrayals of actors performing to a director's interpretation of characters invented by an author for books which were, even in their own time, deliberately drawn larger than life. And even then, most of the membership still finds that it needs further stimulation!

He visualized the crowded Halls, each area set up to

extend or enhance the sensory perceptions of the hallucinators, and each centering on a particular sense, tactile, audible, visual, palatal, olfactory or interior, with overlapping areas. Somehow he had always managed to find his high points without resorting to boosting Trippers, after his enforced testing and initiation in Junior High. His Basecard showed him to be nonaddictable to any drug or stimulant, from alcohol through the barbiturates on up to and including the latest Argadian groups, and so he was safe to indulge, and had no physically morbid distastes.

He came out of his thoughts as he heard Thomas, in his role as M, call upon him.

"Doctor No. Hoi, Doctor No! The Bondsmen await your report on the next High Adventure that you've planned for the Chapter."

Forcing himself to take a firm grip on the existing circumstances, Al rose to his feet and marched to the desk, smoothing down the white smock which was part of his character, and smoothing his face into the pseudo-Oriental blankness that his role demanded. In front of the desk he first snapped to attention, then bent himself in an obsequious bow.

"As M decides, so shall it be," he said. "I have the utmost honor to announce that this otherwise unworthy being has prepared a program which, in this humble one's opinion, will whet the exquisite appetites of our membership. A program, a planned happening, which includes elements designed to unjade the desires of our most satiated Adventurers."

Thomas stirred in his leather seat. "Your absorption into character, Doctor No, is much to be esteemed; but I think it is the feeling of the meeting that a straightforward account of the facts would be more appreciated at the moment. The extent of your practice is recognized, Doctor; but a little more semantic surgery would be desirable at this time."

Al clicked his tongue to acknowledge the wordplay and continued. "I've set up a Thunderball barbecue, down in Baja. There will be mixed teams in opposition, headed respectively by myself and Largo over there."

The large, handsome Italian with the big nose, bursting through his skin with debonair domination, nodded and smiled.

"Largo will make his own confidential plans, of course, but his main purpose will be to defeat *our* attempts to raise the treasure—the location of which he does not, as yet, know. I have arranged for scuba equipment and have rented a flock of submarinettes for the use of both sides. Simulated sharks and barracudas will be present, and underwater mines will be laid. Statedets have been alerted and will oversee the entire operation, and the plan has been cleared through the Nat-Feds. The beach chosen for the barbecue is private, so the membership can do as they will. There is an undersea grotto in the immediate area which has been well stocked with semiprecious stones from Jewel Beach, and non-participants in the Adventure proper will be notified of its precise location." He hesitated, then continued, "As usual, therefore, the Adventure will be divided amongst those who wish to turn on to the unreal, and those who pretend to a search for the more concrete aspects of our culture."

"*Real* treasure?" asked Thomas.

"Real treasure. Gold. But not enough to upset the spirit of Keynes and disrupt society. Our funds can stand it."

"Ah, Keynes," mused Thomas, his eyes studiously fixed on the Bond waximile. "The gross prophet of the capitalistic world."

With an accompanying sign of disgust Al clicked his tongue and concluded.

"The Statedets have approved the plan and have found no antisocial elements involved. Bureau Chief Flanders even regretted that he was not thirty years younger, so that he could join us. I gather that he was originally one of Kennedy's New Frontiersmen, and is an avid reader of The Books."

"Thank you, Doctor No. You may retire into your laboratory and continue to dream of ways to change the world."

16

Thomas waited until Al had resumed his seat, then rose from behind the desk.

"Fellow Bondsmen, and Handmaidens! All reports have been heard, and I take it that there are no Specters among us to give the Nay to any of them. Yes? O.K., then I will conclude by asking you all to ratify the new Constitution of the Chapter, as required by the Nat-Feds and the Statedets. I am certainly glad to learn that its new Chief is almost one of us. A copy of the new draft is before you, and I will wait until you have read it before asking for your vote."

He sat down. Al glanced at the recordogram in his hand.

CONSTITUTION

Article I
The name of this society shall be: The *"With Love From Russian Hill"* Chapter of the International Bondsmen.

Article II
The purpose of the society shall be the study and where possible the enactment of The Books.

Article III
All persons, regardless of sex, color, race, or political affiliation, who pass examinations in The Books set from time to time by officers of the Chapter, and who are otherwise, by reason of their reported and self-admitted habits, considered suitable, shall be eligible for entry into the Chapter.

Article IV
The officers of the Chapter shall be: an "M"; a James Bond surrogate; and a Miss Moneypenny. The duties of M shall be those commonly performed by a President of a society.

The duties of James Bond shall be those commonly performed by a Secretary-General.

The duties of Miss Moneypenny shall be those commonly performed by a Secretary and Treasurer.

There shall also be, from time to time as appointed, those officers whose duties shall be to organize, control, and suggest activities suitable to the nature of

17

the Chapter, numbering at no time less than five nor more than seven.

Membership

At no time shall a Bondsman or Handmaiden be considered in default; but a grant shall be made by Her Majesty's Treasury, through the Chapter's Treasury, to provide for such needs and requirements of the member as shall be deemed fit by the Officers.

All Officers and all members shall be at all times subject to the laws of the Sovereign State of California, and their representatives (The Statedets); the Nationale of Northern America (The NatFeds); and the World (The IntFeds).

At all times, and in all places, no Officer, and no member shall cause to bring into actual physical or psychic danger the body, mind or person of any personality under the jurisdiction of IntFed.

To the nonsurprise of Al, used as he was to the ever-encroaching power to subjugate of the IntFed authority which ultimately decided what was in reason to do, all of the Officers drew their blank-shooting Walther PPK's and fired, rather than reaching into their shoulder-holsters and letting go with the sawed-barreled Berettas.

All of a sudden he felt sick, and with the barest nod to Thomas, got up and returned to the bar, which by this time was all but deserted. There were still some late-comers at the Dispensorium, down by the left wall, but these were scurrying with the intensity of disgodded religieux for the temporary security of the mystic-making Halls.

He signaled for another pint of malt and threw his head back to let the liquid pour outrageously down his throat. He coughed as a large hand struck him between the shoulders, and looked up to see the saturnine Thomas smiling down at him.

"I thought that the good Doctor No . . . I beg your pardon, my good friend Albert . . . took no stock in stimulants? Albert, my boy, I want a word with you, and here is just as good a place as another."

18

For perhaps the thousandth time, Al wished that his friend would get over the name hang-up, and call him just plain Al. Because one didn't want to be called Tom was no excuse to lay the whole formal nomenclature on every acquaintance. ("Tom is the name of the thief, the Piper's Son; of the confreres of Dick and Harry; of the naïve schoolboy Brown; of Bedlam; of little, manipulated manikin o' Thumb; of poor, downtrodden soldier Atkins; poor Tom-fool of the acceptors. I am Thomas, descended from the Doubter, through Aquinas the Thinker, to me. Me, *me*, ME . . . Thomas!" said he once cynically to Al.)

Al shrugged a hand around the scene. "I don't know. This. These people. I feel bored, up to my brainlobes in a kind of fog. The feeling's been on me for several days; and I suspect for several weeks before that, down in my real depths."

Thomas smiled. "Probably just the usual four-month blues, Albert. Let's see, how long is it since you started your off-time?"

"Five weeks. And another thirteen to go before I'm due back at the desk. But it isn't that. Or at least, it's what's behind the whole thing. Here we are, with a guaranteed four months in every year free from jobbing and on full pay, so that we can get on with any real work that we want to do, or to loaf around if that suits us better. But what *is* there to do, for most of us? We don't want to paint, or sculpt, or write, or compose; we don't have the talent to invent; we're just part of the ninety-five percent who can do a job well, and perhaps can think and dream. Savio's New Freedom Declaration was a good thing, I admit . . . it put the economy of this world back on a level plane, and on the face of it the idea was humane and just what the world had been crying for. But where is the fun in life any more? Some of us escape . . . look at them down there, all about to escape into their own heads. But they can't do it forever; they have to come back to this level eventually.

"Before New Freedom a lot of us *did* manage to get into our own worlds on a long-term basis. They called us mad, insane, mentally disturbed, but the fantasy we,

19

they, created was as real to them as the world we see around us! If a Psyche from the 'sixties were to go into any one of our Sensoriums now, he'd say the bods there were out of their senses, temporarily insane. And so they are, every last one of them, out of five senses and into the other one. But a few hours later they come down into full and firm possession of *all* their six senses. Back to this world. And it may be a good idea for the artistic and creative types, but what about the rest of us, who are at best mere dreamers?"

Thomas was looking humorously askance. "Everyone expanded. No more major wars. Practically no exploitation of anyone by anyone else. Freedom of the sexes and for the sexes. Sane child-rearing. An indulgent form of government, guarded only against ourselves. A minimum of jobbing, sufficient to keep the world balanced. An unbiased system of interlocking and overlapping constabularies to prevent practically every form of danger, disaster and disease. . . . What else do you want?"

Al sighed. What was the use? How to explain it? He tried.

"You've just said the key phrase, Thomas. We are protected, from womb to tomb. Look at it. I organize an Adventure for the Chapter, and the Statedets have to pass on it. And they'll be there, oho, never fear. They'll check out all our gear, and they'll patrol the area, and they'll scan every cubic centimeter of sand and water that we'll occupy, to make sure that no one can possibly graze his knee on a piece of wood from a wreck, or, goddammit, even get sunstroke or overly sunburnt!

"Thomas, where the hell is the Adventure? What can anyone do these days to pit his life against the unknown? There *is* no unknown, there are no true adventures, there can be no danger. Only these simulated dangers, only these synthetic adventures. We still have bullfights, oh yes; and what happens if the bull looks as though he might win? He gets electrocuted from below ground by the cop at the console. You can still sail a fifteen-foot boat around the world, but all the way you are monitored by remote TriDi so that you don't inadvertently get your pinky wet. And TriDi itself: 'So real you are *there!*' except that you are *not* there! You're *not* in the jungle, or on the moon, or being attacked by Amerinds, or being chased down an alley by IntFeds. You're sitting right in the middle of your TriDi cube, and nothing's going to happen to you! Thirty years ago society was driving people *out* of their minds. Now it's driving them *into* their minds . . . and some of us haven't got a place to hide in, down in there!"

He signaled for another malt, got it, and gulped half before he was ready to continue. Thomas made neither reply nor comment, but blandly surveyed the activities of such Chapter members who were still around in the subdued room. Al swallowed, and went on.

"Fifty, sixty years ago, people could console themselves on their lack of opportunity, or the dreariness of their existence, or the emptiness of their minds, or the meaninglessness of their lives by having faith; faith in some religion or other, some God that would alleviate their suffering, be responsible for their failures, and provide them with a general excuse for being the way they were. The man-god Marx told them that religion was their opiate, and started an earthly religion of his own. Now, with all religions and the biased teachings of any of them outlawed, man has turned to a neo-mysticism of drugs. . . . Opiates are now the religion of the masses!

"O.K. I'll grant you that religion was a bad thing to have taught to irrational, unreasoning children, who grew up bedeviled by a god-myth. . . ."

Thomas stirred and commented, dryly: "It wasn't bad for everyone, Albert. Remember, the wages of sin were a fat living for the priesthood."

With ill-concealed frustration at the interruption Al called for a Bond Special, as indicated, then hurried on: "Sure, sure. It's not cool to sound off like this, but don't humor me, Thomas. Yes, I'm angry; yes, I'm in a bad state of nerves, despite my shots and pills. But I want something—adventure, romance, the call of strange places, the mystery of unique situations . . . something beyond my reach. And so do our members, and so does mankind in general. Man was born to reach upward to

21

beyond the stars for something unreachable. And he wants a thrill that is not vicarious, not planned, not plotted and predicted for him.

"Did you ever read about Lindbergh, Thomas? Didn't the story of the 'Spirit of Saint Louis' capture your imagination? Have you read the accounts of the crowds that turned out to cheer him, and the millions who waited in suspense for his success? Why, Thomas, why? What made him a hero? I'll tell you why and what."

Excited by his theme he finished off his malt and leaned on the bar.

"Lindbergh was a hero because he was one man against the elements. He flew a few thousand miles in a man-made machine, alone and in full control of his circumstances. And you remember what happened when the first astronaut went up and around the world? If you check back the tapes of the time, and read the microfiles, you'll find that the public admired him, and felt for him while he was up there, but in a different spirit. That man was *not* in control of himself and his machine. He was controlled by others, and everything he did had been predicted and plotted and charted and checked out. He might have been another mouse, or a monkey, or a dog. It was the *project* that was admired, and the feeling of wonder was felt not for the man so much as for the 'marvels of science,' and the ingenuity of 'us' men who could plan and carry out this project. He was no Columbus; he wasn't Scott, daring the unknown, the self-reliant. He was only an extension of the machine. Oh, brave enough himself, I admit; but he couldn't capture the imagination of mankind, because he didn't really represent the individual.

"Man was earthbound and yearned for the stars, beyond his reach. But he couldn't put up a sail and take off for up there . . . he couldn't pack a wallet of food, say goodbye, and step out smartly by himself. He had to have the complexity of machines, and became a part of the machine he invented. He was earthbound, and then suddenly moonbound, but that particular bound into space was a jump into lunacy, for having discarded an abstract God whom he thought had controlled his activities he now discovered a very concrete God of wires and lights, and tapes and wheels and currents and impulses that he *knew* controlled him, and to whose laws he had to conform to survive. No matter that *he* had invented this new electronic God; he had invented all his previous Gods too!

"There is nothing for a man to *dare* any more, no risk he can take. He can always find out what chance of success or failure he has in any undertaking by checking out with a computer. And if it is a serious business then he is *forced* to check it out by law, and forbidden the venture if he is liable to be harmed."

He hammered his glass on the bar-top. Thomas restrained him, gently, patiently. Al sighed. "I know, I'm talking too damn much to no purpose."

"Have to get it out of your system. Why don't you try a few days at a Pleasure Dome . . . relax . . . indulge your senses . . . work out your complexes. . . ."

"Pleasure Domes . . . ! What are they except extensions of what we have here in the Halls, with outdoor sense-stimulants added? Guarded by attendants, so that we can't do one another any harm, or do damage to ourselves. That's not what I want, Thomas. That isn't what anyone wants. I want, they want, we all want some real *action*. We want to be pitted against something that will bring out our three parts, physical, mental and emotional, and challenge them in a meaningful way. We want some real terror to chill us, not a monster created in our own minds, which we *know*, deep down, is not part of the physical world. We want some *real* danger to spice our blood with, not some phantom threat. We want nerve-wracking, heartrending, painful experiences, to prove that we are men, a higher grade of animal. We want real Adventures, not Adventures in Bondage! We want to be Fawcetts, Livingstones, Marco Polos!"

FOUR:

Musing in the afternoon sunlight, Al grinned ruefully as he thought of the remainder of his evening. He hadn't given in to the temptation to patronize the Dispensorium and take a quick Trip, that much he could remember clearly. But what else had happened was a blur in his mind. Dimly he recalled Thomas being avuncular, urging him to go home and sleep it off, steering him clear of a dreamy-eyed girl with the remark: "Don't touch that one, Albert. Unmarried mother-to-be. Laboring under a misconception."

Vaguely he remembered some magazines being shoved under his arm, with the advice to stay in bed and browse through them. *Now that was an odd kind of remark to make,* he thought; and looked around the room to see what had happened to them.

He found that by stretching just a little he could reach the topmost of the bundle, and opened it to the screaming three-dimensional color layouts that urged him to invest, invest, invest! With the world shockingly brought up to the level of living of the original United States of North America it was an international buyer's market, but of course one did not "buy" anymore, one invested—money, credit, time, effort.

He riffled through the pages carelessly, until suddenly he noticed a red-crayoned circle around a small classified among the end pages. Surprisingly the circle seemed not to be yet another example of the advertiser's eye-catching gimmickry, but a personal note. Thomas? He read the ad carefully.

Are you really seeking the Pleasure Dome . . . ?
Or is the Golden Road to Samarkand your Trip . . . ?
Or the Yellowbrick Road to Oz . . . ?
If you would sooner DO
than DODGE . . . rather ACT
than ACCEPT . . .
then consult Doctor Mordant . . .
call The Dreamhouse #1,
98638-849-4103
(All Calls Collect)

Al breathed a sigh of remembered pleasure. *Ah, yes; the Golden Road to Samarkand. How did HASSAN go, now? Mmm, yes; "We travel not for trafficking alone;*

24

By hotter winds our fiery hearts are fanned: For lust of knowing what should not be known, We take the Golden Road to Samarkand."

He read the classified again and worked out the call-code. The first "9" made it General World Area nine hours west of Greenwich, in the eighth sub-zone, thirty-eight degrees north of the Equator, which put it . . . which put it somewhere in the middle of the Greater San Francisco Area! Interesting. Mysterious, even. But perhaps just what he was looking for. Certainly he would rather do than dodge, act than accept. And thinking about doing, why not act, now?

Throwing back the covers he rose and reached for the verbiphone. He had refused visiphone service on the grounds that for a man living in one room it could be too embarrassing. Like now, he thought to himself, grinning, aware of his nakedness, as he waited for an answer to his call.

For a welcome change the voice at the other end indicated a human operator, female, instead of the usual recorded voice, but despite his cajoling he could gain no more information other than that the ad was correct, and that he could make an appointment for as soon as he liked.

"Why not . . . ah, say, three hours from now? Or does the doctor refuse appointments in the evenings?"

"No, sir. The doctor will be available at the time you requested. If a patient is impatient, he feels he should be on hand to treat the trait."

"Oh, no; not another punster," groaned Al.

"We find the practice puts our clients in a good humor, and the bad humor doesn't harm our practice."

"Oh God! O.K., O.K. Just tell the doctor I'll be there on time; I'll let no procrastination stand between my progress and his prognosis."

FIVE:

Al was surprised to find the doctor's office in a block of residential apartments. An air-lift took him up six stories, and the corridor led him to the door beside which a modest sign of black script on a glowing fluorescent panel declared simply: *Doctor Mordant.*

Since there was neither bell-push nor knocker he surmised that his presence before the door had triggered a scan-key, and the opening of the door confirmed it, as the panels became transparent one way, temporarily, so that whoever was on the inside could check him out.

Inside was a small reception area, designed as the lobby for a residential apartment, and now doing duty for the office which no doubt lay behind the interior door. A small black-topped platform desk, a conturest for visitors in front of it, a visiphone on its surface, with a videorecorder attachment, a well-cushioned chair for the operator, and a good reproduction of a Marris tri-diactinic placed opposite its projection source on the opposing wall, completed the furnishings of the space. Beneath his sandaled feet a shimmer-shag appeared to stir restlessly.

He stood there for a full minute before the inner door opened and a woman stepped through. She wore the traditional white of a doctor's assistant, plain unornamented 'tards with a brief white armless tunic, and her golden hair was caught up into an invisible but neat and sterile plasti-cap. Even in her heelless slips she was an inch or so taller than Al, but the thing he noticed first was her eyes. They seemed to have a too-cautious, too-alien look, unaccountable to him even discounting the fact that she probably wore contacts. Although the eyes seemed amused, it was not from the same amusement that broke her face from its professional mask into its professional smile.

"Mr. Jones?"

"That's right."

"The doctor is waiting to see you. Please come straight through."

No preliminaries? No credits to be established? No tapes to be punched and recorded?

The inner room had evidently been a living area, and even now there were few signs that it was being put to use as an office. Low couches, with multicolored cushions of foamite, were scattered about the floor, each resting on its air-jets. To one side was a naturalle, complete with small shrubs, a waterfall, a pool and rocks, with one clear plastic side to the pool in which exotic fish could be seen. An artificial sun was set in its tracks across the ceiling, and a cool wind came from the diffusors in the corner. The picture window which filled the far wall was now closed and screened, and displayed a moving jungle scene, through which could be glimpsed various bright tropical birds. Immediately before the window was the only evidence that this was something more than a living room, a large semicircular desk, in a deep blue, with a cream trim, in the top of which was set a console, and which probably concealed the various sensory tape-machines which the doctor would require.

Behind the desk sat the doctor.

Al's first thought was that the doctor himself was in need of medical assistance of some kind. Into a lean, clean-shaven face, sallow to the point of darkness, were set two glittering eyes, each floating in a pool of shadows, shadows caused both naturally by the play of sunlight on the face, and by the unnatural duress of stress and exhaustion. A muscle twitched spasmodically under the right cheek, and the skin between the high cheekbone and the edge of the temple, at the corner of the eye socket, seemed set in a permanent mesh of lines, like a map of the Mississippi Delta, giving the impression of the frozen end of a wink. A saturnine, intelligent face, but the lines around the mouth denoted humor.

"Mr. Albert Jones? I am Doctor Mordant. Please sit down."

Al fingered a couch to the front of the desk, and relaxed back into its softness. The doctor touched keys on his console and the almost imperceptible hum of recording equipment filled the room. Mordant asked a few questions regarding Al's background, education, employment, hobbies, nodding from time to time as something about one of the replies was to his particular liking. Now that he had more time to study his interviewer Al noticed that Mordant was older than he at first appeared to be, probably around sixty or so. He had a trick, while talking, of running the thumb of his right hand around the perimeter of his lips, slowly, as though in the depths of great thought.

Finally the doctor slapped close a set of console keys and sat back. During the interview his hand had at times slipped below the level of the desktop as though toying with something concealed there, and now as he straightened and leaned back, a small black kitten climbed from his knee to his chest and clung there, while its master continued to fondle it absentmindedly with his left hand.

"Well, I think those are all the general facts I need to know, Albert. I may call you Albert, I trust?"

"I would prefer Al, if you don't mind, Doctor. And, may I ask two questions before we go on?"

"Certainly, Al."

"Well, in the first place it seems odd to me that you haven't yet asked me why I came here, what is wrong with me, my reason for calling you."

Mordant smiled as though at a private joke. "You could only have read my little advertisement. If you read it, responded, and came here to see me, then I am sure I know exactly what your needs are. We'll return to that in a moment. Your second question?"

Al leaned forward. "Just what are you a doctor *of?* There are no initials after your name on the door, and this"—gesturing around him—"doesn't look too much like a regular doctor's office."

A shadow passed over the other's face.

"I hold doctorates in several fields. . . . Philosophy, psychology, sociology and, once, in medicine. Unfortunately, for reasons I will not go into now, I am forever barred from practicing in the last area by my erstwhile fellow-practitioners. I have been . . . disbarred, unfrocked, de . . . medicated as it were. However, I can assure you that you need have no fear of anything harmful happening to you through listening to me, or taking any advice I might offer. I prefer conversation with a minimum of jargon, so you will understand exactly what I am talking about. And you can always get up and walk away, yes?"

Al nodded. The proposition seemed fair, and something about Doctor Mordant and his manner intrigued him. Nothing to lose by merely listening, surely.

"I thank you for your trust, Al. Now, will you please tell me, in your own words, just why my advertisement appealed to you. Do you merely feel inactive and jaded, or was it the romantic connotations of the Golden Road that drew you?"

Slowly at first, but with gathering speed and lucidity as he felt the doctor's interest grow, Al plunged into a recapitulation of all that he had said and thought the night before at Morgans'.

Mordant was a good listener and only nodded now and again and interjected a few "Ahs" and "Uhuhs." The kitten purred contentedly. In the middle of the monologue the blonde woman quietly returned, and sat unobtrusively near the naturalle, also listening attentively.

"Just so, just so. Man is overprotected, and has lost his one and only birthright, his decision to die if he wants to, his choice of continuing on in the world or of ending his neither richer nor poorer, wiser or more ignorant, existence."

"Well, yes," said Al, "but it's not exactly that. I think you're implying a death-wish in my fight against being overprotected, Doctor. I don't think of it in those terms, actually. I hope to go on living, but I want something to make the living sweet. I want the contrast of a real risk of death to make me aware of the mere satisfaction of being alive. And I find that the contrast offered by the purely sensory worlds is only one between what my life might possibly be, if expanded continuously, and what it actually is. Those worlds don't excite me, don't . . . thrill me."

"Exactly! Exactly!" Putting the kitten on the desktop, Mordant walked around and clapped Al on the shoulder. "That is precisely what I had hoped you would say. You are quite right; it is not a secret death-wish. A wish to defy death is very seldom to be confused with the genuine morbid death-wish, in the same way that most criminals did *not* steal just to be caught in their theft, punished, and thus recognized by society. Man, as the most naturally weakest of animals, without natural protection against the elements, without natural weapons, without sufficient natural warmth in his body, even, is the one animal that has been forced to adapt himself to his environment and his environment to himself. He has, first and foremost, to have been adaptable, since nature has not pampered him in the same way as the other beasts, and to spur him on to survival he has instinctively invented the mechanism of *challenge*, an abstract concept. Nature always rules!"

Al looked up, startled by this last statement.

"You sound as though you thought of nature as some kind of sentient being, a god, almost. . . ."

"*No!* That would be a paradox. Here, Teri, fetch me a Webster's from the shelf." The woman rose and left, to return immediately with two fat volumes. Mordant took one, feverishly turning the pages.

"Ah, here we are. Listen. 'Superstition—any belief or attitude that is inconsistent with the known laws of science or with what is generally considered in the particular society as true and rational; especially, such a belief in charms, omens, the *supernatural*, etc.' You see? A belief in the supernatural. Now it is obvious, surely, that there can be no such paradoxical thing as the *super*natural. Anything which *is*, is natural. Therefore anything which is *not* comes under the heading of 'superstition.' Since there is no need nor any place for any kind of god, and belief in it is *un*natural, then a belief in a god would be superstition, and there again be *super*natural. Nature *cannot* by definition be *super*natural, and so nature cannot be god!"

He slammed the book closed triumphantly and let out his breath.

"No, Al; when I talk of nature, I don't talk in terms of natural 'laws,' but in terms of series of happenstances that have occurred biologically, botanically and howsomever in such a way as to perpetuate themselves by the simplest method. The first thing to learn about nature is that it is lazy, and highly conservative, requiring a good deal of prodding before developing something new. And the gods that man invented for himself were anything but lazy. Who could stand a lackadaisical deity?

30

No, gods were one particular branch of mankind's sentimentality that they could well have done without."

Retrieving the kitten, Mordant wandered absently over to the naturalle and fingered a couch near it. He nodded to Teri and she went out. Al turned his own couch to face the doctor. He was beginning to feel stimulated, and though he could not see where this conversation was going to lead them, and furthermore felt that it was irrelevant to his problem, felt that it might give an insight into the character and personality of the man who was apparently offering to help with those problems.

"Come on now, Doctor. You make sentimentality sound a virtue. How do you fit irrational sentimentality into your scientific pragmaticism?"

Mordant's eyebrows fired up at the challenge. He thought for a second.

"One of the best definitions of sentimentality I have heard is this. Ah, wait a minute, first." With a sardonic grin he took the kitten by the scruff of the neck and held it over the naturalle's pool, where it hung, squealing.

"Now, why shouldn't I let it drop into the water here, and see it struggle and drown?"

Al thought and shrugged. "No real reason, I guess. Just would seem a pity to kill a kitten for nothing."

"Very well. I have known this kitten since birth, and it has amused me, and I have become attached to it. You have known it for perhaps a half-hour, and it means nothing to you. If you had never met me, and were not here now, it would mean less than nothing to you. In fact you would know nothing about the event, presuming that I did in fact let it drop and drown. If I, too, were not here, and the animal were to somehow climb up here and fall in unobserved, would it mean anything to anyone at all?"

Al shrugged again, and smiled. Mordant retrieved the kitten and soothed it in his arms till it purred again, as he continued.

"As I was saying, one of the best definitions I know of sentimentality was by R. H. Blythe, who said: 'We are being sentimental when we give to a thing more

31

tenderness than God gives to it.' Now, bring me the Webster's, if you will."

Al took the volume from the desktop and over to Mordant, pushing his own couch nearer.

"Hm, what does Noah have to say about sentimentality? Here we are: 'Sentimentality—the quality, character or condition of being—sentimental,' which is . . . 'one: having or showing tenderness, emotion, delicate feelings, etc., as music, poetry, etc. . . . two: affectedly or superficially emotional; pretending but lacking true depth of feeling; maudlin; mawkish. . . . three: influenced more by emotion than by reason; acting from feeling rather than from practical and utilitarian motives; moved by emotional factors. . . .' Yes, yes, and here, 'synonym—*romantic* suggests emotions aroused by that which appeals to the imagination as it is influenced by the *idealization* of life in literature, art, etc. . . .' Right.

"To take Blythe's definition for a moment—it offers a comparison between man's feelings and 'God's.' So, since there *is* no God, in any sense at all, then *any* feeling, by this standard, is sentimental, since nature just doesn't care at all about the life, living, death and manner of dying of any of the organisms—and you can stretch that word's definition as far as you like—nature has no thought, no mind, no intelligence, and so *cannot* care in any way. So we are left with the proposition that *all* feelings are artificial, in the sense that they are *unnatural*. But we have already seen that nothing can actually be outside or supernatural!"

He paused for breath, and the woman Teri returned, with a small portable bar-and-dispensorium.

"Have a drink, Al. It will, I think, be your last . . . for several days. You prefer . . . malt, I remember. Sorry to sound pedantic, but it's a carry-over from the days when . . . I used to lecture to a class. Ah well, where was I?"

With a smile Teri handed him a drink, and with a slightly different, more subtle expression, passed a malt to Al. Mordant took a quick swallow and cleared his throat.

"Yesssss! Right. So why is there such a thing as feeling, or sentimentality, at all? My contention is that it is man's saving grace or, more specifically, his saving factor. If there is no tenderness in nature then there is not one particle of a *reason* for anyone to care about any other person or thing. Only by the application of the coordination of man's three parts—physical, mental, and emotional—to the problem of survival has he been able to adapt himself to his unfeeling, uncaring environment. He has had to balance his intuition with reason, and this alone would long since have made him quit and abdicate his right to live. But to level the balance he has invented—or nature has invented for him—the concept of sentimentality. Compassion, pity, love, greed, jealousy, ambition, anger, despair, stubbornness are all parts of his invention, but the greatest has been compassion, to use a small word for a large area of feelings. Compassion encompasses, among other things, what are called 'community spirit,' or 'true humanitarian feelings,' but there is no line, as you will now agree, between these and any other kind of sentimentality. If he is not 'sentimental,' man is lost, he will not survive. And the word includes its synonym of 'romantic!' "

He swung suddenly and nailed Al with his finger.

"And isn't that exactly your problem? Don't you wish for 'romance' in its broadest sense? You want your emotions aroused by that which appeals to your imagination, as it has been influenced by your idealization of life, through the books you've read, the tapes you've heard and seen? You await appeals to 'duty,' 'honor,' and 'loyalty,' abstract concepts which have no place in your real world out there. And I can give you that chance for 'romance.' Follow me."

In a great surging roil of activity that burst through the room like a hot tempest, he thrust himself to his feet and imploded into what had originally been one of the three bedrooms of the suite. Caught up like the dust- and spore-laded tail of a comet, Al and Teri followed him, as he decanted kitten and declamation in his wake.

"See! Come, you luster after knowledge that should not be known! You dramatic, theatrical seeker of sentimentality and romance. Let me unfold my . . . conception, my prophecy . . . my fantasy in which all humanity can sublimate its ultimate fantasies. Come, see how you can live the life you would have wished to have led, the life which you and mankind have been committed to realize!"

The inner room had been stripped of all furniture and decor, and was just about the most functional, utilitarian and starkly purposeful room Al had ever seen. Smack bang in the center was a white-enameled diagnostician's couch, with the addition of a contour-molding mattress which overflowed the edges. Mordant had snapped on the room's only light, a bright 500-watt overhead, set in a highly polished reflector. At the periphery of the room stood and squatted a series of consoles and machines whose purpose Al could not even begin to guess at. Some twenty pieces of equipment were strewn around, each connected, with the rest in a vast cluttered complex of wiring, and each with at least one set of cables leading toward, and plugged into, a master console situated near the pillowed end of the couch. The guts of several of the mechanisms were displayed outside the body of the housing machine, and it was obvious that equipment had been perverted, cannibalized, and reconstructed to suit the peculiar ends of the doctor. A separate complex of switches, dials, buttons and controls of one sort and another was sprawled across a white steel table beneath the heavily curtained window, and a swivel chair stood in front of this table. Multicolored wires again led from this to the various machines, and to the console at the couch's head.

Mordant went to the only chair, sat heavily in it, staring at the black window-drapes, then swiveled around to face Al.

"You have asked me to present a challenge to you, one which will perhaps cause you to risk your life; but at the same time you have not asked me what my fee might be. Very well; I will perform my part, and show you how you may risk your life, in more ways than one. At the same time I will deal honestly with you, and tell you that my fee will either be your life, if you accept the risk and fail—or nothing, if you should accept my proposition and win through. However, I will tell you in any case, even if you should lose the 'life' which you *are* at the present, you will not 'die'!"

"You speak in paradoxes, Doctor. If you disbelieve in paradoxes, since they are unnatural, perhaps I should refuse to accept here and now."

"You accept my philosophy, and summation of the situation of mankind?"

"Yes."

"You admit that you are a romantic, and that you seek adventure?"

"Yes."

"You agree that there is no kind of hereafter to trouble your mind and conscience?"

"Ye-essss."

"I am about to offer you a 'heretofore,' as it were . . . a new life, in the past, in which you will eventually die, or from which you will abdicate in order to return to this particular present."

Mordant paused for a few seconds while Al digested this, then added: "Do you know much of Robert Burns?"

Surprised, Al replied that he knew a little of the poet.

"Good. Supposing I borrowed from Burns and said to you: 'He either fears his fate too much, or his deserts are small; who will not put it to the test, to win . . . or lose it all'?"

Al gave a wary grin. "I'd say that I'd go along with the sentiments expressed. With the addition that a man has to know what he is gambling for or about before he puts up his stakes and wagers."

"Capital, capital! I shall therefore be honest with you. What you see around you, in this room, constitutes the labor of some fifteen years. This is the heart, the soul, the body of the first Dreamhouse. Here, on this couch, a man may go to sleep and live his dreams. From this launching pad, if you will allow me the privilege of dramatization, one can soar away to discover new worlds of inner space, or, at least, the old worlds of one's imagination, since one can never take out of one's mind more than one has put into it."

"But, Doctor . . . surely this is no more than just another escapist plant . . . just another way of living vicariously. I have to take you seriously, I guess, in all this, but what is essentially new? I'll admit I don't see anything comparable to the TriDi screens, and perhaps you don't operate with drugs, but . . . ?"

"No, Al, my young friend, you're entirely wrong. With this equipment I can put you to sleep, into a very deep sleep, and while in that sleep you can literally live out a dream life in which you will risk real danger, even to the point of death and including it. You see, I started with the theory that the real world is uninhabited by man."

"What!"

Mordant chuckled hugely. "When you perceive an object in the real world which surrounds us, you actually perceive only the memory of it. When first in your life you touch a blanket, you don't know that it *is* a blanket. You have to develop a frame of reference which allows you to know that this particular material is different from another piece of material—a sheet, say—and sooner or later you learn the name for it, you have to give it a label. In later life you see another blanket, and you recognize it for what it is only because of all the other blankets which remain in your memory, and to which this new blanket bears a resemblance, from its looks or its texture. Now, another person can also arrive at the conclusion that this later object is a blanket, but *his* set of memories of previous blankets encountered will not be identical to the information stored in *your* computer-mind. These memories can never exactly overlap, d'you see? And so with every object in this real world. Although objects exist, and would continue to exist whether or not there were any sentient being to identify them, to label them, they at the same time have completely separate subjective existences in the minds of every sentient being in the universe. If n is the number of sentient beings, then there are always *n-plus-one* worlds.

"Now then, consider the mind as a computer, which contains as facts, as information, all that you have ever *experienced* through your senses, including what you have read in a book, listened to or viewed on a tape, or heard in conversation; that is, third-hand experience, transferred from the experience-banks of the mind of one man, through the imperfect medium he selects, to your mind. Since no two people can have *identical* experiences, it follows that each of the *n-plus-one* worlds must be unique.

"Furthermore, as one gets away from the present, in either direction, past or future, then the degree of similarity between these worlds decreases, since both past and future details can only be extrapolated, predicted or deduced from the information in the mind-computer at the present."

As the doctor paused for breath, Al took the opportunity to interrupt.

"I think I begin to see what you are getting at. Since the future and the past are necessarily a kind of illusion, a sort of picture drawn from fancy in each individual mind, then an imagined dream world would be as real to the senses as the existing world of the present."

"Not *as* real, but *more* real. Because any new factor unearthed from the past, or discovered in the future-as-it-becomes-the-present is something that the mind-computer has to assimilate; a piece of knowledge which does not jibe with the real world of the present as we have expected it to be. But a dream world based solely on the contents of the mind-computer cannot contain undiscovered *new* information to upset its axis of 'reality.' "

He broke off abruptly. "Teri, fetch me a drink, please. But none for our friend here, unfortunately. He has to be drained and empty of energy for tomorrow's . . . expedition. That is, if he is prepared to go through with it."

"I'd like to know a little more before I commit myself, Doctor. I think I trust you, and I expect you can explain exactly how this thing works, but . . . uh . . . well, have you tried it out before?"

Again the thumb was making its elliptic course around Mordant's lips, and Al was keenly aware of the aura of restlessness which emanated from the man. He got up from the chair and paced rapidly up and down the limited area beside the couch, then swung around to gaze at Al, leaning against the couch, arms folded. He considered.

"I'll be completely honest with you. After all, I owe it to you to explain the very real risk which you will be up against. I have myself tried out this equipment, with Teri as my operating assistant, and Teri has allowed me to use her. And there has been one other. As you can see, Teri and myself have suffered no harm or ill-effects of any sort. And you will have to take my word for it that the other . . . dreamer . . . is also as alive as you see we are."

He reached for the drink that Teri had returned with. The strange blonde woman stood next to him, absently gazing over Al's head.

"Well, let's explain the technical details, shall we, Teri? If you will just lie on the couch . . . oh, you'd better take off your tunic, my dear, though there's no need to strip for the purposes of this demonstration. Now, Al, come over here."

Al moved to the couch and gazed down at the woman who lay there in her 'tards, eyes closed, hands resting lightly on her abdomen, legs slightly apart and relaxed with the feet wilting outward. The doctor busied himself with the ends of the various sets of wires and connections leading from the console, and began attaching them to Teri's body as he continued to speak.

"Basing my research and experiments on my original thesis, I learned all that I could of the various techniques for manipulating the brain itself, and by a stroke of luck stumbled across a paper in the journal that dealt with brainwaves. This was a theory that all sentient beings emit a kind of radio signal, a discharge of electrical energy, whenever the mind-computer is being used. I may add that this paper attempted to correlate such phenomena as telepathy, clairvoyance, the powers of psychic mediums, mass hypnotism, the reason for supposed 'hauntings' and so on and so forth. However, I was able to use this theory in parallel to my own. To cut a long and very technical story short, one which I could not possibly tell without confounding you with a lot of jargon, I have constructed a receiver which can pick up the emitted wavelengths of the subject to whom it is linked, and by means of an amplified feedback itself transmit to the receiver of the subject's mind.

"In effect, what happens is that a thought which embodies an idea is picked up and fed back into the area of the mind which can expand upon that idea, stimulating those sensory areas in the same way as if they had been affected by sense reactions from the real world. Thirty-odd years ago the surgeons had begun to approach this result through physically manipulating the brain, but this was, and remains, a clumsy method which is both dangerous and unrefined.

"To get back to my own system, then, which is not dangerous in the same way, and which is perfectly refined. If you think of a color, or a particular odor, then your thought will be picked up, amplified and retransmitted so that you will then actually seem to see that particular color, or smell that identical odor that your memory has conjured up.

"You go to sleep, and you begin to dream. Beforehand we will have discussed in general terms the type of dream and background you wish to experience. These basic bricks of the fantasy, as it were, will be fed through this console as a program to the small computer which is here connected with the transmitter-receiver, and so the reception areas of your mind will be stirred. From there on you will be on your own, and your mind begins to take over the program.

"Now here, where I have attached these wrist- and leg-bands, are some of the other mechanical devices which will merely record such minutiae as heartbeat, pulse-rate, blood-pressure, respiratory rate, temperatures, both oral and rectal, perspiration rate, graph of your brainwaves, and possible chemical changes in your body. There are other attachments, of course, for some of these things, but we needn't demonstrate them all at this point, I think."

Al stirred uneasily. "But how long will all this take?" he asked. "Surely this will require a lot of setting up for what I guess will be a few hours sleep at the least?"

"Well, some of the equipment is by way of providing a safety factor, so that we shall know whether we need wake you. And also I want to maintain as complete a set of records as I can, with the idea that eventually I shall have enough material to be able to predict a set pattern for a certain type of dream, and so be able to produce what will in fact be a predetermined dream."

Teri stirred on the couch and opened her eyes. "Tell him about the movies," she said, not looking at Al.

Mordant slapped her lightly on the thigh. "Yes, yes!" he declared. "I had almost forgotten. Thank you, my dear."

As he began to disconnect the various pieces of equipment he continued to explain. "Once you have gotten into your dream you will be somewhat in the position of a combined producer-director-cameraman-scenarist-art director-actor in a motion picture for TriDi. Unlike the normal dream, where you would drift from scene to scene without any apparent relevance, you will find in your dreams that you'll build your own continuity. You will almost certainly not live every second of the subjective time of your dream but, for instance, if you need to 'sleep' within your dream then, subjectively, you will go from one second of wakefulness across the gap to the next second of awakening. But just as in real life you have no memory of the time you have been asleep, you will be 'aware' of time having gone past.

"The strange thing is that since you are in fact writing your own pre-edited script, you will sometimes be in the position of knowing what is going on in another area of your dream, even though as an actor in your dreams you will *not* have this knowledge. At first both Teri and myself found this mildly disturbing, because what happens is that after you have, as it were, 'lived' through the section of the dream of which you have had prior knowledge, but which you do not 'remember' as it occurs to you, you have a sense of déjà vu. I was first to experience this, but when Teri went through the process, having heard my story, she found that this helped her to keep a better grip on 'reality.' In other words, she was better able to keep in a corner of her mind the fact that she was actually dreaming, though this knowledge did not obtrude into her dream-consciousness."

Teri swung her long legs off the couch and touched his arm at this point, and he ran to a halt.

"Yes, yes; well . . . that's about it, I think. Any further questions?"

"Well, you haven't really explained the timing of all this. Just how long will I be asleep?"

Mordant drew in a deep breath and exhaled slowly, motioning the other two to return to the main room.

"Time is subjective. In your dream you will seem to live at a faster rate than you do on this 'real' earth, and it appears from our researches that each person has a different subjective time sense, and that this also varies within the individual. I have not managed to discover why. On my first trip, for instance, I dreamed that I was in my dream-world for something less than a day, and in 'objective' time here I was asleep for five hours. On my second venture I was 'away' for three days and slept for twenty-two hours. Teri was away for a week or more, but slept only fifteen hours. I might add that while in this particular kind of sleep the body's metabolic processes slow up enormously, the heart beats at about a fifth of its normal rate, and other functions act more or less in proportion.

"You will be completely emptied before you undergo the experience, and if you sleep long enough, then we will feed you intravenously as required. You will have cause to curse us before we begin tomorrow, for not only will you not eat, but we will also steam as much perspiration as we can out of you . . . but there are some compensations, as Teri will show you later. Hmph. Now, I think that you should go to bed as soon as possible, and rest. You might try to prepare for yourself the sort of background you would prefer for your dream, so that tomorrow, bright and early, I can feed it into the computer."

So saying, he waved Al off to follow Teri, who had meanwhile redonned her nurse's tunic, himself sitting

41

down by the naturalle, pouring a drink, and watching the fishes, the kitten on his knee. His thumb returned to its orbiting.

SIX:

The evening began with a rather unpleasant and somewhat embarrassing time concerning the ruthlessly efficient nurse and an enema. He was then told to bathe himself, and philosophically he planned a long, relaxed soak for himself. He knew that a couple of phone calls to his landlady and to Thomas would take care of anything which might turn up in his absence, however long it happened to be, and since he was on his four months' off-time from jobbing there was no employer problem.

His musing was not for long, however, as without a sound the lavorium door opened and Teri came in, her expression as inscrutable as ever, but wearing only a *cache-sexe* and her plasticap. Al practically instantaneously sat upright, forgetting that this was one of the new adjustable baths, with the consequence that water spouted over the lower end of the bath like a miniature combined Old Faithful and Niagara.

"Wha . . . ?"

"Please relax, Mr. Jones. I'm only here to get you completely cleaned up."

"Mr. Jones! For God's sake, I think you might call me Al, at the very least. What are you going to do?"

"If you will just relax there I will go over you carefully, and massage you to get rid of any little knots you may have."

Al let the bath bear his relaxed weight. Starting at the crown of his head Teri began to soap and shampoo him, kneading every square inch of his skin. She was an expert masseuse, and he soon began to feel drowsy and comfortable, and by the time that she had climbed in to straddle him, he was almost asleep. He watched the light play on the rhythmically moving muscles of her shoulders, all but hypnotized by the steady movement as she worked over him, and he was on the

42

knife edge of sleep itself when she was ready to turn him over. He was really dozing while she made a final examination of his feet, pedicuring his toenails, and then she was done with him, and stepping from the bath. Taking two towels from a warming closet she slapped him on the shoulder and offered one.

Completely happy, drugged with the warmth and the good feeling the massage had engendered, he came out of the bath and began to dry himself. Her voice penetrated his haze.

"Tomorrow morning, early, you will be placed in the steam bath, and any remaining wastes you have in you will be disposed of. For now, you will go to bed. Your room is next to this. You will find whatever you need on the coverlet."

Unexpectedly she smiled at him directly, the first human expression he had seen in her. She added: "Don't think that I am too terrible. It's just that I have a job to do, and I must remain professionally alert to my duties. The doctor needs me very much at this time . . . Al."

Al smiled back. "Yes, I noticed that he seemed to be a trifle overwrought. I hope that he knows what he is doing, since I'm to be entirely in his hands."

"And in mine. That is why I must be always at my utmost efficiency. He is under strain, and is overworked. He relies on me and so"—with a shrug of her magnificent shoulders—"I must remain reliable. But don't worry . . . you'll be as safe as we were."

She slipped out of the room as she was, throwing the towel casually into the sterilizing-oubliette in the corner. Al soon followed, but more modestly wrapped the towel around his waist. Not that he was ashamed, or embarrassed, but, well . . . a guy felt just so *naked* without his clothes.

SEVEN:

He ignored the bedwear on the coverlet and slipped naked into the cool bed, his skin alive to every sensation. With his arms under his head he lay back and began to think of the day's events, then, as he felt sleep moving in on him, tried to think what basics he should feed to the machine tomorrow. He opened his eyes with a start as something cool and silky tickled its way across his face, and the bed beside him sank slightly. Teri's long blonde hair veiled his sight as she lowered her head to his.

"All waste products," she murmured.

"Waste?"

EIGHT:

When he had wakened earlier, before the torture began of losing four pounds of evaporation in two-and-a-half hours, the pillow beside his head had been empty, and it had been Mordant himself, a quiet smile on his twisted lips, who got him started on the day's routine. Now as he rested on the couch, feeling as though he were about to float off it altogether, Teri stood beside the doctor, wearing her professional uniform and expression.

After their lovemaking was over she had kissed him lightly and told him that indeed this was just part of her official duties, and of his preparation for the adventure, and that he was to think of it as nothing more, enjoyable though it had been for both of them. He had thanked her for the experience and returned her kiss, then slept, with her head on his shoulder.

As he looked up at the two of them he couldn't forbear to wink at her. She smiled slightly, but Mordant, intercepting the motion, was not amused.

"Just try to save all that for your dream-life, Al. It's entirely up to you what you do with your time there. You could have chosen to be a Sultan, with a thousand and one wives, and a thousand and one Arabian nights to tell them stories in, for all I care. But you didn't, apparently. I think we'd better run through your program once again, to check that the machine will feed you the proper initial stimuli. Teri, will you please read back from the list?"

He went over and sat on the chair by the console. The woman drew a pad from her tunic pocket and began to read.

"Subject wishes to retain full use and memory of saber-fighting. Subject . . ."

"Ah yes, Al; I meant to ask you, just out of mere curiosity, why you selected the elements you did."

"Oh, back a few years ago I got interested in a bunch of cut-and-thrust stories, by Sabatini and Orczy and others, and decided to take up fencing as a hobby. But it turned out that I was better able to handle a saber. Of course I've never had any need to use one in real life, so I'd like to use one now. Though actually I shall be using something like a narrow-bladed scimitar, I imagine. You know, Doctor," he added with a grin, raising his head from the couch slightly, "for the first time I'm beginning to get excited about this project. I guess it's all happened too fast for me."

Mordant said nothing, so after a short pause Teri continued.

"Subject wishes to start his dream somewhere on the Malayan peninsula, in such a way that he can begin his dream-life naturally, without being 'pitchforked into the middle of some melee that I don't know the reason for.' "

"Yup, I've read a few books about that area of the world, but there are no real names on the surface of my mind, so I'll actually be living in a complete world of my imagination. And it seems to have been the kind of place where a man could be a man in his own right. And, well, it sounds kind of exotic and strange."

"Subject wishes to be a 'foreigner' in the country, but to be able to speak the local language."

"Naturally."

"Subject wants to dream of a time exactly 700 years ago."

"That's the time when that part of the world consisted of a lot of small kingdoms and independent states, after the Indian Empires had about collapsed, and before Europeans had got there. Seems to me that it was just before the first known Western traveler arrived in those parts. That was . . ."

"Enough, I think." Mordant rose and approached the couch. "Those are the facts fed into the computer, and you are ready to go, as soon as Teri injects a little something into you to calm your nerves and induce you to sleep deeply and soundly."

He stopped, and once again his thumb rose to his lips. He looked even more worried and under pressure than he had the previous night, but still a certain kind of sparse but definite confidence seemed to radiate from him. He took two quick turns up and down the narrow space, brushing past the nurse, before coming to rest alongside the couch. Putting a hand to each side of Al he leaned over him, staring earnestly into the latter's puzzled eyes. With a sign he concluded his searching gaze and stood upright.

"I must be fair to you, boy. There is one great risk which you must prepare yourself to take, over and above all else we have discussed. Oh, the precaution against it is simple, and you may even care to disregard my warning and still come to no harm. Actually there are two things to bear in mind. You remember my little anecdote regarding the kitten last night? Well, just keep in mind, in the 'aware' part of your brain, that the people you meet in this world of yours are your creations. So don't get sentimental if it comes to harming them, either physically, mentally, or emotionally. Mind you, they will be real to that part of you that is dreaming, and they can certainly kill you, if you let them. That is, if you do not will yourself to wake up in time. But that is a risk which I have already explained to you. But don't let sentimentality trick you, as we have already defined that word.

"Secondly, there is another factor which neither Teri nor myself have had to face. That is, what happens if you meet a real historical figure; someone who is known, as far as anything in history *is* known, to have lived in this existing world. I have a theory, which I admit may be wrong, that if you *should* get yourself into a situation which exists in the mind of but a single person in this present now, then you may be irretrievably lost back there in the past of your dreamworld. Alternatively, my theory allows that the mere fact that you yourself know of this person, or this situation, will block you into the reality of the history of this present now, else you would be forced, in the 'aware' part of your brain, to doubt the *real* existence of the person or situation, since you know that you are dreaming. Either way, your brain might lock you into that past. I didn't tell you this last night because you might have chosen the future instead —as you still may, if you wish, of course—in which case the circumstances could not arise, since nothing of the future of this present now is actually known as a fact. And neither Teri nor I have visited the future, and so could not vouch for what might happen there."

He looked straight into Al's eyes, and when the would-be adventurer turned his head slightly to get away from that worried yet somehow beseeching look, he met that of Teri. She, too, was beseeching and at the same time urging him with her eyes. He closed his own and thought briefly of the world outside of this room, as he knew it. Of all the synthetic problems that faced today's mankind. Of all the escapist answers to those problems. Of all the incessant, in-circling talk of what a wonderful and safe world man now lived in. Of all the rationalizations for the lack of ethics, morals and responsibilities. Of the cloying atmosphere of protectiveness which surrounded every step of life. Of the lack of any real sense of comradeship or meaningful cohabitation. Of the lack of any true challenge to the mind, the body, or the spirit.

No, nothing to stick around for. The chances seemed to be that he would return, as the others had, and if so then he would have had one real goddamn experience to savor. And if by some fluke he was stranded somewhere in the depths of his own mind, then Thomas was the only person or thing that he would regret having lost. He opened his eyes and looked into the no longer evasive regard of Teri.

"I will go as I am, as planned."

He felt the sharp prick of the needle in his arm and without any awareness of time passing . . .

47

ONE:

. . . floated out into a blue-tinged void, a sea of air, Mediterranean blue. Through which golden insubstantial streamers flowed with a high yellow glint of a flute-like sound. At the periphery of his vision came a darker blue ambience of a plucked cello which felt of hot wet velvet to his touch. He rolled into this new sound and wrapped himself in its color, pulling the cobalt over himself. With a taste of brass a trumpet note ripped apart his protection; and afraid and turned-out upon himself he dropped slowly down, supported only by a jasmine scent of green, which became darker as he fell. Desperately he struggled up into a crimson drumbeat which reached out to catch him, then turned to umber and orange flames of pizzicato violins, tasting of honey. A dry white wine pressed against him, saturated him, flooded him, flashing intermittently around him like a choir of harps. Clubs of magenta began to beat on him, as other iridescent bubbles frothed with brazen clangs and silkiness, exploding out from him. The odor of freshly percolated coffee chirruped silver-like around and through, bearing him up with a cold scarlet slash of greed. Angrily he burst out to the surrounding horizons, drunk and dizzy with the harsh texture. Maroon stars ululated with a rotten stench that he bit into bravely, as sweet rays of yellow buffeted his feelings of grand and gray compassion. Midnight and the moon smelled of pure water as he crashed blindly through the tintinabulation of thorns and ivory incense and jealously breathed the hot blinding turquoise smoothness of waves susurrating hopelessly. Giant sunflowers, flecked with hot bursts of laughter, gripped him as in a vise, and suffocated him into blackness. The blackness grew, and the pressure filled his every pore with it, until finally he could feel, taste, smell, touch and see only the rich polished hue . . .

. . . and the color relaxed, and lightning split blue and gold crackling down the air, and thunder roared and slapped at him, and cold blinding rain slashed through him, and great combers below him raced dementedly across a pale green ocean of slate and marble. Dimly he made out a ship, tall sparred, high at bow and stern, proudly painted and gaily caparisoned, but beaten down now, with deck-planks writhed upward and floating overboard to be instantly carried off by the coarse thieving waves. A groan he could scarcely hear above the howl of the storm presaged the fall of the mainmast and the weight of its imbalance brought one bulwark below the water level, and the torrent rushed into the vessel, capsizing it in a matter of seconds. As the remaining mast hit the water it, too, snapped . . . and a great jolt whiplashed him into unconsciousness.

TWO:

(The sea is a bright blue transparency, topped with quick-stepping miniature white circus ponies. It is cool and desolate in the just post-dawn sun, and stretches out emptily to the horizon, darkened to green there in the shadows of a few scattered clouds. It is not quite empty, though, for presently the teams of horses begin to drag with them a bright yellow spar, splintered and wrapped with trailing rope and a snatch of waterlogged canvas. The body of a clothed man, white and black in the blue water, is enmeshed in it.

The wreckage is being nudged toward the shore. Glaring white sand, as fine as sugar, puffs scurrying in a breath of wind, fringing like milk around a saucerfull of green gelatine the thick, wet mass of the jungle. A few solitary coconut palms have dared to advance a little way down to the beach, perched uneasily on their exposed clumps of roots, ready to flee back to the jungle if the sea encroaches further upon them. One end of the visible beach vanishes into a cluster of mangrove shrubs which have edged themselves well out

49

into the water, but keeping a firm roothold on the earth beneath the sand below the sea.

Round this bushy promontory swims a second figure, stroking with an inexorable slow strength. The distant head rises from the water, sees the wreckage, and swims toward it with an increased speed. The mast snags on the shallow shore and the second figure rises to its feet and plunges through the shallows like a water buffalo in fright.

The water beating back from the immense thighs makes an intruding noise which in turn arouses and alarms birds and monkeys in the trees, who move through the fronds and branches cawing and chattering.

The former swimmer cuts impatiently to the shore and runs along its edge. He is enormous, perhaps six feet six inches, with a large, bony head set on a short neck which links it to a pair of shoulders worthy of a professional wrestler. Heavily muscled arms end in two great powerful blades of hands. His rather dull face is at the moment apprehensive, strained; but with an eager look in his large dark eyes. Most of his features, however, are concealed by a bushy black beard, streaked slightly with gray. A sharp, high-arched nose thrusts out from the beard like the scar of a landslide on a wooded mountain. He wears a coarse, uncollared shirt, with one sleeve missing, and torn and split, and discolored white pantaloons in similar condition. What can be seen of his skin is black, with purple highlights as the sun plays on his exerting flesh. He is barefoot, and leaves giant prints in the white sand.

Reaching the wreckage he drags it ashore with one great effort, and pulls free the body which still attempts to cling to it until the last possible moment, unconsciously clasping the safety of the wood and ropes which have supported it. The big man turns the other on his back and feels quickly for heartbeat and pulse. A huge smile lights up his face, and he turns and bends outward toward the sea, as if praying. He puts his ear to the other's mouth, hesitates, then slaps his cheeks, but with no result. With a squeeze of the stunned man's shoulder he rises and trots off to the edge of the jungle, looking for something.

The man he leaves on the beach is short, around five-eight, but well built, with slim and hard muscles. He is much younger than the other, and would probably be handsome; but his present greenish-sallow complexion is ugly in itself. His skin, elsewhere, is the dark brown of black coffee in a glass, evening's shadow tinged by the red of the dying sun. He wears the remains of a richly embroidered silk shirt, open from neck to navel, the ends of which are tucked into black velvet trousers which, although now wet and clinging to him, would be tapered out to a bell bottom, but these ends are now caught up into narrow leather puttees. Despite his rough passage through the water his shirt is still snug to his waist because of the broad crimson cummerbund he wears, which has also allowed him to salvage the narrow-bladed scimitar thrust through it on the left without benefit or protection of scabbard or sheathing. His hair is long and jet black, matching the short chin beard and pencil moustache. The sun catches a glint from his ears, in which are inserted two plain hoops of gold, and sparkles from several rings on his fingers, clutching at the sand, brown on white, and from the great purple jewel set in the hilt of his scimitar.

In the jungle the big man enters a small clearing and listens. He hears the sounds of birds, still welcoming the sun, but over this sound he hears the tinkle of water dropping from a rock. He goes toward the sound and pulls aside broad green leaves to discover a spring bubbling up through a crevice in a large boulder, and overflowing into a pool at its foot, vanishing into the ground again a few feet away.

Cupping his hands, he is about to kneel when his foot strikes a half-coconut shell, legacy of the monkeys. Joyfully he throws it up in the air, catches it, fills it at the pool. He returns through the jungle with the shell all but hidden in his massive hands.)

THREE

(Wrecked. I was wrecked. Yet I fell through the air. And now I'm here. On a beach. And that must be jungle. Is this where I wanted to be? WANTED to be? What do I mean? And what is it I must remember? Something about not meeting some other traveler. But who would he be? What am I thinking about? Who am I? Of course, I'm Al . . . Al . . . Al . . . Ali, that's it. I'm Ali!)

Ali opened his eyes to find himself supported in the arms of his body-servant, who was at the same time attempting to force water into his mouth from the coconut he was holding, but managing to spill most of it over his master's face. Ali was completely exhausted and closed his eyes again immediately, to find himself dumped back unceremoniously on the sand. Through slitted eyes he watched as the other, with a disgusted expression on his face, padded to the sea's edge and scooped up a shell-full of seawater. Before Ali could think to protest the contents of the coconut were flung into his face, and he sat up, sputtering.

"Wooooosh! Sssssshhhhhwaaaahh! What the devil . . . ?"

He shook his head free from water and looked up to see his burly companion standing over his head with a happy grin on his face.

"Bakar, you villain . . . ! Why throw seawater at me? You know I've been half-drowned in the stuff since we were wrecked last night."

Bakar said nothing, merely bending down, with happiness radiating from him, to help Ali to his feet. The latter brushed sand from himself, looked at the wreckage on the shore, and gripped Bakar's arm.

"Well, anyway, I'm glad to see you are alive, thanks be to Allah, though I fear none of our companions could have been so fortunate. It's a pity the Rajah, my father, will have no way of knowing that I am alive, but it will be a long time before he begins to worry about our non-return, since we are still several thousand miles from India. But who knows, Bakar, who knows? Perhaps with luck we shall hit upon a way to return before long."

He looked around him, at the blue sky, the transparent sea, the white shore, and the green jungle.

"Before we begin to think of getting back we have to find out where exactly we are. If we drifted to the south, then this is probably the island of Sumatra, and if westward, then this will be one of the tributary states of the Malayan peninsula. Any ideas?"

Bakar shrugged, and nodded his head.

"Ah, I forgot, my poor dumb Bakar, even if you did know anything you couldn't tell me."

Ali stretched himself in the sun, trying out his strained muscles. "Hhhmm! Feel a little bruised, but nothing seems to be broken at all. And you? Good. Well, let's away into this jungle, for there seem to be no footprints on this beach other than our own to show that anyone else ever has come this way."

Feeling to see that his sword was secure, he started up the beach, searching for an opening into the dense undergrowth, striding with a proud agility despite the faulting sand. Bakar caught up the shell and stuffed it into the remains of his shirt before following, gaining rapidly on his master. Overtaking him, he plunged into the gap he had made on his first search and led the way to the hidden spring in the clearing.

Both men drank deeply from the shell, and Ali sat back to rest on a fallen trunk. He looked around the open area, feeling the fresh dewed grass under his feet, looking up at the birds, who returned his gaze curiously, with cocked heads and staring beady eyes.

"Ah, that was good! This is a pleasant and secluded little grove you have discovered for us here, Bakar, but though I'd like to rest up I feel we should push on and try to find some place we can sleep without guard. I don't trust whatever beasts may lurk behind this green curtain. Unless I misrecall, they have tigers here as fierce as the ones in our own country. I don't know too much about the people, but I'm prepared to deal with humans if not with animals. I bless the day I decided to learn the language of these confounded savages, to ease my collection of the tribute for my father."

He got up and began to make his way out of the clearing, but Bakar suddenly clutched at his shirt.

"What is it?"

Bakar pantomimed a richly dressed Ali swaggering along, flaunting his rings, then imitated a stealthy follower coming up behind and stabbing down, then the stripping of an imaginary body of its finery. Ali watched the performance with some amusement, not unmixed with admiration.

"Not bad, not bad at all! It's a pity you can't talk, else you'd make a fortune on the stage. Your idea is excellent, too. I think I'll leave all this stuff here, near the spring where we can mark it, so that we tempt no robbers. And we'll keep my royal status secret also, so we encourage no ransom attempts."

He slid the rings from his fingers, and took the gold chain from around his neck. Bakar's remaining shirt sleeve served as wrapping, and the bundle was stowed carefully among the plants at the foot of the rocks. He drew his sword, and glanced at the jewel set in the handle.

"What to do with this, though? My sword I need. We'll just have to risk the ruby, unless . . . Bakar?"

The big man took the sword and gripped it between his knees. His face contorted in exertion and concentration, he clasped the handle of the sword in one hand, and, with a sudden grunt, wrenched the jewel from its setting. He returned the sword to Ali and hid the stone with the other jewelry while his master thrust the weapon into his sash, slapped him on the back, and strode off into the jungle, away from the beach.

(*And with a quick blink of the eyelid of the mind . . .*)

The sun was noon-high in the sky and shone clearly down through the tops of the now more widely separated major trees. The going had been easy for some time since the undergrowth had thinned out, and now Ali and Bakar rested at the foot of a broad-bladed Durian tree. The prince was eating at the soft white flesh of the fruit with gusto, but the rotten stench was more than

Bakar could stomach, and he contented himself with wild bananas that grew in a clump some little way off.

Spitting out a smooth black seed and wiping his mouth with the back of his hand, Ali laughed at his dumb companion.

"Whatever strange country that we have come to, the fruit is even stranger. You may turn up your nose, or hold it against the offense of the smell of this fruit, but by Allah, it has a royal flavor. There is a subtle tang hidden by the chimeric of the odor. That's true of many things in life, you know that, Bakar? Even your brute strength hides a tender heart, yes?"

Bakar grinned back at him to show he understood, but he would not come near the fruit Ali offered him. The young Prince slapped his thigh and guffawed with amusement. "You miss a lot in life by not exploring, my friend. There are a great number of important clues, and tidbits of fact to be discovered behind the curtains of doorways, and between the covers of beds and books."

With his eyes half-closed in ecstacy he returned to the eating of the Durian, his lips drooling as he held the melon-sized growth in both hands.

FOUR:

(*Strange. I don't remember how we arrived here. Did I finish eating?*)

They were hacking their way through the jungle, Ali using his sword and taking care not to dull the blade on any hidden rock, while Bakar used his strength to force a passage. The sweat was pouring from both of them like water from a spring, and each had contrived a sweatband to twist around his brow, using portions of Bakar's shirt. The squashed remains of myriads of greenflies and mosquitoes plastered their skin and clothing and Ali's hands were a mass of scratches and cuts from the leaves which slashed at them.

Ali paused for breath, then stood listening.

"Bakar, can you not hear the sound of a river?"

Slowly the big head turned this way and that, then

an arm pointed unerringly to the left, and they changed direction, moving a little faster with hopes of relief urging them on.

The river turned out to be at least a hundred yards wide, and though they went up and down the bank for quite a way there was no apparent narrowing, though it seemed to meander on its path. At the side where they were it was quite high above the river, but not dangerously so, and the stream appeared deeper here, with a strong current. The farther bank was shallow with a long sandbar sticking out a little below them, and there were others further up the river. Bakar seized Ali's arm and pointed to the upstream spits.

"What? Those balks of timber? Oh yes, I see now. Your eyes are sharper than mine. They're crocodiles, sure enough, but I think they're too far away to bother us. We should be able to get across without any trouble. Come, that looks like a man-made track over there."

Bakar jumped down the low cliff and began striking out with powerful strokes. Ali took a short run and made a clean dive into the muddy brown water, surfacing to see his servant halfway across already.

(In their nests underwater beneath the cliff crocodiles hear the splashes, and one slides out through its cave entrance and silently thrusts itself upward until it is only just submerged.)

The current was stronger than Ali had anticipated, and his progress was hampered by the sword which slipped around in his sash and became entangled with his legs. Treading water, he set about securing it more firmly, not without glancing upstream to reassure himself that the somnolent beasts on the sandbar had not moved. Bakar was already in the shallows on the far side, slightly above him, and was walking out of the water.

Cursing to himself, Ali resumed his struggles with his sword, and (so does not see Bakar turn and notice the sinister black log lithely coming up behind his master. Horrified, the dumb giant assesses the distance and decides he cannot swim back in time. Desperately he looks around him and espies two large, thick branches on the bank behind him. Seizing them, he swings one rapidly over his head, letting it fly out over the river as if released from a slingshot, to fall with a great splash just behind Ali who has) decided to hold the sword in his hand. Turning in surprise he saw the crocodile begin to dive no more than six yards inshore from him. Taking a deep breath he, too, submerged, going down as far as he was able, hoping to come up under the monster.

At first he could not see through the murky depths, but an ominous shadow gliding between him and the ceiling of light that was the river's surface soon showed him the enemy's position. Kicking upward he was barely able to touch a rear leg of the beast with his sword point. Immediately the tail convulsed and he was only just able to escape the steel whip as it cracked toward him. As agilely as a tropical fish in a tank the crocodile began to turn, but Ali followed it around in a spiral, coming up for a snatch of air to see Bakar standing waist high in the water, brandishing a piece of timber as a club. The Prince turned to see his enemy had also surfaced, and was approaching him with upper jaw opened. He forced himself vertically downward and the beast paddled over his head, unable to close its upper jaw quickly and unable to submerge without taking in water.

Ali felt his feet touch bottom, and let himself come to a crouch in the obscuring mud his descent had caused. He clasped the handle of his sword firmly in both hands and waited. Sure enough, the crocodile had turned exactly in its traces and came back now just a little below the surface, looking for its elusive prey. With a strong thrust and a fervent call on Allah, the young Prince straightened his legs and shot up off the bottom, aiming the point of his sword for the soft spot of the neck, where the under jaw was hinged. The blade cut straight through and lodged against the top of the skull. As he rose to the surface he had to ward off the scrabbling claws as the crocodile sought vainly to rid itself of the sword, but in a few seconds the body floated upward, lifeless, and began to drift downriver. Diving again, Ali tried to dislodge the sword hurriedly, expecting that at any moment the reptile's companions would descend upon him, but the blade seemed immovable. Swimming with one hand, the other clasping the sword hilt, Ali dragged the creature to shore, where he collapsed, exhausted, in the shallows.

Bakar came thundering through the water and dragged beast and man to shore, and while Ali drew in drafts of fresh air, tugged the sword from the crocodile and pushed the monster back out into the stream where it was immediately the scene of an orgy of cannibalism as its brothers threshed the water to foam in their desire for food.

Bakar washed the sword in the water, then returned to present it to his master, who took it, kissed its blade, and thrust it into his sash. Ali pointed to the melee in the river. "There but for the mercy of Allah goes one lost Prince of India! Allah and the sword, both. It's not the first time it's saved me, eh? (*Is it? What have I used it on before?*) That little spot of excitement was a refreshing fillip to the day. The creature was a little too stupid to be a worthy antagonist, but it was better than fighting . . . than fighting . . . (*Simulated sharks! Simulated sharks???????*) than fighting. Strange, Bakar, I can't remember the comparison I was about to make. But let's not stand here talking. The sun is getting lower, and we must find shelter for the night."

So saying he led the way along the bank where there was a faintly discernible path which became more definite as it turned away from the river and passed into the mass of low scrub.

"I think this track was made by man, so let's go find the man who made it."

On this side of the river there were no towering jungle trees, only miles of low bushes and tall plants, the omnipresent green now broken more frequently by vivid splotches of color as strange blossoms signaled their presence. Nature appeared to have banished sound for sight here. No birds fluttered and sang among the dense undergrowth; no animals stirred; no insects chittered. No mosquitoes, even. As if bound by the same interdiction the two trudged on silently along the well-defined path, which curved and turned upon itself for no apparent reason, and so did not allow them the minor pleasure of seeing their destination.

The hot sun continued to lay its rays across their backs with whips of heat, uninterrupted now by the trees which had shaded them on their morning's trek, and gliding slowly down the sky.

It was still well before dark, however, when the path abruptly disgorged them into a large clearing, at the other side of which the semi-jungle thinned out, and in the center of which stood an enormous pile of boulders, evidently the results of the elements' erosion of the jagged chunks of rock that thrust themselves out of the ground like gigantic teeth.

"Ssshhhwwwaaahhh! Let's rest." Ali threw himself to the ground in the shade. "We'll cool off for a moment and then we can climb up here and see . . . whatever there is to see from the top."

Bakar grunted, but stood out in the sun, looking warily around, sniffing the air. Ali watched him disinterestedly through half-closed eyes as he finally shrugged and turned to join his master. As he did so there came a loud yell and a figure leaped off a rock from the side and launched itself on Bakar's shoulders. Despite his bulk the big man dropped instantly to a crouch, thrusting his head forward and down so that his attacker flew over his back to land shatteringly on his own back where he lay stunned and winded. Ali, struggling to his feet, dragging out his sword, had only time to notice that the assailant was dressed in black trousers and a red neckerchief, before eight more men, similarly clad, appeared from behind the rocks, some running out to cut off their possible retreat back along the path.

As Ali moved toward Bakar two of the figures leaped to the spot he had just vacated, so that the two were surrounded.

"Back to back, Bakar!"

Ali leaped to his position and swung his sword, while the big man spread his legs and held his makeshift club before him in a defensive stance. While the attackers closed their circle Ali noticed that while they were all

59

identically dressed, their weapons differed, two bearing broad-bladed arms similar to machetes, two were with clubs, and three of them holding foot-long daggers with peculiar, flat, snake-like, double-edged blades. One, distinguished from his fellows by the large circular earrings he wore, carried an ornate scimitar and by this Ali judged him to be the leader.

Swinging his sword easily Ali struck out and down against the leader, to draw him out and watch his method of handling the scimitar. The other used his weapon with both hands, with a very controlled slicing of the air immediately in front of him, the blade not heavy enough to swing him around into an exposed position. The rapidly moving scimitar acted like a shield and Ali could see no way to penetrate the guard, but a downward blow at a moment when the opposing weapon was slicing down served to break the flow of movement and allow him to make two quick jabs at the other's breast. His blade did not strike home, but the attack caused his opponent to withdraw. Ali dared not advance, for to do so would mean exposing both his own and Bakar's back. A flicker of movement on his right caused him to turn his head and catch sight of a dagger-armed figure advancing, crouched, upon his flank. A lightning thrust and circle of his own blade clipped the man's lower arm, sending the dagger flying into the air and the attacker, clutching his arm, to the sidelines.

Behind him Bakar struck out once, twice, with his club, catching one assailant on the head, knocking him senseless, and another on his shoulder, causing him to drop his machete, his arm numbed.

With a yell two men dashed in on Ali's left, one with his broad blade high over his head ready to slice downward, the other coming in low with dagger in his outthrust hand. As Ali turned to meet this threat, the leader, still using his scimitar as a shield, took a step closer, suddenly letting the blade come circling out in a blow calculated to slice at the Prince's legs. Ali leaped high in the air to clear this attempt, at the same time kicking out to catch the dagger wielder under the jaw as he crouched and, off balance, the latter staggered backward against his companion, whose great chop at Ali thus fell short of its mark. Coming to earth in a crouch of his own, to avoid the following high swipe of the leader's scimitar, he struck out at the machete-man. His fine Indian steel narrowly missed the man's fingers but cut through the wooden haft of the weapon. A quick movement of his foot brought the handleless blade toward him and he kept his foot on it. His would-be attacker stepped back out of sword range, looking for a substitute weapon.

Bakar was using his club now for offense, keeping a whistling wooden barrage against the snake-like thrusts of the remaining dagger bearer, and now for defense, holding his club at each end to ward off the other club handler.

Ali's late attacker had found the club dropped by the man that Bakar had disabled and resumed his pressure on Ali's flank. Meantime the leader had taken up a dueling stance before the Prince, and the scimitar and the sword rang together like hammered anvils in the hot afternoon sun, neither weapon gaining an advantage for its owner. All of Ali's skill was required to defend himself against the leader, for whom a kind of grudging respect was building in his mind, a respect changing to admiration as he noticed the other signal for the club-man to stand off and not interfere.

As the dust rose around them and settled on their sweaty bodies, Ali strove to aim his sword at the other's head as the scimitar swung downward, but each time the grinning, mocking face of his opponent would dodge aside, or be hidden fractionally behind a surprise up-sweep of his own weapon.

In a sudden switch he threw his sword to his left hand, hoping to take the leader by surprise and sneak in under his right arm, but the grinning fighter was ready, and with both hands clutching the handle of his own weapon, sliced vertically down. With no time to change grips again, Ali was forced to hold the flat of his blade against his right palm, and take the chop of the scimitar against the middle of his blade. As the shock of metal on metal ran up his arms his opponent stopped

61

dead for a second, but by the time Ali had taken his sword into his right hand again and thrust forward he was ready for it, and with no time to parry, let the two weapons slide up each other until they were hilt to hilt, wrist to wrist, face to face. As the sun hammered down to be shiningly repelled by the gold handles, the steel blades, and the dusty, dusky planes of their faces, the two stared into each other's eyes.

Mutual liking, the liking of a fighter for another fighter, the recognition of one manly spirit by another, filled the air between them, as they struggled silently each to force the arm of the other away and down. Teeth gritted, lips curled back in effort and concentration, they swayed and strove, but both were nicely balanced. With a piercing yell that momentarily discomposed Ali, the leader disengaged, leaped back, and swung single-handedly in a body-blow, which the Prince barely escaped from by springing aside. With the other now exposing his flank he pressed home the attack, causing the man with the scimitar to slowly retreat.

So engrossed was he in this private duel that he forgot he had now left Bakar's rear exposed. A grunt, intermixed with cries of triumph from behind him made him turn his head to see the giant, his legs knocked from under him, topple over to be engulfed in a breaking wave composed of the remaining attackers. Although his gaze had been distracted for but a moment it was sufficient time to allow the leader to step forward, swinging his scimitar, and to knock Ali's sword jarringly from his hand. The point of the Arabic weapon came up to press into his throat.

Ali froze, shrugged, and held his arms apart, palms outward.

The grinning leader let his point fall, and made Ali a salute with it, and the Prince in turn half-bowed to this worthy opponent. He turned his head to see that, even outnumbered, Bakar was still valiantly trying to rise from beneath the host of enemies.

"Enough, Bakar; I fear this is the end, for the moment, and it seems we are not to be killed—at least not immediately."

The giant was allowed to rise as he desisted from his struggles.

So that his command was understood by the enemy Ali had spoken in the best Malay he could muster, knowing his servant's rough knowledge of the language would suffice to make him understand. The leader touched him with his blade and spoke in the same tongue. "A wise order, my fiery friend—I should have hated to slit the throats of two such mighty warriors."

Warily, Ali made no response but stood waiting for the next move to be made. Bakar came to his side, looking disgusted and mutinous, but Ali motioned him to reluctant obedience. The young leader walked over to Ali's fallen sword and regarded it closely before thrusting it into his own belt. He glanced at his captives.

"This is not a Malay weapon, and unlike any I have ever seen; and you use it in a manner strange to me. You interest me, my friends. We will question you at the camp."

He turned to his men, who were still recovering from blows received in the battle. "Tie their hands and bring them with us. Bakri, Ahmed—you remain here on guard. Let no one pass from the river path. Karelman, Ishka—scout down the path to see whether these two have any followers or friends waiting their return there."

The company moved off into the rocks and Ali, in their midst, wondered what was dreamed up for him next.

FIVE:

(A large fire burns in the center of a clearing, the tall surrounding trees almost meeting overhead to form a cave of timber. Rocks and stones, perhaps the ruins of some ancient temple, lie strewn along one side of the clearing and before these are two smaller fires over which men are cooking spitted meat, and boiling rice and water. Some thirty men sit around the large fire, or among the rocks, waiting to eat. One or two of them are whetting their knives on the rocks, others are talking in small groups. They are of all ages, and the trousers and occasional tunics and sarongs of all are worn, torn and patched. The flames of the fires glint fitfully on their brown faces.

The clearing's size is partly artificial, as numerous stumps and a low, protecting wall made by placing trunks of palm trees one upon the other in the places where the jungle undergrowth is less dense, testify. On one of the stumps near the main fire, the center of a small group, sits a big, heavily bearded and powerful-looking man, gross around the body, but not fat. His beard is coarse and untrimmed, and grows from his chin only, straight and lank, contrasting with his short, black, close-curled hair, and looking more like some strange parasitic growth than a natural attribute. His large eyes are red rimmed and half-hooded by the lids, giving him a hunted, haunted stare which sits ill with the forced joviality which has carved a grin around his lips. With the aid of a twig he is picking his teeth.

A smaller man, and older, bearing a shallow-bowled platter of wood in which some hot liquid steams pleasantly scented, comes now from the fire saying, as he approaches the group: "Here is your soup, if you will drink it here, Chief Achmed."

However, as he draws closer, concentrating on the balance of the soup in the flat bowl, he stumbles against the legs of one of the men and the liquid slides out in a flat, wet, hot mass and spills on Achmed who immediately roars and jumps up. His full height reveals him to be a head taller than most of his companions. With his left hand he seizes and proceeds to shake the little man, lifting him off the ground with ease.

"You clumsy fool. Can't you be careful, or was that deliberate? That soup was hot, but I'll find something hotter for you, to teach you caution!"

So saying he shakes the man and with a backhand throw pitches him into the small fire where, dazed, the cook lays sprawling for a few seconds. Then with a scream he jumps up and runs off to a small stream which runs chuckling through the far side of the clearing, his clothes smoldering, bursting into flame as he runs.

Achmed, hands on hips, puts his heavy head back and roars with laughter in the momentary silence his action has created. He stops suddenly and grins evilly at his companions who pick up the cue and immediately start to laugh with him as they catch his eye, some rolling on the ground in mirth.

With a smile of satisfaction Achmed sits down again on the stump, reaching for his neighbor's bowl of soup without opposition, and he is about to sip when there is a call from the clearing's main entrance, where a ragged guard with a wooden spear stands.)

"Who approaches?"

The group, with Ali and Bakar in their midst, trod silently forward along the narrow trail leading into the clearing. The young leader halted to reply: "Hassan, with two prisoners!" The group passed the guard and entered into the circle of firelight.

Some of the men around the fire rose at their approach, Ali noticed, with hands on their weapons, and he began to think that perhaps he should not have so easily accepted the situation, and should instead have tried to escape on the way here. He and Bakar were thrust forward toward the big man sitting on the stump, who did not look up until Hassan stood before him. Ali observed that although the younger man seemed to recognize the authority of the other he was not subservient and seemed to be on some terms of equality.

"No signs of any enemy anywhere toward the coast, Achmed."

"And who, then, have you brought here, that they are tied? If there are no enemies then you have a strange way of treating our friends."

"No friends of ours, and perhaps no enemies, for they are strangers; I suspect, though I have not yet interrogated them, that they are even strangers to our country, no less than to this kingdom, for the accent of this young man is foreign to my ears. And there is this."

Hassan handed Achmed the sword which had almost defeated him earlier in the day. Achmed handled it lightly, tossing it end over end to test the balance, as the fine steel shone in the flickering light of the fire. Presently he looked up from under his prominent brows and pointed the sword at Ali.

"This weapon is not of the style or manufacture of this country, stranger. Who are you, and from where do you hail?"

"I am a man, and I come from afar."

The other's eyes slitted.

"As to the second statement, I am sure you speak truth; as to whether you are a man, it is yet to be decided. Now, lest you wish me to test the latter point—speak fair!"

The voice came as a growl, but Ali was not to be intimidated by words alone. He shrugged and, with some mockery in his eyes, replied: "It seems I must. Well, then, I am a trader from India, from beyond the sea. Washed overboard together with my unfortunate dumb servant who stands beside me here, while the ship sailed on through the storm. No doubt my father searches for me now."

"Your story has the sound of truth, though your eyes belie it. If it indeed be as you say, then no doubt your father will wish to ransom you. But hold, how is it that you speak our language, Indian?"

"As a trader, and the son of a trader, I have been to your coastal ports before now. And there I was received with greater courtesy—but then, of course, I was dealing with men, and not such great fat animals as yourself."

Ali had made his speech with all civility of tone, his accent one of deprecation, so the significance of his last sentence took a few seconds to sink into the minds of his audience. He noticed several of the men, especially those who had captured him, regarding him with some admiration, and Hassan seemed to be hiding a quick grin. Achmed rose to his feet and struck Ali across the face with one great hand, rocking his head back on his shoulders.

At this Bakar let out a howl, breaking his silence for the first time, and lurched forward, restrained hurriedly by the guards. Blood oozed from Ali's mouth but he shook his head free and kept a mocking grin on his lips and in his eyes, staring up at the man before him.

"It seems your bloated carcass is as empty as your words, that you must needs have your enemy tied before you dare strike him!"

A shocked hush fell over the whole mob as the words rang out. Slowly Achmed let his arm drop back to his side, and a wary gleam shone in his eye.

"Carcass, eh? I think we shall see who is, or who will be, a carcass tonight. Release this young cockerel who crows so well without his spurs yet hard, and clear a circle around us. I wish to take a little exercise, and pluck a chicken for my supper."

He stripped off his sleeveless tunic and tightened the waistband of his trousers. Someone behind Ali cut him free, and he stood for a while massaging his wrists while the crowd fell back to leave the two men alone in the center. A new log was thrown on the fire and sparks rocketed upward toward the leafy roof, throwing stronger gleams on the shining bodies of taunter and taunted.

For a full minute they just stood and looked at each other. Ali slowly drew off the remnants of his shirt, wondering whether Achmed would have any system for wrestling or if he would only rely on his greater height, reach and weight. He got his answer as the Chief yelled, "Hail!" and fell into a crouch, advancing step by step, legs spread far apart, hands performing circles in the air before him. Achmed had a method, and was not about to take any chances with his younger opponent.

Since there was no point in postponing the start of combat Ali suddenly stepped forward, leaning forward from the hips toward Achmed, and feinting with his right hand at the latter's neck, making sure to keep out of the clutch of those brawny arms. As Achmed grunted and closed his guard Ali let fly with the side of his left arm at the other's biceps, below and in front of the shoulder. Although he saw the numbing shock register on the man's face Ali was not to escape unharmed, for Achmed turned as the other went by him and let his own left come slicing down against the Prince's leg, behind the knee, in a hamstringing motion. Ali saw the blow about to start and managed to deflect most of the power by a chop of his own at Achmed's wrist, but he was still knocked down on to one knee.

As the Chief rushed him from behind to take advantage of his position Ali seized a groping hand and ducked his head, dragging the great body over his head, but since his approach had lacked a deal of rush the Chief fell more on top of the Prince than past him, winding them both for a moment. And by the time Ali was out from under and up on his feet his enemy had scrambled to his, and was facing him once again in the same crouched pose. Then with a heavy, stamping approach Achmed drove in on him, hands flickering in and out with an agility surprising in one of his girth. Ali was hard put to it to fend off the blows of the other with his own hands. Falling into a new tactic Achmed continued to advance, more slowly now, with the same circling motion of the hands as before. With a yell of his own Ali leaped forward, striking downward with both his hands, then sliding them outward to seize the other's wrists, continuing to press himself forward, and Achmed's arms back and out.

The two stood chest to chest, legs apart, arms out to the side. If he could only get a slight advantage and get his opponent's arms moving slightly backward behind him, Ali knew he could force the larger man over and to the ground, but the Chief's strength was at least equal to his own.

Suddenly Ali relaxed his right hand, letting go, then moved his hand over to Achmed's right arm, behind the shoulder, and slid his palm up and back under the chin, at the same time dropping to one knee and turning to his left. Achmed flew through the air in a vast, ponderous somersault, and crashed dully down.

Ali noted to his surprise a low cheer from some of the rest of the crowd gathered around, which was quickly suppressed. He sprang over to the other to receive in turn a kick in the chest which sent him staggering back. Before he could recover his balance Achmed was up on his feet, rushing at him, then putting a leg behind his own to send him sprawling on his back. He quickly rolled aside as the Chief dropped his great weight on the place where he had been, but once again could not take advantage of the position, both catlike up on their feet at the same time.

So it went on for several minutes, with Ali using the weight of his opponent against him for some earth-shaking throws and Achmed, apparently never the whit bothered by this, eternally seeking to come to grips so as to use his superior strength to crush this darting adversary. At one point Ali feared he had forfeited any chance of winning, for Achmed had him in a potentially bone-cracking grip that was only failing because of Ali's elbow pressed up into the "V" of the Chief's breastbone, so that any increase of pressure merely served to drive it further home. Achmed dragged the Prince closer to the fire and began to bend him back over it, so that he could feel the flames scorching his shoulders. In a bold move he let himself drop, forcing the heavier man to break his grip to keep his face from the fire, himself sliding lithely out from under the falling body, and off the fire.

Ali seized a brand from the flames as he rose, and belted the man across the buttocks with it, which raised an unexpected laugh from the onlookers, who recalled an earlier event. The crowd was by now becoming wildly excited as the fight wore on.

Hair singed, chest scarred red, face scratched and blackened, Achmed threw himself from the fire and ran at Ali, all sense of style or method lost in the red anger which burned in his eyes. He charged down on the Prince like a wounded buffalo. Feinting as if to dodge, Ali instead prepared to stand the shock and, fists above his head, toppled himself into the Chief's stomach. His feet slid back from beneath him as the impetus of the charge transferred itself to him, but he fell into a crouch to see Achmed slowly doubling over toward him, mouth open in pain and surprise. As he crumpled, Ali moved to one side then leaped up to land, knees down, in the small of the other's back. He put a headlock on the gasping giant and shouted in his ear: "Enough?"

Achmed, with his air supply cut off, feebly patted the ground with both his spread-eagled hands and Ali stood up, panting, his muscles quivering beneath his skin in nervous release. A roar went up from the crowd and Hassan approached him, turning him to face the men, two of whom slipped forward to raise the prostrate Chief, who hung between them, retching for breath. Hassan gestured for silence.

"This is the first man ever to defeat our Chief, Achmed."

"Yes!" "A brave challenge!" "A true defeat!" cried the gang, and once again Hassan had to motion for silence.

"When the leader of the elephant herd is defeated, his conqueror becomes the new leader."

"Yes!"

"I say that if Ali the Stranger agrees, then he shall lead us."

"Truth!" "We'll follow him!" "Let the Stranger fighter lead us!"

Shaken to the depths by this unlooked for turn of events, Ali smiled helplessly at Hassan, who returned him a friendly and admiring grin, before turning to address the waiting crowd.

"I am in truth a stranger, but if you can trust and accept me, then I can do no more and no less than to trust and accept you. I feel that whatever it is, your cause must be an honorable one."

From the corner of his eye he noted the partly recovered Achmed calling the little gathering of his own cronies around him to be silent, as he continued without interruption. "What your aims are, I do not know, but I name Hassan here as my personal lieutenant, and he will guide me."

There were nods and shouts of approval at this suggestion. Taking confidence Ali held up his hands for quiet.

"Since I do not know your country, and need able men to assist me, I propose to make Achmed my other deputy second-in-command."

At this there were only muted cheers, noticeably from the group of men around the ex-Chief, and Hassan looked as though he were about to say something, at which Ali shook his head at him almost imperceptibly. He turned toward his late opponent and called across the clearing. "Achmed, do you accept?"

With a conciliatory smile on his coarse features the big man shambled across to him.

"I shall be proud to serve under one who can defeat me."

The eyes of the two men met and held, but Ali could see only a shielded blankness, no challenge, no acceptance. Bakar, who by this time had also been released from his bonds, came over at Ali's gesture to stand beside him. Still holding Achmed's gaze with his own he announced his last decree. "And this is Bakar, who is my bodyguard and personal aide. You will treat him as I do." He turned his head and smiled at the crowd.

"Now let us forget past quarrels, and celebrate!"

With a jerk of his head Ali called Hassan to follow him as he and Bakar moved through the crowd and reached a fallen log. The three sat and waited, making small conversation, as members of the gang brought food, mutton broiled on sticks, fruit, boiled rice, hot spiced soup, and a variety of nuts and berries. Hassan pointed out various specialities of fighting or trickery characterizing his men, but volunteered nothing of real importance. Ali's body was fatigued and the plentitude of food put his mind into a stupor.

Around the fire some of the men were beginning to sing, beating out a rhythm on the ground, or on pieces of wood. A few of them rose and began an intricate dance, in which one partner of a couple would initiate a series of steps which his opposite number would have to duplicate almost instantaneously. Listening to the sounds of dance and singing, with Hassan now fallen silent over his food, Ali felt himself drifting away into a doze, and he let his mind carry him off. Casually he observed that Achmed was sitting apart from the main group around the large fire and was surrounded by a small knot of his own who took no part in the festivities of the others (and is talking softly to them, saying: "Don't worry, my friends. I did not agree to follow this unknown upstart for nothing. There will come a time when I can take my revenge and recover my position, and when I do, by Allah, these other dogs will be sorry." He glares his hatred across at the dozing Ali and his set, and happens to catch Hassan's eye. The young Lieutenant quietly nudges Ali to wakefulness) and whispered: "I do not trust Achmed, friend Ali, and I feel that you made a mistake when you made him second-in-command. The inferior position will sit heavily upon him, or he is not the bullying, ambitious rogue I think him!"

Ali laughed softly and gently, touching the other's hand. "I do not know him, save that he is not the smartest brute I have known. But he can fight, and commands the loyalty of some, and by giving him position here it should make him loyal to me."

Hassan shook his head, stubbornly unconvinced. Ali clapped him on the shoulder. "Come, Lieutenant; do not be so gloomy. You should be cheered that you outfought me, who outfought Achmed!"

"Not so, Stranger. We captured you through weight of numbers, and a moment of surprise. One against one, and with your swordplay alone you would easily have defeated me."

"I think you could all do with lessons in my style of fighting. I do not know, still, against whom I am supposed to lead this band, but you must tell me in the morning. On the morrow I will start to train you and you can tell me more of your followers and your plans. Meanwhile I wish to sleep, for I have not had an easy day."

"As you wish. I'll wake you early."

They rose and stretched, and as Hassan moved toward the circle of firelight Ali and Bakar sought shadow and sleep.

SIX

"No, no; you don't hold it with both hands. If you bring it up like that then I can—hah!—stick you with the point while you are open."

Ali had twenty of the men drawn up in two lines facing each other, about fifteen feet apart. Using weighted lathes of timber, or the broadbladed *parangs* some of them owned, he was teaching them the elements of saber fighting, getting them to think in terms of footwork, point, and blade, instead of the face-to-face two-handed slice and single-handed cut they normally used.

"That's it, stand sideways, so you present a thinner target to your opponent and keep your heart away from him. No; use *both* legs as a team, not one to move and one to balance with. And remember, if you can, all of you—save your breath and don't yell. If your enemies are used to shouts, your silence will disconcert *them.* All right, keep at it."

Bakar sat on the grass, watching the drilling with an impassive face. Ali strolled up the center of the aisle of men to where Hassan made the last man in his file. The Prince-incognito stood opposite for a moment. "That's excellent, Hassan. Soon you might be up to my standards."

His voice was dry and bantering and Hassan, foregoing his look of concentration, looked at him and replied in the same vein: "Might be? Why, I think I can beat you any time now at your own game."

Ali raised his eyebrows. The other men paused to watch, grins on their faces.

"You really think so? Very well, let's have at it."

Using his Indian blade against the other's self-made wooden practice weapon he drove forward, and they parried and thrust with great vigor. It was soon obvious that Ali was toying with Hassan but the young lieutenant was giving him a fair amount of opposition, considering his short amount of training. Finally Ali stepped in and with a circling wrist movement whirled the piece of timber out of Hassan's hand. The latter grinned and held out his hands in mock surrender. Ali stretched himself lazily in the sun, which was not yet high in the sky, its rays glancing off many cool green leaves before engoldening the still dewy clearing. Sauntering smoke climbed from the green-wood fire across the azure sky, bearing with it the belly-stirring smells of roasting meats.

"That was good exercise, and good sport. We'll break now, and practice some more this afternoon."

The men sketched salutes with their miscellaneous and makeshift weapons, and strolled off. Ali took Hassan's arm and led him to where Bakar sat, chewing on a grass-stalk, and flopped down into the cool grass on which the drops of dew were each a miniature blue arc of sky, uncountable, true and separate. Ali sighed. "That took more wind out of me than I like to admit. I'm out of condition."

"I'd hate to be up against you when you *are* in condition, then. By Allah, but you are master of your blade. But tell me, who are you really? I'll wager no trader ever learned to fight like that. He'd be more likely to use his bags of gold as weapons."

Ali laughed and gave his questioner a friendly, disingenuous look.

"My dear Hassan, men may trade in many things—food, goods, materials of all kinds, curios; even in countries, and names. A trader will do as well as any other title to describe my . . . vocation in life. But now, tell me at least your story, and of this band I am supposed to lead."

Hassan closely studied the other's look, and slowly shook his head to acknowledge he knew Ali was concealing something, and would accept it. He looked down, paused, then apparently decided to trust his chosen leader.

"Well, you are a stranger . . . and a strange man. I have seen the men of China, and I have seen those of your own country, of many hues. And once I saw an Arab trader, from some other land far beyond yours. And I have heard, but a few days since, of a stranger touching shore on the East Coast, north of here, with a crew of Chinese. But he was taller than they, it is said, and spoke an odd language, for all that his garments were part patterned after those of his men. Mayhap he will venture south and we shall meet with him . . ." (*There is a man you must not meet. Someone . . . but what is his name; and what am I thinking?*) ". . . but I have met none so strange as you, who speak our language. And yet you are of Islam, for I have heard you cry upon Allah. Ah, well; perhaps one day . . ."

He grinned again at Ali, then lay back upon the grass, remembering. "This land, and these several islands make up the Kingdom of Srivijaya, though there is some talk of the Madjapahit fighting on the eastward islands of Java. But our country here pays only a small tribute, and rules itself. Until little more than a year ago we were ruled by the Sultan Mohamed, a good and peace-loving man who reigned from his palace in the City of 'Dak Betul. . . ."

As Hassan continued his tale it seemed to Ali, drowsy in the scents and sounds of the glade, that he could picture the events related. . . .

SEVEN:

". . . He had governed well and wisely for two-score years, but now at last the ungovernable had reached out to claim him. He lay in his bedchamber, his body raised from the hard planks and mats by a mattress of cushions designed to ease his last hours. . . ."

The gentle-faced man was in his sixties, a year for every traced line on his cheek and brow. He slept fitfully, his breathing shallow. By the low bed stood the Mentri Besar, first Minister of State, with two other Councillors. Near the head of the bed stood Hassan, relaxed but mentally alert, on duty but expecting no incident. On his head he wore the silver-embroidered stiff-cloth headdress which marked him as Captain of the Palace Guard. A blue tunic, with silver edging, falling outside his blue and silver sarong, girded up for action, completed his dress, save for the sash into which was thrust his scimitar and snake-bladed *keris,* sheathed now in its wooden scabbard.

One of the men muttered, "Our Sultan is old; yet I cannot see a reason for his dying."

His companion, a doleful-looking, slit-mouthed man, answered him in a low tone, glancing at Hassan. "It would not surprise me to find Abdul the Red One behind this somewhere."

The Mentri was sharp voiced. "Cease this talk, I request you. I too fear that the Sultan's cousin has a hand in this, with his dark doctors and his darker dreams. But it is not well to speak of these things unless one has proof."

The old man on the bed slowly opened his eyes and began to whisper. Hassan interrupted the Mentri. "His Highness is awake, Sire!"

The three ministers moved closer to the bed and made obeisance. The Mentri lowered his ear to the old man's mouth, then turned quickly to Hassan.

"He wishes to see his granddaughter, the Princess Meriam. Fetch her, Captain."

Palms together, head bowed, thumbs against forehead, Hassan backed from the room. Awaiting his return the old men talked.

"Ah yes, Princess Meriam; a great pity that her father, the Prince, should have died with his wife."

"I have heard it said that Abdul the Red One caused the fire that destroyed them both."

"Lucky it is for the country that an heir survived, when the Princess escaped the holocaust."

"The maid, Saripah, was courageous in rescuing her. . . ."

"And the good Captain Hassan of the Guard was royally rewarded for his part in it. But here they come now."

Scimitar drawn, Hassan hurried into the room, making perfunctory obeisance, and followed by a petite gamin of a girl, enormous black eyes set into a pretty ovaloid of pale brown, framed by a black lace head scarf which matched the long, wide-skirted blouse worn over the black and gold-figured sarong. In her arms she bore the two-year-old Princess. The Mentri bent to the Sultan's ear.

"The Princess Meriam comes, Sire."

Dragging himself back from scenes of a far-off country, the old man opened his eyes. Saripah, the maid, boldly sat herself down on the edge of the bed, holding the Princess up to stand against her. The Sultan, her grandfather, with what was obviously part of a confirmed game between them, weakly raised his thumb for Meriam to hold. Abruptly she fell to her knees and stroked the old man's beard. Saripah made as if to restrain her, but he gently shook his head, and let his eyes wander from face to face before speaking, his words stumbling, but his voice gaining strength.

"My friends—and all of you are friends, I know—I am forced by the will of Allah to take leave of you . . . and of my people. I entrust *their* future welfare . . . to my granddaughter . . . Meriam, who is to rule after me. It will be long years before she is able to rule . . . and in that time I entrust *her* welfare . . . to you."

His tired gaze dropped fondly to Meriam, who cooed at him, oblivious and uncomprehending of his condition, and while the hushed audience watched, the last smile froze on his lips and his eyes closed.

Saripah gently picked up the little Princess and held her close, tears brimming into her large eyes. Quickly she slipped from the bed and sat cross-legged at its foot. The Mentri and the two Councillors busied themselves reverently with the Sultan, covering his body and head with a white linen cloth. Hassan went down on one knee and made his last salute to his late lord, and raised his eyes to see Meriam looking up at him from the shelter of Saripah's arms. Stiffly the young man rose, went before her, and fell on one knee again. Palms together, thumbs to brow, he held her eyes and slowly spoke to her, while she watched entranced.

"I hereby pledge my life and my allegiance to none other than the Princess Meriam, and swear to protect her person at peril, if need be, of my own."

77

As if suddenly aware of the full meaning of the moment the little Princess reached forward and touched his hands with her own.

EIGHT:

"We did not know, then, Saripah and I, just how perilous our task would be, to keep the Princess Meriam from harm."

Hassan's voice recalled Ali to the present. Dreamily he watched as a blue and golden parakeet, orange-eyed and yellow clawed, its breast as green as the palm leaves, flung itself from branch to frond above, to stare accusingly down, scolding incoherently, at the intruders disturbing the natural idyll below.

"We didn't know it then, of course, though we suspected, but Abdul the Red One, cousin to the late Sultan, was already plotting to usurp the throne. . . ."

Against the red-tinged screens of his eyelids, back-lit by the sun, a gorgeous scene of decadent decor played before Ali's mind's eye. There was a richly decorated chamber, over-full of furniture, with walls, floor and ceiling too-elaborately embellished with cloths and brocades, silken drapes, and tasseled cushions. Carpets covered every inch of floor and what little light penetrated the large window spaces was colored and diffused by ornately patterned rice-paper panes.

One corner of this room was raised, with three long and shallow steps leading up to it, and at the center of this dais rested a divan screened on three sides by hanging laces. On the divan, propped upon one elbow, lay a figure which seemed at first sight to be the epitome of opulent and indolent grandeur, wrapped about in scarves and shawls and a sarong and over-sarongs of gold-thread-worked many-colored cloths. But this impression was negated as soon as the face was observed, eagle-eyed, hook-nosed, powerful, ruthless. The upper lip was ornamented by a drooping moustache, which hung like two bloody rattails each side of the thin, cruel mouth. The startling thing was their color, almost orange, matching the long thin hair which dangled loosely from below the high, stiff-clothed turban. The skin which ill-contrasted this orange was itself of a greenish-brown complexion, into which the pale blue eyes were set like fungoid mold in pools of filth.

Below this man, who could only be Abdul the Red One, sat another, soft and fleshy as a Persian cat, fingers beringed, and arms entwined in silver bracelets, which he seemed never to cease turning and studying in a quiet ecstacy of self-admiration. At the foot of the steps sat two others, younger men, plainly dressed, studiously not listening to the conversation behind them. The red-haired man was speaking.

"My dear Karim, you don't follow me at all. After we have reduced the taxes on our landlords, and have thus swayed them to our side, we increase the taxes on the commoners, thereby regaining our lost income and re-plenishing the treasury but, what is just as important, with the assistance of the eager landlords, who will then take the brunt of the commoners' complaints."

The dark man he addressed tore his eyes from his bracelets for a moment and looked with a wet stare at the other. "Brilliant, Sire! The idea of a genius of government, Sire!" He returned his regard to his rings too soon to catch the disgusted sneer of Abdul.

"Yes, well, that's as may be. But it all depends upon the message from the palace, and my future control of the throne."

He was distracted from continuing by the sound of bare feet padding down the corridor outside the room, and he looked up to see a man come panting in. The two men at the foot of the steps rose as one and drew their *parangs*, but the man flung himself breathless on the lower step, saluted, and looked up at Abdul.

"I have news from the Istana, Sire!"

The Red One leaned forward eagerly. "Yes, continue. Never mind these others. You can speak freely. What word from the palace?"

"Sultan Mohamed is dead, Sire."

"And?"

"He has named the Princess Meriam as his heir, and
79

entrusted her to the care of the Mentri Besar and Hassan, the Captain of the Guard."

"What!" Abdul swung himself from the divan and stood, to reveal a tall and heavy figure. "May Iblis take his soul! He has tricked me to the end. I was sure of the Regency!" Striding up and down the dais he pounded fist to palm. "He must have suspected I poisoned him. But as I broke his body, so I'll break his spirit and defy his last utterance. I'll have the Regency!"

Karim stood hesitantly on the lower step. "But if you have not been named as Regent, Sire, the people will not accept you."

"I know that, you fool, but there has to be a way. There has to be a way. There always is a way to get around the intentions of honest men."

Karim shrugged at the others as the redhead paused, caressing his moustache in thought, his thumb following the line of his lips. Suddenly he swung around, pointing. "You, messenger. Fetch the Princess Latifah here!"

Saluting, the messenger left at a run as Abdul sank back down onto the divan and smiled at Karim. "The people will not accept me, perhaps; but they will accept Latifah, the cousin of Meriam. She is obligated to me, in a certain way, and will do as I say."

"But still Meriam has been named as heiress, Sire!"

"And how many people know that? It cannot have been publicly proclaimed yet. You two! Go and see that nothing is made known. Tell the Mentri that Princess Latifah wishes to speak with him first. Go! Ah, here comes the Princess now. How pleasant to see you, my dear. We were just talking about you."

The departing messengers had almost collided in the doorway with the Princess, who came forward now to stand below the steps. Karim obsequiously prepared cushions for her but she dismissed his efforts with a scornful glance. The servant who had summoned her had effaced himself beyond the door, but the young girl looked around her as though expecting to find others in the room. Her hair was long, black, and undressed, but although her tight-fitting, low-necked baiju and sarong were plain and simple, and no ornaments adorned her person, her strong features bore the unmistakable stamp of regality, compassionate yet self-impassioned, self-centered yet not selfish. Her fine dark eyes were hidden by long lashes, but her tone revealed the scorn she felt.

"You sent for me, Uncle? Yet I do not see your dark men of medicine here, so perhaps I am to leave here in good health. With your creature Karim here I perceive that I am excellently well chaperoned."

The sycophant shot a glance of pure hatred at the girl, and the redhead could not forgo the luxury of a slight smile at the thrust, but instantly he replaced it with a mask of gravity. "I'm afraid I've sent for you to inform you of bad news, my dear Princess. Your uncle the Sultan has just died."

The girl bit her lip but said nothing. Abdul rose and continued his pacing of the dais. "The news will come as a shock to you, I have no doubt, as it came to me, and I join you in condolences for his soul, for I know you loved him, and he, you. In fact, you are to be his heiress."

He swung around at this to observe her reaction but her face remained expressionless as she asked: "And what of Princess Meriam? Surely she is more nearly in the line of descent than I?"

"Ah, that is the thing of which I wish to speak. I think it only right that you should rule, my dear. You are older, and can soon govern the country yourself. It is no task for a child of two."

For the first time the girl looked up at him as he stood above her. "You mean, *you* wish to rule the country, Uncle? No, don't bother to deny it. I know your ambition, and I know just how much power would remain in my hands . . . and I suspect for how long, till I had named you my own heir. And one thing I am as sure of as I am sure that you would conceal it if you could . . . and that is the Sultan *must* have made Meriam his heiress!"

"I am surprised and hurt by your suspicions, my dear. I had hoped that by now you would have come to know me better."

"I know you too well!"

"Come now, don't you think you owe me something?

Have you forgotten that your late father was banished from the country, and that I raised you? You have been living on my charity ever since you were born!"

The Princess flung her head back and laughed in his face. "You have other news for me, Uncle? You have been reminding me of my dependence upon you every day since I became your charge. What did you do for me? You plundered my father's lands and converted his money to your own uses. He died in exile, and you diverted the little he left me into your own treasury. . . ."

"The law says a rebel may not leave—"

She swung around to face him again; at that, her waist-length hair flying about her head to give her face the appearance of the moon seen through dark storm clouds.

"The law! *You* designed that law. A rebel? *You* designed that charge, and pressed it home on evidence the Sultan was loath to accept. And still you say I owe you something? No, Uncle; I don't know what deep and devious schemes you may have in mind, but be sure I will never help you."

Abdul had waited impassively and patiently for her to finish, not unaware that the disturbed Karim was trying to catch his eye. He made a little bow to the Princess and continued to smile down at her.

"You've quite finished, my girl? Good. Now listen to me. You love your cousin Meriam, don't you? And you would hate to have her die, wouldn't you? And you would not want to be the cause of her death, through some silly little action, would you? I have listened to your ravings; now attend to my words, and attend them well!"

He bent and seized her chin in his hand, forcing her to gaze at him. "Mark me, Princess Latifah. If you do not agree to my plan, if you do not follow my every step, and walk with apparent enjoyment, then I will have the Princess Meriam killed by one of my several methods. I think that you have learned by now, if you have learned nothing else about me, that I have a certain skill in obtaining the ends I seek, and it could be that I would arrange to have you accused of the crime, and so encompassing two of my aims and tying them into one knot. I tell you this because you know I speak the truth, and because you cannot prove the utterance."

He thrust her from him with a twist of his wrist, and she tripped over a cushion to the floor.

"If you agree, then I will spare her. If you do not . . . The choice is yours."

Her hair obscured her face from his view, and he could not tell whether she cried or not for her voice, low that it was, remained steady. "What can I do? I must agree, it seems."

As he turned to smile contemptuously at Karim he could not see that her face had paled to a firm resolve, that her fine eyes were bitter, but not resigned.

NINE:

(*I like this Princess Latifah. A girl of spirit who does not, like others of her sex, escape the situation into a flood of tears; and of evident and obvious beauty. But how can I know that she is beautiful? How is it I SEE her beauty, since I have not met her? No, of course I have not met her. But then . . . How . . . ?*)

"Hey, Ali; I believe you've fallen asleep on me. Is my tale that boring to your . . . trader's unexcited ears?"

"No. I felt just a little dizzy, that's all. The story is fine and you tell it well."

Ali shook his head and opened his eyes to find all as before; the green glade, the distant moving men, the blue sky overhead, the leafy palms, the birdsongs falling through the clear, pure air. He took a deep breath and turned to his companion who was observing him quizzically. "No; carry on, please. What happened then?"

Hassan settled himself back and plucked a sturdy blade of grass, balancing it across one finger. "See that? See, if I turn my finger slightly one way or the other this grass will roll and tip, so . . . and fall. Well, that's how precarious things were for the next hour or so at the Istana. If one thing had gone wrong, well . . . I wouldn't be sitting safely here telling you this story, for one.

"Of course, I didn't know all that was happening at the time. It was many weeks later that I learned that as soon as Abdul the Red One had delivered his ultimatum to her, the Princess Latifah sent for her maid and charged her to go to the Palace and warn Princess Meriam's maid, Saripah, to take the child and escape from the City. I had already warned the girl that she might have to leave in a hurry, having a premonition, by intuition, of what might happen; and so when she received the message from Princess Latifah she wasted no time but slipped immediately from the Istana.

"And by all the names of Iblis I wish I knew where she had gone!"

Ali was surprised by the vehemence of his tone and looked at him curiously.

"Ay! Apart from the safety of the Princess Meriam I have the thought that I might seal our joint guardianship a little more strongly. The wench was not without her attractions, and regarded me not unfavorably."

Ali laughed. "Your cause is not altogether an altruistic one, then, friend Hassan! But continue your story."

"Well, I had noticed Abdul's man go running off, to advise him, I suspected. The dog had been hiding behind the door. The Mentri agreed with me that we should be prepared for possible trouble, since the Sultan's wishes were not those of Abdul's. We decided to post a full guard on each door to the Istana and so I went to call the off-duty men. When I returned I had only found ten extra men I could fully trust, which was not enough to withstand any great attack. Abdul's man had returned with his master's message and the Mentri asked me what I felt he should do. We were still wasting time trying to come to a decision when Abdul himself marched in, with thirty men of his own. I confess my heart was cold when I saw them line up around the great hall.

"The red devil marched up the center and would have gone to the throne, no doubt, and sat himself down, but I stood in his way. He looked over to the Mentri. 'I wish to speak with you, Mentri. Call off your Captain and dismiss him,' he demands, cool and smooth as silk. But the Mentri was not to be outfaced. 'What you have to say can well be heard by the Captain,' he says. I still stood there, with my hand ready to draw my scimitar against him, for all that he was of royal blood, but he didn't give me so much as a look. 'That is what I wished to talk about, Mentri. Now, it is reasonable to assume that, in his last few moments, the old man, Allah rest his soul, was not too clear about certain things. To put it bluntly, I would like to think that he was sane enough to name the Princess Latifah as heiress to the kingdom, as the older cousin.'

"For all that he wasn't giving me the notice of a gnat I spoke up then. 'We have already sworn our allegiance to Princess Meriam, and accept her as our ruler. The Mentri Besar will act as Regent, and later advise her. The girl Saripah will tend to her upbringing and care for her as she needs. And I will guard her until such time as she needs no champion!'

"Well, this sets him back a pace, and he looks from me to the Mentri and back again. I was still a little too puffed-up at myself to think clearly, or I would have seen what was in his mind. He stood off and stared at me. 'So,' he says. 'We will have to take measures. Guard, fetch Princess Meriam from her quarters.' Before I can make a move one of his men runs out of the hall. The Mentri, poor old man, moves before I can warn him and jumps down from the throne dais, trying to run to the little doorway near him, but another of Abdul's traitorous gang stands in his way. I begin to move and have my scimitar out to go to his aid, but I catch a nod from the Red One and his man cuts down the Mentri with his sword.

"My people had begun to realize what was happening and jumped to form a ring, facing outward. Abdul had moved back out of reach, and his men started to close in on us. I tell you, Ali, I didn't expect to get out of that place alive, nor my men. We started to press for the main door but even though mine were the better trained of the two groups, three to one was too heavy

85

odds. What saved us was the messenger who had gone to get Princess Meriam returning to say that the child and Saripah were not to be found.

"For a moment the Red One was caught undecided, and his men waited for a space for his orders. Taking advantage of the pause I let out a roar, and we charged down the hall, *parangs* flying like steel wings, and out through the great door. Once we were through I had to halt our retreat. We were at the top of the steps which lead down into the courtyard, and across that to the gate-keeper's lodge and the closed gates were at least a hundred yards without cover. At the top of the steps we could stand for a while and cut down any who tried to come out of the doorway, but I knew that a minute or two would see them come around from behind us. So far I had lost no men, while we had cut down several of the enemy. Luck wouldn't hold with us much longer so I called out, 'To the main gate, boys. Retreat on the double.'

"We took to our heels and ran like mouse-deer toward the gate. I looked back and saw, as I had expected, that we'd caught them flat-footed, for now they were jammed into the doorway like fish in a funnel.

"There were two short walls leading back from the gate, like an alley, with a platform behind each so that invaders could be flanked from above. I had my men defend the entrance to this and called up to the gatemen: 'Are you loyal to Sultan Mohamed's wishes?' There were four of them, and they shouted back as one man, 'Yes!' My heart leaped for such loyalty. 'The Sultan is dead. Meriam is named to rule. Abdul would destroy her and us. Will you help us?' Again they cried yes, and three of them dropped down behind us while the other pulled on the ropes and wheels that opened the gate. By now two of my lads were down, but the rest were holding off the enemy at the alley's entrance. So soon as there was room I urged them to slip through the narrow slice of gate, one by one, the three gatemen going first, all unarmed as they were.

"I and three others held the rearguard, and I felled two of the dogs before I slid through to safety, and cut the head off a third as he was improvident enough to venture to follow through the slit of the gate opening. Above us the remaining gateman cut the weight free that swung the gate closed, but as he leaped down from the outside wall to join us a spear took him in the back and he fell at my feet.

"My uncle it was. A brave man, and an honor to my family.

"But there was no time for mourning. A hasty glance told me that with the three gatemen we were twelve men remaining, some wounded, but all with two feet and two arms. 'Run, you sons of Iblis, or you'll be with the houris tonight!' I cried; and we raced off through the end of town and into the jungle.

"Like a good leader I led the flight, for they'd have been lost with me speared behind them, and I had a higher loyalty.

"And so we came into the woods, and have been named as outlaws ever since, though there are those who would aid us if they dared, and a few brave souls who have already joined us."

Hassan sat up and took Ali's arm. "I swear that's the truth of the matter. Are you with us? Or rather, are we with you?"

Ali smote the anxious Hassan on the back. "By Allah, I am! There is nothing I enjoy more than a good hard fight in a good clean Cause. There's nothing better to take the sickness out of a man's soul, or put a light into his heart, or add purpose to his arm!"

"Not even a smart piece of trading, putting a smart deal over in the way of business?" said Hassan, distending cheek with tongue. Ali clapped him on the back again, a good hard blow of friendship.

"I have a question or two more," he said, "but you must be dry. Bakar! Go fetch some water."

The two rested in a comradely ambience while the giant went to the encampment, filled a large beaker with water, and returned.

Hassan drank, and inquired: "What else do you need to know?"

"This Achmed, my it-is-to-be-believed trusty second-in-command. It strikes me that he owes his first loyalty to himself rather than to a child Princess, unless I mistake in my judgment of men. How does he fit into this scheme, and how was it that he became your leader instead of his following you?"

He drank in turn, as Hassan explained that in the early days, when the outlaws were still few and unorganized, his band had met with Achmed's, professional rebels against authority, and had enlisted them to the Cause. "Not without some trouble," added the young ex-Captain. "It was mainly the promise of great rewards after we had overthrown the Red One that gained Achmed's sympathy, though several of his men, I think, are genuinely interested in our Cause and are loyal to it. Since Achmed's men were the larger group originally, and wiser in the wild ways of the jungle, it being their home, it seemed both sensible and expedient to let him lead, with myself as his lieutenant. Though I have had cause to regret it from time to time."

Ali shrugged. "Expediency seldom offers a worthwhile solution, short-term or long. You say that Abdul the Red One is a tyrant and a usurper. Well, I have never liked those who abused their power, whether Princes or Parliaments, Ministers or the masses. I'll lead you in this, with the greatest pleasure in the world, but I insist that I train them, with your help, in the ways I think best."

"But in this country, merchant, you must learn to fight with our weapons. That is only sense!"

"Your weapons, hah! Give me a straight dagger, instead of your dainty, waved *keris*, and I'll undertake to beat any of you with it against your weapon!"

Hassan grinned and rolled over. "Come and try, then. Here, Ishka, bring me one of the meat-knives."

They waited till the man brought over the short, dagger-like knife, and Ali tested it in his hand. "It's not the best, but I don't aim to kill you with it, so it will do. Now, let's see you put your hand where your tongue was!"

The two men began to circle around the invisible pivot that would be their meeting place. Ali held his dagger out and before him, his left hand as a balance behind him as he moved, but he soon saw that Hassan's method was radically different. The Captain held both hands out slightly before him, and moved with a springy crouch, swaying from one leg to the other, poised and waiting. Ali took the initiative and leaped forward, right hand extended to the full toward the other's throat. Instantly Hassan's left hand came up and out, striking down the dagger-blade, his own *keris* coming in low and upward. Ali dropped to one knee and as the *keris* slid over his shoulder, moved his right hand up to the Captain's heart, at the same time rising up to hit his opponent's right arm with his own left shoulder.

The second part of his maneuver succeeded well enough and Hassan's blow went wide of the mark, but again the Captain's left hand shot out against his wrist in a sharp cutting blow that paralyzed his arm and made him drop the dagger and stumble into his adversary's body. "Hai!" cried Hassan, and Ali felt the point of the *keris* touch the back of his neck, then the small of his back, in quick succession. Grinning ruefully he stepped back and picked up his dagger. The Captain was jubilant. "You see, the *keris* wins!"

"Fairly fought, friend Hassan. I see I have something to learn after all. But I think I'll stick to my sword in the future. With that I feel I'm invincible."

The victor put his arm around Ali's shoulders and they began to walk back to the camp. "You see, with us the *keris* is a weapon that we learn to use after we have mastered our art of self-defense, so that we use both hands together, whereas it seems to me that you start from sword fighting and then use your dagger as a short sword."

"Yes, but if you find me a good dagger I'll show you how I am used to fighting, with a sword in my right hand and a dagger in my left. I think if your men can be taught to use a *parang* and a *keris* in the same way then we will have something to surprise Abdul and his pack with."

TEN

(Where's the sun? WHERE IS THE SUN? How is it we are near the fire, in the dark? WHAT HAPPENED TO THE SUN? WHERE DID THE TIME GO? Somebody said I would go from scene to scene, like . . . like WHAT? WHO said?)

Ali blinked his eyes again and hammered the hard ground on which he lay in the warmth of the fire. The silent Bakar touched him with his foot, and, startled, he looked at the man, not knowing why he was startled (*Does he KNOW? WHAT is there for him to know?*) and then his mind was clear. He turned to Hassan, sprawled easily beside him.

"Hassan, I have been thinking (*WHEN?*) and have come to a decision (*HOW?*). I cannot hope to make plans for our success until I know something of the ground on which we have to fight. Apart from your story, I know only that Princess Latifah . . ."

"Is probably an unwilling assistant to her uncle, Abdul the Red One."

"And the Princess Meriam . . . ?"

"Is alive, hopefully, with Saripah. There has been no report that the Red One has her, and indeed he insists that they are with us."

"It is obvious to me that eventually we must take over your city of . . . ?"

" 'Dak Betul."

"Yes, 'Dak Betul. Well, then, I propose that we three —you, I and Bakar—start off for the city tomorrow to spy out the land, leaving Achmed in charge of the camp."

At the mention of Achmed's name Bakar stirred and turned to look at his master. In mime he played out the part of a man who would willingly stab another in the back, with a smile sketched on his face. Laughing, Ali reassured him. "Don't worry; Achmed can do us no harm. This might be a good time to test him. Now, be ready for him when he returns from foraging, and tell him I would like to see him."

Shaking his head dubiously, and grimacing gloomily, the giant went off. Still with a laugh on his lips, Ali turned to Hassan. "Bakar is as faithful as a shadow to my wishes; but occasionally he tries to think for himself, a tendency I have to curb in him. But he's as necessary as a shadow to me, also. He's a tower of strength at my side, literally."

"And he'd be a terror of strength if he were not *on* your side! Come, let's rest till Achmed arrives."

That night Ali slept. A deep, dreamless sleep.

ELEVEN:

They came out of the jungle at the top of a small rise, with the city of 'Dak Betul spread before them. It sprawled over about a mile of each bank of a narrow river, with a "T" of roads leading through the center, the stem parallel to the river.

To Ali's unhurried gaze there appeared to be few large buildings, and these in any case were not tall. Only the Istana raised itself above the single-storied leaf-roofed huts on the nearest bank, while across the river the finger of the muzein's tower pointed to heaven against the fist of the mosque.

Below them a wide track wandered from further along the forest wall to join the bankside road before it led into the first scattered groups of houses. There was no wall around the town, and in fact there were no fences or separating barriers of any kind, save only a high palisade surrounding the Istana and another containing a large compound with several small huts and one long, low, wooden-roofed house.

"That's the Red One's compound over there. He still keeps it up, though he spends most of his time at the Istana," said Hassan.

"I'm interested in the marketplace, where the commoners are. Let's see what gossip and information we can pick up there. Will we pass muster?"

Hassan regarded the miscellaneous collection of disreputable ragged clothing in which the three were wrapped. "We look poor enough to become rich on charity before the day is through," he grinned.

"Then let's go see how we fare. My trader's blood calls out for money in my palm! Come, Bakar."

The large dusty square which made up the market-place was thronged with people, though Ali shrewdly noted that there seemed to be more bargaining than buying. Most of the stalls were lightly constructed, being little more than planks laid over trestles, with a framework above from which depended cloth screens to keep the dust from the goods. Bolts of brightly colored cloth, earthenware utensils in shades from black to white and variously painted, sarongs and the baggy-legged *seluar,* brooms and metalware were on sale in one corner, where a snake charmer played his flute before the stalls, and hoarse-throated men cried the value and quality of their goods.

To one side were stalls of vegetables and fruits, lush melons, orange yams cut for display, egg-fruit, carmine pomegranates and green and black and purple grapes; red cabbages and greenstuffs of every kind; lean string beans and brown, knobbed leaf-haired pineapples, multi-faceted and jostling with rough-bearded coconuts and their greener younger brethren, half-hidden by hanging stands of bananas. Sights and smells and sounds assaulted the senses of the three companions as they wandered, inconspicuous, through the crowd. An itinerant metal-worker brushed by them, rattling his string of square brass plates to draw attention to his trade, and small boys with wooden castanets clicked like so many crickets around their heels, crying the kinds of food their masters sold.

With a "Hai! Hai!" a milkman parted the throng for his long-horned water buffalo, large jars of brown pottery slung pannier-like across its back, he himself perched on its shoulders. Dust rose in his wake like heavy wings. Hassan spat: "Let's go over here and find some coffee." They made their way past aromatic stalls where curry powders were displayed in wicker baskets, and a low shed under whose roof were gathered the meat-sellers and their fresh-slaughtered carcasses of venison, cattle and sheep. Near a small stage, where a puppet shadow-play was being performed against the white cloth screen mounted upon it, they found a coffee stall; the seller squatted on the ground surrounded by the paraphernalia of his enterprise, brass urns and bowls for washing, a large jar of water, a sugar-juice mill, copper dippers and big wooden ladles.

The three men sat on the low stools and ordered, covertly regarding the scene as they waited. Just behind them was a *satay* seller, with the small pieces of mutton and chicken broiling on their twigs and skewers over the open charcoal fire, with several customers waiting for the morsels. As they sipped their steaming coffee Ali eavesdropped on the conversation amongst the *satay*-eaters and presently nudged Hassan to listen.

One of the men, a little, wizened fellow, was speaking. "Well, friends, I'll pay for this round of *satay*, and then I'm off, with empty pockets." His companion looked up. "Why? When we last met, a year ago, you were settled with your little vegetable farm, surely?"

"Aye, but that was before that damned Abdul had my land seized for the taxes I hadn't paid. Truth to tell, I *had* paid 'em, but the collector had kept 'em for himself. Now all my vegetables go into the palace free."

A third man nodded. "I would join you in your travels, comrade, but I have a score to settle first."

"This is a poor time to worry about creditors, brother!"

The man spat, then opened his tunic to reveal a chest freshly scarred. "This is one debt I reckon to repay in full, comrade. One of our beloved Abdul's noble friends fancied my daughter. When I tried to prevent their taking her, the Red One's guards seized me on his orders and forced me to watch while they had their sport of her. Then they had me whipped, and left me for dead outside the gate. But I've marked the men to whom I'm debtor and I'll give them a full tally before I leave this city."

Ali glanced at Hassan and raised his eyebrows inquiringly. The young Captain nodded and moved his stool back to speak to the men, but just then a disturbance arose at the far end of the square, and they turned to see a small procession making its way through the crowd, which had fallen silent at its approach, all haggling ceased.

Two great wooden chairs were borne litter fashion on the shoulders of sixteen men, clad in a matching livery. In the first sat an arrogant orange-haired man who could only be Abdul the Red One; but the second was lightly screened by floating veils, and Ali could not make out its occupant. A band of spear-armed guards surrounded the group, breaking a path through the rapidly scattering throng. The silence was sullen, broken only by the hoarse shouts of the soldiers and the creak of the litter poles. As the first litter went by Ali bowed his head to avoid any possible recognition in the future, for already a plan was running through his head; but as the second drew abreast he raised his eyes to get a glimpse of its passenger. The veils parted in a sudden breeze to reveal the face and figure of a beautiful girl whose eyes alone betrayed a sense of sadness mixed with fear. She stared straight ahead, with no glance to left, to right, or below, as if trying to vanish the crowd and her surroundings from her perception by sheer mental effort. But all unregarding as she was, her face struck a dual chord in his mind, the one of present beauty (*the other of beauty past?*) (*the past perceived?*) and he remained looking after the litter till a blow on the shoulder with the butt end of a spear recalled him to the situation. Without thinking he began to rise, with a growl in his throat for the guard who had unconcernedly gone by, but he was restrained by the pressure of Hassan's hand on his arm.

As the procession went out of sight they sat back. Ali rubbed his shoulder and one of the men at the *satay* stall muttered, "That damned Abdul, may Iblis take him!"

His companion struck in. "I pity the Princess Latifah. They say she is practically his slave, a prisoner in her own palace. I wonder what witchcraft his dark men of medicine have used on her?"

"Truth indeed, there must be some reason. I have

heard it said that she would help us poor people if she could."

Ali whispered in Hassan's ear. "I think we may have some recruits for our band there, my friend. If they wish to join, then have them wait for us at the jungle's edge tonight, and we will meet them after I have visited the Istana."

A bright moon shone down as the three men, staggering slightly, and laughing inanely among themselves, came across the narrow green in front of the Istana's main gate, attracting casual attention from the two guards who stood without. The wicker door was open, and inside Ali noted an officer giving some orders to two more guards who were posted at each side of the far end of the fenced alley. Continuing their apparently aimless stroll they followed the stockade wall along, keeping well out into the moonlight so that they would arouse no suspicion. Between the gate and the next corner patrolled two more guards, and the heads of two more could be seen performing a similar function above the level of the wall on the inside, evidently walking along some platform.

The next stretch of stockade was considerably higher than the other, some twenty feet in all, Ali judged, and this faced out on a small plain unbroken by cover, except for a few rocks which at about the center became the foundation for that part of the wall, which marched over it.

The three companions paused and began to argue among themselves as if unsure in which direction they were headed. They remained long enough to see that there were only two guards performing sentry duty along this section, the length of their beat allowing several minutes between their meetings.

"This wall seems to be loosely guarded, Hassan?"

"Yes, it is considered too high to be scaled, and this cleared ground before it prevents a secret attack. And unless the Red One has added something, there is no platform on the inside of this wall, for beyond it are the private royal gardens."

"Right. Now I want to study those rocks. As soon as those two fellows have met and passed again, and have their backs to us, take my cloak here and hang it between you, so that to the casual eye it will appear that three of us are walking off to the jungle there. Wait for me. I don't intend to be too long."

"Good luck," whispered Hassan, but the guards were past and Ali was running silently toward the rocks.

On this side of the Istana the wall cast a heavy shadow on the ground and the rocks up which he lightly climbed. At the top he was still some ten feet below the top of the wall, but he was high enough to be out of sight of the guards when they passed below. He turned and with his dagger began to cut away at the padding between the upright logs which formed the stockade until he had made a chink giving him a full view of the interior.

Immediately below him, at the foot of the rocks projecting inside, was a small pool with a raised rim, on the surface of which floated lilies, weirdly green in the full moonlight. Beyond this lay a small area filled with shrubs and flower beds, with a narrow path winding through it leading from the pool to the palace buildings a few hundred feet away. All this Ali caught in a glance, but his attention was drawn inevitably to the poolside, where sat the girl of the afternoon, the Princess Latifah. She sat with her hair unbound and with her full-skirted sarong spread around her so that she looked herself like a lily-flower, pale of face as she looked up at the moon, surrounded by the shining green stuff of her dress.

He was struck to the heart by something infinitely sad even in her unmovingness. Breathless, he watched as presently she looked down and began to finger the lavish gold brocade edging of her sleeves, the other hand playing idly across the surface of the pool. Now he could see that there were goldfish in the water, their scales glinting as they passed from shadow to moonlight and back again.

The Princess began to hum, and soon, to sing softly to herself. By straining his ears he could just make out the words, a trite little thing comparing the imprisonment of the fish, in their golden uniforms, within the confines of the pool, to her own predicament, clad in fine clothes trimmed with gold and free only to swim around under restriction. The world could come and admire, but each was really a prisoner with no means to communicate the true position to the audience.

Trite enough, yet true enough, as most trite things are, mused Ali. A voice returned his attention to the scene below and he looked to see a maid approaching, calling her mistress to come and attend upon her uncle. With a last wistful look at the goldfish the Princess rose and followed. He watched her go for a moment then, making sure that the guards had passed below, jumped down and sprinted wildly for the jungle's edge, his heart pounding for more reasons than one. (*But that is sentimentality. And what is wrong with sentimentality? What is dangerous about sentimentality? What is DANGEROUS...?*)

TWELVE:

A bright, sparkling morning, with the dawn's chill still in the air, though the sun had been up for several hours. The glade was hidden among the trees, with mossy banks forming a natural wall around its saucer. The sun seemed to drift smokily through the tightly packed trees and sprawling shrubbery, as lazy as the day it lit, with a pillar of light standing all but solid beneath a storm-torn hole in the leafy roof.

Ali swung and sliced, thrust and withdrew, feeling his muscles become once again a part of him instead of an extra set of extensions. He drew in the raw, green-scented air in steady drafts, the heady pureness of it intoxicating his mind and filling him with a quintessence of the sheer joy of living for living's sake. The cool grass warmed under his bare feet and thrilled his skin like clean linen sheets. The sky was an inverse sea, with absurd islands of white cloud drifting across it, blown by some high wind that did not descend to stir the palm fronds and branches of the jungle.

The long steel blade struck through the air like gold and silver lightning, beautiful but dangerous, a golden eagle solid in its whirling rapidity. He plucked a handful of grass, and as the blades came drifting down, cut through them without hardly disturbing their passage. He heard the sound of voices approaching and sped silently to the safety of a tree-trunk, cautious until he recognized the tones of Hassan and some of the band, who came into the glade bearing bundles on their backs. As Hassan stood staring around him, Ali stepped from behind and touched him lightly on the shoulder with his sword-tip.

Hassan swung around, dropping to a crouch, hand on *keris*.

"You must guard yourself better, Hassan. You'd have been a dead man by now!"

"It's only you! I had expected to meet you here. I have brought the goods you asked for, though it was not so easy to suit Bakar."

"Well, let's not waste time talking, but start to prepare ourselves. Get those bundles unwrapped. Did you get the jewels?"

"Baker showed me."

"And Achmed?"

"He gave me an argument, but I think I managed to reassure him. He knows nothing of the jewels, of course. He does not know exactly what we are planning, and I left him in charge of the camp. I only hope he remains there and doesn't get any ideas of his own, like moving out, or following us."

"We'll just have to trust that his curiosity will keep him there till we return, I'm afraid. Come on, let's get ready."

Just before noon the usual bustle of the market-place was interrupted by the blare of trumpets, ringing out above the multifarious noises of the multitude like a fox's bark in a barnyard. As the fanfare died the crowd turned to see a procession making its way into the open area, its novelty cutting a clear pathway for it. Though small in size the party's precision and compactness made it an object of some note, and it was manifest that a unique impression was formed in the minds of the spectators of its content and intent.

Twelve armed men marched step by step, and at the rear of the group, eight more carried on their shoulders a litter whose very simplicity of design lent it a richness not otherwise apparent. Within the litter sat cross-legged a man who bore himself rigidly, seated upon the one black cushion that occupied it. On his head he wore a white turban unlike those headdresses of local royalty, and in its center it bore a great red jewel. His black velvet tunic and trousers were modestly embroidered with silver thread, and his eyes looked neither left nor right.

It was remarked that his face was uncovered.

The guards, the litter-bearers trotting lightly under their burden, the dapper man who seemed to be chief of the guards, and the giant who walked by the side of his master, all wore strange headgear which completely surrounded the face in white cloth and which included as an integral part a cloth which veiled the face from just below the eyes.

Like their master the escort looked only straight ahead, as though assuming that the crowd would naturally part before their course, with an inherent insolence. The citizenry fell back amazed indeed, and as two of the escort raised their trumpets in another fanfare the party passed from the marketplace and approached the Istana, leaving behind a wondering mass of mutterings.

"Did you see that sword laid across his knees?"

"That was no Malayan sword!"

"Those were not Malayans, in those uniforms."

"Who can they be?"

The crowd returned to its coffee and soup, bargaining and blandishments, curries and conversation.

Meanwhile the well-disciplined caravan had reached the gate, where its appearance caused as much consternation and surprise as in the market. The two sentries outside crossed their spears before the cavalcade and were hastily reinforced by two more who ran out from the interior. The guards' cries of "Who comes?" went unheeded, until an officer of the guard joined them and added his voice to those of his men. At the appearance of this man the leader of the visitors' escort turned to look back questioningly at the man in the litter.

Ali, for such of course the latter was, for the first time moved his gaze to look at his silent interrogator. "*Annamaran sumbaragan ushtuvthan!*" he declared, imperiously.

Hassan, playing the dual role of escort leader and interpreter, spoke to the officer in heavily accented, stumbling Malay. "My master, the Prince Ali of Bohongistan, desires entry to the palace of the Lord Abdul."

The officer asked, deference creeping into his voice, "From whence comes your master; and yourself?"

"We have but lately arrived from India, to which country the fame of your own has spread. The Prince has hastened here in advance of the main caravan, bearing gifts, which are yet unloading on the coast."

Ali had assumed a supercilious and blank expression, but his eyes and ears confirmed what he had expected, that a show of richness would prove to be a sure passport of entry into the Istana, for with an almost obsequious salaam the officer bowed before him, then turned and impatiently ordered his men to open the gates wide and let the royal guests in. So soon as this had been done the fellow whispered a few words in a guard's ear, which sent him running off to the main Istana building. Hassan-the-interpreter blandly turned to learn his master's will, and Ali gave him a quick wink which instantly dissolved into the haughty, patronizing expression he had adopted for his role.

By the time they reached the foot of the Istana steps and the litter had been lowered, the orange-haired and moustached, olive-visaged Abdul was hastening down to meet them, with the plump, wet-eyed Karim following anxiously after. With Hassan's assistance Ali rose from the lowered litter and impassively faced his host-to-be. Without turning his head, he spoke. "*Shehara ademkinagun surrunaminum.*"

"My Lord, the Prince Ali of Bohongistan, gives you

his respects and craves your hospitality," gravely intoned Hassan, interpreting this nonsense.

The Red One inclined his head, the mask of a smile on his face.

"Prince Ali is most welcome to share the meager facilities which we here in 'Dak Betul can offer. In the name of Princess Latifah, I, her uncle Abdul, welcome your master."

"Your caravan follows?" asked Karim, fingers toying with bracelets; a remark which drew a sharp warning glance from Abdul.

Hassan translated. *"Inharadan kandahamadan Abdul suri venum, dentirivegum dentirivega mandahamini Latifah. Balakrisna hamad."*

Ali let a slight smile rise to his eyes, and bowed his head. *"Vendrahanchapan kaldaharanum parsum."*

"The Prince Ali thanks you, and asks that your men show similar hospitality to his men. And the caravan will follow in two days."

"Certainly, certainly . . . and never mind the caravan. Be sure we will welcome your men equally. Come, take my arm, Prince, and let me lead you into our humble palace."

With a certain repugnance that he was hard put to conceal, Ali took the proffered arm and they went in together, while Hassan dismissed the guards and bearers who were now surrounded by a group of inquisitive soldiers and servants, before turning on his heel and hastening after Ali, to reach his side and interpret. As Karim also turned to follow he caught the grim eye of Bakar, who all this while had been standing like a pillar. Meeting that stare, Karim ventured a fleeting smile. Bakar reached up and pulled aside his face-cloth, the while continuing to study the other. At the sight of that craggy physiognomy Karim hurried up the steps and into the hall, Bakar striding firmly after, as rigid as an automaton.

Some little time later, after the preliminary courtesies had been exchanged, Ali was installed on a divan similar to Abdul's at one end of the Great Hall of the Istana.

Behind them two servants fanned gently with palm fronds, and below them crouched two others. Karim sat near his master's feet, whilst Bakar stood stiffly to one side of Ali. Hassan, in his part as interpreter and intermediary, hovered between the two principals. *So far everything is smooth,* thought Ali. *I only hope our men will be as successful, and play the part of strangers to the country without suspicion.*

Abdul's dry voice broke into his musing, though he managed to turn a deaf, uncomprehending ear to it.

"So your master has been on a trip to collect tribute for his father, the Rajah, from his overseas possessions?"

Hassan did not bother to interpret this, but replied on his own. "That is right, my lord. He was but now returning to his country with a shipload of gold and jewels, costly gifts, spices and rare perfumes, tribute and taxes from his subjects, and presents from his Governors. And now the ship waits to be watered and provisioned for the next stage of our long voyage to India."

"And you say that a small caravan is on its way here from the ship, with gifts for me . . . for the Princess, that is? There are dangerous rebels in the jungle. Perhaps I should send an escort to protect your men?"

Ali started at this, but Hassan replied, off-handedly. "I think that will not be necessary, my lord, for our men are armed and well-disciplined, and I do not think your rebels could ambush and attack them with any success."

"Ah, well, then; tell your master the Prince that he is welcome to enjoy my hospitality, such as it is, until his men arrive."

"Ankadrum parabellum Abdul kanawar."

Ali nodded graciously, wondering if there might not be someone who could understand the Indian language, and hoping against hope that their trickery would not be uncovered. He smiled politely at Abdul, and prayed inwardly that it did not appear to be as false as the one he received in return. Karim touched his master's foot, and muttered something to him.

"Ah, yes," said the Red One, turning to Hassan. "If

you will follow my servant, he will show you your lord's quarters." There seemed to be no alternative but to obey, and the Captain left to go after the servant. Silence fell. Ali waited for something to happen. Silence continued. Finally Abdul beckoned the remaining servant and told him to inform the Princess Latifah that she must make herself ready for the dance, for he wished her to entertain his royal guest. Abdul smiled at Ali, who returned it blandly, and in an aside to Karim added, "Were this deaf fool not royal it might shame us for the Princess to dance before him; but it is time that she received another reminder that it is my hands alone which prevent her destruction, and that of Princess Meriam, when we catch the brat. And in any case, the dance will distract him while I talk with you. I am beginning to see a scheme before me."

Abruptly, as though aware of being impolite, he bowed slightly to his guest, who exchanged the courtesy, afraid that his empty expression would somehow reveal the excitement he felt at this last revelation. The Red One offered a plate of sweetmeats which Ali studied thoughtfully before accepting one and popping it into his mouth. His mind was already turning to thoughts of possible poison attempts. Treachery was about to be launched into the air, that was sure. He only hoped that Hassan would not return prematurely, so that he could continue to eavesdrop on the intended conversation and unconcealed confidences of his double-dealing host.

At this moment the sounds of drum and pipe were heard and into the hall before them came four musicians, beating and fluting, who settled down to one side of the steps, keeping time and melody for the troupe of dancers who followed. Some twenty dancers filed in, all girls, as Ali noticed, though half of them were dressed in male clothing, with their hair hidden beneath the stiff turbans of the Malay. In the center of the group, which opened out into a circle, was the veiled figure of a girl.

In a way the dance was a disappointment to Ali, for it seemed to be nothing more than a formalized national ritual of some kind, with intricate steps and movements which apparently symbolized some courtship myth. The central figure was graceful and skillful enough, but performed with modesty and discretion. In another way he was glad of the somewhat boring performance, for the snatches of conversation he overheard between Abdul and his henchman provided heady entertainment. Glancing to see that the guest was properly enthralled by the dance, Karim began.

"My lord, you are hoping that Prince Ali's gift to you will be large?"

"I care not for his presents and gifts; I plan to take all the wealth he bears!"

"But how will that be possible?"

"If I understand aright—and bear me out in what I say—then nobody in his own country knows of his visit to our shores. I take it that this trip here was merely capricious, and was for water to replace that stored in leaky barrels, and for provender to replace that which had rotted."

"That is as the interpreter related it."

"Then I will endeavor to persuade this Prince to send for his ship to come up the river here to 'Dak Betul, so that he may board it without the troublesome journey back through the jungle. And when his ship, his men, and his wealth are all here, we will sink the one, kill the other, and make ourselves rich. His father will undoubtedly surmise he has been lost at sea."

"And if he will not be persuaded?"

"I think the Princess Latifah will help us in that."

Ali could hardly repress a grin of sheer satisfaction. He had been wondering all along how he might get the Princess alone, and now it seemed that the opposition was about to play right into his hands.

The dance was meanwhile coming to an end, and one of the "males" reached forward and stripped the veil from the central dancer's head. As he caught sight again of that beautiful young face he felt a shock go through him, and his heart seemed to sing like a plucked harp string, a thrum of something more than mere desire, though indeed the girl was desirable enough, with her coal-black hair now plaited and coiled by each cheek, and her loose open-necked overdress falling forward from her shoulders as she curtsied deeply, to reveal the upper reaches of her breasts. Rising, she caught Ali's eyes upon her, and blushed slightly before disdainfully turning her head.

Hassan had quietly returned by now, and as he approached, Abdul told him to inform his master that he would introduce the Princess Latifah to him. While the Captain "translated" this, Abdul beckoned to the Princess who came forward to him with a wariness hardly apparent.

"My dear, this is the Prince Ali of Bohongistan, from India. I wish you to show him the courtesies of the court, and entertain him . . . in any way you think fit."

Ali stood and bowed to the girl, then muttered to Hassan, who turned to Abdul.

"Prince Ali wonders whether the Princess could show him the gardens, sire; he feels a need for fresh air."

"Certainly, certainly. Latifah, my dear?"

With a reluctance ill-concealed the Princess smiled at her uncle and at Ali, and waited for the latter to join her. As Hassan was about to follow his master, whom Bakar was already joining, Abdul caught at his sleeve and whispered, "And you may tell your royal master, oh, discreetly, of course, that should he wish for, let us say, a more intimate form of female entertainment during his stay—perhaps tonight?—then I will gladly provide him with whatever he desires in that direction."

Hassan nodded and hastened after the others. As he caught up, Ali dropped back a pace and murmured, "I'm anxious to learn something of the rest of our band. I hope that they are playing their parts without fear of detection. Later, when we are in the garden, slip away and check."

The four walked along several corridors to a doorway which led them out into what Ali realized was the garden that he had spied into earlier. Through Hassan he had exchanged pleasantries with the Princess and he was confident that she thought him no more than a polite and ingenuous nonentity. With a warning gesture he indicated that the other two should drop behind, and meanwhile he continued to stroll with Latifah through the unelaborate shrubbery until they came near to the fish pond. As they meandered the girl started to say something to him, but then, realizing that he could not understand, pouted in exasperation, the while he smiled courteously at her, as though thanking her for her attempted good intentions. They stood alone for a moment at the pool, the Princess tapping her foot. Then he could have sworn a grin of devilment swept over her face, before she glanced to see that they were out of earshot of the others, then looked at him. *Has she found me out?* he wondered.

However, it seemed that the Princess Latifah was in a mood to assuage her bitterness with some amusement at the expense of her victim. She pointed to a small flower growing among the rocks and said, stressing each separate syllable as though addressing a child, "This—is—a—palm—tree. Palm . . . tree. . . ."

Repressing a grin of his own, but playing to the hilt the role he seemed to have been chosen for, he nodded gravely and repeated, "Palm—tree. *Dega. Deeee-gaaa.*"

She pointed to a sprig of some grassy plant and said, "Co-co-nut."

"Co-co-nut. Mmm, *kam-par-i-tan-ni!*"

With no hint of a smile on her face the girl pointed to her own body.

"Cat!"

Laughing inwardly at the thought of what would happen if he expressed his desire for a girl to Abdul the Red One after this lesson, Ali pretended to misunderstand her intention entirely, and made as if to embrace her. The startled Princess cried "No! No!" causing Hassan and Bakar to look sharply at them from across the garden. Surreptitiously Ali waved Hassan to vanish, looking disappointed and crestfallen for Latifah's benefit. He noticed Hassan's quiet departure and hoped to himself that all was well.

It wasn't until much later, after the action was all over, that he learned from Hassan what had happened.

Meanwhile, however, he continued to amuse himself at the expense of the Princess, who herself was intent on getting back at him for his earlier miscalculation. Pointing at a coconut-sized rock, she said, "Your head."

Ali almost gave himself away by repeating, "My head," but he caught himself in time and repeated the phrase correctly. Then, deciding to take a bolder hand in the game, he pointed to one of the swimming goldfish and said, "La-ti-fah!" She glanced at him with a hint of suspicion in her voice and repeated the name with a questioning lilt at the end. As though not understanding the cause for her note of inquiry he nodded gravely and said again, pointing to the fish, "La-ti-fah!" She decided to take this as a compliment of some kind, apparently, and dutifully simpered, but her expression changed to one of outrage as he pointed to her back, mimed a fish flicking its tail, with his hands; then swayed his hips extravagantly, all the while smiling sweetly at her. "La-ti-fah!" he repeated, nodding. She turned away, but not before he had surprised a flash of annoyance in her eyes. He followed her from the pool and caught up with her along the path.

Attracting her attention he pointed in a circle around the garden and inquired, "Kindah?"

"That is 'bo-dy,'" she replied.

"Ah, bo-dy. Mmm." Then, pointing at himself he asked, "Kinidah?"

"Oh, that," she answered immediately. "That is called 'garden,'" pointing to her own body.

Ali regarded her with his assumed expression of patient inquiry, and in Malay said, "You have a very beautiful 'garden,' and I would be most happy to be its gardener."

For a few seconds the remark made no impression upon her, as she automatically started to work out in her own mind whether the Prince was talking about her "garden-garden" or her "body-garden." Then it struck her like a blow that the supposed foreign royal dignitary had just spoken in her own language. Her eyes grew wide with alarm and astonishment, and her hand flew up to her burning cheeks as she realized the possible results of the foolery she had been up to. Ali continued to gaze at her with his air of bored politeness. Her own

107

expression changed to one of fear and, putting her fist to her mouth, she turned to run, but he caught at her arm, dragging her to him.

"Fair sport, my Princess. You cannot deny that we have scored equal points in this little duel?"

"Who . . . who are you, that comes as a stranger, and reveals himself as two-tongued? Is this another plot of my uncle's?"

"Two-tongued, perhaps. And this is a plot *against* your uncle, with your assistance. I am truly Prince Ali of India, but I have set myself to destroy Abdul the Red One, and to restore the Princess Meriam as ruler of this country."

She had regained her composure now, though her cheeks were pale. She snatched her arm from his grasp. "You lie! This is another trick of my scheming uncle to find out whether or not I am loyal to him. Else why should he warn me to pay special attention to you?"

"Because he plans to use you to hold me here until he can assassinate me!"

"I cannot believe you!"

Ali was racking his brains for some solution to this impasse, some proof that he could give this lonely girl that friends were abroad, when the door into the garden burst open and Hassan dashed in. Running up to Ali, with the alerted Bakar close behind, he looked at the Prince and the Princess, surmised correctly that Ali had revealed himself to her, and blurted out, "Ali! You must come quickly, and get out of here. We have been surprised in the marketplace, and our men are fighting with Abdul's guards!"

THIRTEEN:

When Hassan had first slipped away from the garden (he recounted later to Ali), he had found that their band had wandered off to the market, no doubt to be shown off as curiosities to the populace by Abdul's guards. Some of them were eating, being introduced to many "strange" foods by their hosts, and gradually "learning" odd words of the Malay language. As instructed they had intimated by gesture that the covering up of their faces had some religious significance in their country and now, when they ate, they were careful not to disarrange their face-cloths.

Hassan had signaled for two of his men to join him, to learn whether they had picked up any useful information, and the three sauntered over to the snake charmer as if intent on his performance. Recognizing the erstwhile interpreter, one of Abdul's men, the off-duty guard commander, came pleasantly over, and Hassan guessed that he, too, was to be mined for information.

It developed, however, that there was no time at all for such exchanges.

The trouble started casually. The commander, speaking slowly, pointed to the snake charmer and asked, "You—like—to—see—this?"

Hassan nodded, not taking a great deal of notice, but, not to be rebuffed so easily, the other continued, "In—your—country—you—have—many?"

Hassan nodded again, a little impatiently. But the next slow remark shook him to the roots. "This—man—comes —from—your—country!"

The Captain began to sweat, and wondered how in the name of Allah he could change the subject, or leave, without arousing any suspicion.

But before he could get a chance to think of something the friendly commander clutched the sleeve of his tunic and drew him forward to the snake charmer, saying to the old man, "Hey, Babu; here is someone who speaks your language."

The old man looked up, pleased and startled both, and burst into a rapid spate of Indian. Hassau attempted to stammer out some kind of noncommittal series of grunts, but the more he nodded and grinned, the more the Indian continued, until at length the snake charmer stopped in surprise and indignation. The look of shock and distaste on his wrinkled visage was such that the commander looked sharply from one to the other of them. All might have gone well, perhaps, even then, but one of the two men with Hassan, sensing the situation and too eager for his own good and that of his companions, dropped his hand to his *parang*. Despite Hassan's warning gesture it was too late; the commander had seen the instinctive move. With a face shocked into wide-eyed suspicion the officer tore off Hassan's face-cloth and gasped out, "Hassan; the Captain of the Guard!"

Throwing all caution to the winds now, Hassan bent quickly, scooped up the basket of snakes, and flung the whole thing into the commander's face. Then, drawing his scimitar, he cried above the sudden-stilled throng, "For Meriam and liberty! To me, to me!"

At this rallying call the rebels drew their *parangs* and backed to Hassan's side. Luckily Abdul's men were partly unarmed, as they were off-duty, but those that were with weapons greatly outnumbered still Hassan's small group. Some of the others from the palace grabbed up such improvised arms as metal soup-ladles and vegetable-choppers and joined their comrades in a great semicircle. Fortunately for Hassan his party was at one end of the market near the street entrance, in a fairly open section, while Abdul's soldiers had to advance through the still uncomprehending citizens and the haphazard stalls. Quickly deciding that in this case, at least, attack was the best defense, the Captain led his group to beyond the first row of stalls and made his line there.

For several minutes the fight raged hot and furious, with stalls knocked to the ground and the produce under foot. Melons and coconuts rolled treacherously among the legs of the men, and eggs and vegetables made the footing even more slippery and insecure.

Chickens, forced from their coops, fluttered in and out amongst the fighters, and feathers, dust and oaths filled the air in about equal proportions. With a deafening clang a stall full of metalware toppled and sank to the ground, burying a couple of the guards, while another soldier, with a scream, was knocked into the coffee-seller's boiling cauldron. One fellow was sent reeling into the watching crowd, and in a glimpse between the wrecked stalls, which by now looked like some storm-tossed armada grounded on a reef, Hassan saw a town-man's arm sneak out and hit the hated tyrant's man over the head with a copper pot.

Hassan fell back and reformed his thinned ranks a few feet on the open side of the line of stalls, giving the enemy just enough encouragement to try to gain sword-swinging room between his men and the wooden shambles. There was no hope of final victory, but he needed time to warn Ali. In a temporary lull he told the man next to him to hold out where he was for as long as possible, and then retreat only so far as the end of the street, and hold that position at all costs till he returned.

He dashed through the Istana gates, which were not in sight of the marketplace, and shouted to the curious gate-keepers that on no account were they to move from their posts till their master, Abdul, gave the word. He gave the same message to the guards at the Istana steps, then sped by the back passages he knew well to the garden, where he blurted out his message.

Ali thought quickly, while the Princess, for whom events were moving too fast, stood immobile. Turning to her he made her face Hassan, whose face-cloth dangled at his throat.

"Look, Princess, do you recognize Hassan, late Captain of the Palace Guard?"

"Of course," she said, startled. "Why, Hassan, what . . ."

Ali had no time to waste. "He is with me. Now do you believe?"

"Yes. . . . I do not understand, but . . . you are in danger?"

"Right. I had hoped for more time but it seems I must somehow arrange to come back yet one more time. For now, I leave you."

He took her hand and kissed it, then spun on his heel and was about to dash from the garden when she called: "Prince Ali! I must trust you. If you want to find the Princess Meriam, tell Hassan to take you to the wood-cutter's hut near the great white rock to the north of the jungle."

He stared fixedly at her. "Remember, we too must

111

trust you. I hope that your information is true. I shall return here, have no fear, and if you have lied, then . . ."

"The Princess Latifah never lies!"

He made a mock bow and laughed at her. "Only about gardens and bodies, eh? Well, we shall see. Until we meet again, may Allah protect you!"

Hassan and Bakar were waiting anxiously near the garden door, and he was about to join them when a thought struck him, and he looked back at the rockery near the pool. On this side of the palisade it came to within six feet of the top, built up artificially. With a whistle he called the other two over to his side. Like cats they scrambled up the rocks, climbed the fence, and perched on the top, checking to see if the guards were near.

"You had better disarrange your clothing and claim that we forced you not to cry out," Ali called back to the watching Princess, in a low voice, and then dropped to the rocks below to join his two companions.

He had hoped that the alarm had not yet been sounded at the Istana, but as they approached the corner of the wall they discovered that the sentry on this beat had deserted it to run to the main gate, where his fellows were excitedly conferring. There was no other way to get to the market save past the gate. The three at first attempted to run in file close to the stockade, so as to get past the guards before they were seen, but while they were still some thirty yards short of their goal a troop of a dozen or so men came out through the gate, obviously intended as reinforcements and surprise force, to take Hassan's band from the rear.

With ululating cries, Ali sprang forward, his sword out and flashing in the evening sun. With a yell, Hassan was alongside, his scimitar in his right and his *keris* in his left. A glance to his left showed Ali that Bakar, too, with his great club, was pacing him.

The men at the gate swung around at the shout and the three companions were upon them almost before they could draw their *parangs*. The fierceness of this surprise attack drove Abdul's men into the jaws of the gateway itself, and in that compressed space only a few

112

of them at a time could face the three. With Bakar in the center wielding his knotty timber in vast swooping circles which made a bay in the shore of blades against them, Ali and Hassan picked and hacked away at the headlands. Ali lunged, his sword flickering, keeping the two who opposed him directly at a respectable distance. A stamp and a thrust and one of them was permanently dispatched, but in the second it took him to withdraw his blade, the other sliced at his head, so that he crouched, off balance. As the too-eager soldier rushed in for a final blow Ali plucked loose his sword and in a mighty upthrust took the man through the heart.

The rushing body fell on him and he went down under its dead onslaught, so that two more guards rushed forward to revenge their comrades. Crash! came Bakar's club, streaking sideways in his fist. The nearest man stumbled, unconscious, into the other, and Ali's sword was out, in, and out again almost before Bakar had brought his club back into its regular circular swing.

Bakar had already taken another man on his own account, and another lay crumpled and still at Hassan's feet.

Six of the enemy had fallen in ten times that number of seconds, and now the remnants of the band drew back warily, afraid to approach these master killers. There was a whispered consultation at the end of the alley leading in from the gate, and one of the men went off, the remainder standing their ground as though fearful that these three would attempt to storm the palace by themselves. With little to do but maintain his position, Ali debated with himself whether to beat a hasty retreat or not. Obviously there was no point in entering the palace grounds again, apart from the fact that once they were past the alley's end they could easily be surrounded. On the other hand, if they just turned and fled, a volley of spears might soon catch them. Fortunately spears had not yet been brought into action, though he remembered Hassan's recital of his first escape through this very gate.

At the thought of the gate itself, and Hassan's previous adventure, his mind began to work in other direc-

113

tions. If somehow they could close the gate behind them, the delay would give them enough time to make good their escape now. He eyed the wooden leaves as his hand kept up its continuous thrust-and-cut. Above him and to the left he could see the ropes which must lead to the pulleys which operated the gates. These must work on the principle of sheer gravity. Left alone, the gates would swing tight shut against an attacker, and would have to be wound back by the pulleys to be opened again. His thought was cut short by the sound of hooves.

From behind the Red One's men came galloping three horsemen, and the defenders parted to let the three animals charge side by side through the slot of the alley. If before they had allowed themselves to be drawn into the lure of this same alley, then now they would have been finished as the great beasts came thundering down on them. As it was, both Ali and Hassan darted quickly to the shelter of their neighboring walls, but with a shock of despair Ali saw that Bakar remained where he was in the center, crouched down, as if spell-bound and hypnotized by the charging horses.

Ali closed his eyes sickly against the inevitable death of his servant and friend but he was forced to open them again at the sound of the terrified neigh of a horse. To his amazement he saw that the giant had sprung up immediately before the center horse, swinging his club. At this sudden, unexpected apparition the beast had reared up, forelegs pawing at the air, but at the same time decanting its startled rider to the ground behind it. The two flanking horsemen had gone rushing by, unable to do more than control their mounts in the confining space of the alley, and now Bakar flung himself to one side as the flailing hooves of the riderless horse came down. As soon as the animal was back on all fours, the giant took two steps and with a bound threw himself up onto the saddle blankets, seizing the loose reins.

All this happened in seconds, and Ali took it in at a glance. And then the idea hit him and he began to run, urging Hassan after him. The two remaining horsemen had to rein hard and turn their steeds in a tight circle to return in their tracks, and as the beasts were almost at a halt, Ali and Hassan ran around to the blind side of the busy riders and leaped up, pulling each man to the earth. Ali stamped on the throat of his man, catching at the reins at the same time, then vaulted into the saddle in time to see Hassan galloping at full stretch down the road after Bakar, who was himself urging his newfound mount on to further efforts. Swinging around, Ali made a brief sortie at the gateway, driving back those few brave spirits who had dared to attempt exit, then, standing tall in the rope stirrups of his steed, took one tremendous slash at the ropes above the gate. As he lay flat against the neck of his mount and pursued his comrades down the road he heard the gates fall to with a resounding crash.

His was the fleeter beast, and he caught up with the others just before the three of them swept into the market. Only ten men remained of their original band, and they had fallen back across the road behind a couple of stalls that they had collected in their retreat. As he approached the barrier Ali felt his soul sing with the thrill of action, speed and danger. He gathered his mount under him and they went soaring over the ruined stalls, causing instantaneous confusion among Abdul's guards as he landed among them, swinging his sword like a saber. Hassan came flying over to join him and they wheeled and wheeled and wheeled again, waterspouts of steel in the dusty marketplace.

A quick glance showed him Bakar leading the rest of the rebels off, acting as front flank guard against any possible reinforcements from the palace. With a shout to Hassan he changed tactics, turning his mount sideways to the enemy, advancing crablike with his sword weaving in great circles, the Captain doing the same with his own mount, till the Red One's soldiers, those that remained, broke and ran for the comparative safety of the wrecked stalls further up the square, some of which were now ablaze. Another shout to Hassan and the pair was off in retreat, neck and neck through the air above the barricade, neck and neck, leg to leg up the road, then a swing around to the right, straight into the setting sun, lighting the road ahead of them to golden, glowing embers of the day, the jungle and the rest of their weary band before them.

FOURTEEN:

The rest of the party were already changing back from their hastily prepared uniforms into their usual minimum forest wear when Ali, Hassan and Bakar, leading their horses through the dense undergrowth, entered the clearing. Leaving the beasts on a loose tether to crop the long grass, the Prince led Hassan to one side. The young Captain was intent to know the value of the trip.

"Did you learn anything in the Istana? I learned nothing except that in armed men alone, Abdul's contingent outnumbers us, and that although they would be reluctant to rise in open rebellion at this time, the citizens are for us and the Princess Meriam, against the uncaring tyranny of the Red One."

"I'm glad to have my own feelings confirmed. For the first, I think that our better trained and disciplined force can safely withstand any onslaught from Abdul's men, if we are properly armed, and given only a small element of surprise. And I think that our little foray back there in 'Dak Betul will encourage the citizens, and may indeed lead to an increase in recruits to our cause. On my own part I was able, as you discovered, to bear out my expectation that the Princess Latifah is wholly with us. Or at least, one small point will hammer the belief home for me. Do you know the woodcutter's hut near a great white rock to the north of the jungle?"

"Why yes; but what of it? It is an uninhabited part of the jungle, and the woodcutter whom I knew there was a hermit, trekking into the city but three or four times a year. But he has been dead these past two years, and his hut untenanted. Why do you ask?"

"My lady, the Princess Latifah, assured me that Meriam was there; I suppose in the safekeeping of the maid Saripah you spoke to me of."

"Saripah! Ye—ess. Now why didn't I ever think to look there. I remember having told the wench of the place."

"Well, then, I think that so soon as the horses are fed, watered and rested you had best go and bring Meriam to our camp. If Abdul suspects that Latifah is sympathetic toward us and has the knowledge she has given us, then he may try to force her to tell him; and with Meriam in his hands I fear that we would have to give up our Cause lest harm befall the child. Yes, you and Bakar shall take two of the horses and leave from here, using all due speed and precautions. I will lead the rest of our band back to the camp, and see what friend Achmed has been up to in the meantime."

Later in the day, rested and refreshed, the two men swung up into their saddles and prepared to leave on their mission. Before they left, Ali touched Bakar on the thigh.

"I want to thank you, Bakar, for saving my life, back there at the battle of the gate. You came here as my servant only, and I would have expected only faithful service from you. But you have done more than that—you have offered more than the body of your service. From now on you are your own master, and I shall treat you as a comrade; *a* man, rather than *my* man."

The giant on horseback looked at him silently, and Ali was horrified to see that he was close to tears. Then Bakar reached down, touched the Prince, his ex-master, lightly on the shoulder, then raised his great club in a salute before digging his bare heels into his mount's flanks and crashing off through the thick brush, followed by the surprised Hassan.

Ali watched them disappear rapidly among the trees before throwing himself to the ground, aching for sleep.

As the light from the sun far above him bruised his eyelids in a warm thrum of peace, something began to crawl forward from the back of his mind, an amorphous shape that he could not define and could not bring into

117

clear resolution, for the more he attempted to focus his consciousness upon it, the more blurred became its outline. The wavering vision became an oscillating note which, as he became more drowsy, clarified into words; words which he could not make out, syllable by syllable, but whose intent and content he divined as though by a process of filtering. He received an impression of warning, of alarm, of danger impending.

Blurred patches of fantastic dream came to him, fragments, some related, some irrelevant, some featuring scenes and people he knew, some of a nightmarish quality populated by creatures whose substance and meaning were unfamiliar to him, and frightening.

The final shock came to him on awakening, but in that small stretched second between sleep and full consciousness the beads of dream strung themselves out on the cord of recollection. . . .

(Bakar and Hassan jog along on horseback, going along a little-used, hardly defined track in the jungle, their faces dappled by the shadows of leaves in the late afternoon sunshine. Hassan whistles a meandering tune in keeping with the changing rhythms of movement, scene, direction and mood. . . .)

(Latifah, veiled, dancing in the Istana, her movements graceful but restrained, surrounded by a group of others, the others then fading into the background, beyond the periphery of vision, while a golden light glows around her figure which continues to sway but now has changed to a more sensuous movement that continues to throb until with a sudden wild downslash with the hands before her the costume parts, splits, and floats downward to the floor, leaving her naked and veiled about the face only, while she returns to swaying ever so slightly, imperceptibly turning her body around on the balls of her toes, hands above her head, maintaining the slow undulations of her body, head now fallen down upon her shoulders, face upturned, the cloth of the veil deliberately defining the features concealed, lips parted, her nude body now beginning to

118

lose itself among the mysteriously changing display of colored lights. . . .)

(Bakar and Hassan riding cautiously out of the jungle into a large clearing, in which stands a simple hut. A little girl of about three years of age is playing by herself just outside the door, addressing herself to the task of singing to sleep a crude wooden doll, wrapped in a piece of cloth. As the horses walk silently across the padding grass she does not see them, but looks up, startled but unafraid, as the long shadow of the tall Bakar falls across her plaything. Her eyes fixed upon the two visitors, she calls, "Saripah! Saripah! Saripah! Come see! Two big men here. Come see! Saripah!"

The two men ride toward the long grass at one side of the hut, dismount, leaving the horses to graze, and walk back toward the little girl. The urchin-faced Saripah runs out of the door, clutching the Princess up to her before she looks up to see the men. Meriam squirms around in her guardian's arms to look also, still nothing more than gravely and pleasantly interested, while Saripah's expression changes from one of alerted wariness to one of delighted relief as she recognizes the Captain.

"Oh, Captain Hassan! How did you know we were here, or has some unlucky wind blown you this far from your duties? I thought that we were buried from the world here."

"There would be nothing unlucky about any breeze which wafted me in your direction, Saripah . . . but it is no breeze at all that brings me here, but a storm of protest, of rebellion. I, we, my friend Bakar here and myself, have come to raise you from your burial ground and take you with us back to life."

"Come. Come, both of you; come inside and eat with us, and tell me what you mean. What rebellion do you speak of, and where will you take us?"

"Since you have the kindness to invite us, we will enter and eat, though we do not have time for much talk before we leave. We are hungry and saddle sore, and I thank you for myself and on behalf of Bakar here, who is dumb and cannot thank you for himself."

119

The big man, who has been rolling his eyes in a terrible way at the mock-frightened Meriam, hiding behind Saripah's legs, smiles at the girl. As they enter the hut Bakar gravely offers his finger to Meriam to take, which she as gravely accepts, going into the place as regally as if she were on the arm of a Prince. . . .)

(A strange place, a kind of cube, viewed from inside, looking up, with colors subtly revealed, black for white, pleasant leaf-greens contorted to violent reds when observed closely. Seen through a filter, as though both participating and unseen, and observing yet unconscious. Two grotesques leaning over, looking down, black-clad, black-faced, black-haired.

"Is he gone over yet, Doctor?"

"No, Teri, he is not yet gone over, but he is very near to being over."

"How soon do you think it will be?"

"There is absolutely no way of telling how long it will be, or even if he is to go over at all, as I had hoped you would by now have known."

"Yes, Doctor; I suppose I should know. But we have not had too much experience."

"No, that's true. Only ourselves, and that one other. But do I detect a tone of . . . sadness in your voice?"

"Perhaps a little. He's such a pleasant and somehow naturally innocent young man."

"Now, now, Teri; you know as well as I do that sentimentality has to be viewed correctly, and properly evaluated in any situation. If he goes over, you know, as do I, that he will be no more deprived or exalted than he would be here. And if he does not go over, if he does not meet a real or suspicioned-real personality or situation over *there*, then he will return *here* exalted indeed, but with a counterbalanced deprivation when he sets up his mind's comparison of this and that reality.

"Just at this moment, as the equipment recording his reactions shows, he is balanced on the watershed, and his river of reality can run either way. It will take just that one meeting, that one little incident, to make *there* more real to him than *here*. If his transferred personality remains as true to itself as the profile I designed indicated, then he should have already begun to *feel* over there; to experience emotions far deeper than the crude instinctive reactions of instantly provoked anger and absurdly initiated humor. His physical self is of course in full command over there, with no responses on this side to stir it. At this stage his intellect should now begin to operate on that side, so that only his emotions cause the balance to waver this way or that.

"And once an awareness of the *there* reality impinges on his three parts at once, then he will be wholly gone over."

"And still he barely sleeps here, and dreams there."

"Or sleeps there, and dreams here. . . .")

(Riding back through the jungle, Bakar has Meriam mounted before him, standing upright on the padded blankets that form the saddle, leaning back into his strong arms, her curly head nestled into his chin. On the other horse Saripah is likewise mounted before Hassan, sitting on the blanket pad, seated sidewise, her pretty, barefoot legs swinging gaily to the movements of the animal. She looks slyly up at him, as he sits easy and tight, reluctant, apparently, to take advantage of the situation, and ignoring the warm fragrance which must drift to him from her hair, which flickers occasionally against his breast and brushes his cheeks.

Meriam is fascinated by the dumb Bakar and prattles relentlessly, turning to him for confirmation of some point she is making, while he in turn is pleasantly and rather proudly embarrassed by her admiration. He winks at her and she throws her arms around his huge-sinewed neck. He shrugs helplessly as Hassan catches sight of the byplay and bursts into laughter, bringing a warm smile of liking for the gentle giant to the otherwise pert face of Saripah. . . .)

(An awakening from a sleep to find in his arms a curiously strange girl with oddly shaped eyes, his attention distracted by the sight of weird objects of unknown

121

use furnishing a background to a disturbingly . . . unfamiliar? . . . room . . .

. . . and a memory of long blonde hair, peculiarly unnatural but not unbeautiful, falling across his face in the night . . .

. . . and a maelstrom of sensations, whirling him inward to a blue and placid sea lying at the center of a black and golden storm in which memories were cast up and capsized . . .

. . . including an awakening to the prodding of a spearshaft of sun on a morning yesterday? yesteryear? yesterwhen? in a hauntingly remembered bed . . .

. . . in which never had slept in his arms a Princess black-haired, liquid-eyed as the houries, scented of jasmine and skinned in warm, dark velvet; or a golden-haired girl so soft and white and fair of body that the glow of her health seemed to have as its emanation a clean yet pure yet never sterile essence . . .)

Part Three: The Emperor's Butterfly

ONE:

. . . AND THEN the long-stemmed, brightly-colored flowers of the dreams bobbed and bowed disturbed in the breeze of another awakening (*what day that follows what night?*) on a cool dawn in which the sun had not yet burned off the mists, all rose-pink and pearly and translucent, sparkling and invigorating. . . .

Round the glowing embers of the main campfire some of our men were already gathered, speaking little, speech still stumbled by the night, waiting for water to boil, wiping dew from their weapons, stretching their hands out to the warmth. It took me a few seconds to realize where I was, my mind being a little confused after the heavy sleep into which I had fallen, but here I was, right enough, back at our base camp, with surly old Achmed over there with his particular cronies. I wondered again just how trustworthy he was. I had only been back in camp for a day, for since I had sent Hassan and Bakar on their mission I had sent two of our men into the city of 'Dak Betul again to see what impression our fight had made on the citizenry, and they had returned with glowing reports of our risen popularity, and with a dozen or more recruits, all of whom I had to study and examine for signs of possible treachery before allowing them to accompany us back to the camp.

I'd had a hard day trying to teach them the rudiments of my way of fighting, and I'd hoped to sleep late that morning but what had woken me up, apparently, was the challenge of one of our guards—"Who comes?"

I came quickly to my feet and strode over to the entrance. As I'd expected, it was Hassan and Bakar returned, and they came into the camp leading their horses, with a little girl and a maiden sitting on the backs of the animals. Oddly enough the faces of the two girls seemed somehow familiar, but I couldn't track down the elusive memory as I walked the short distance toward them. As I came up they halted and while Hassan handed the maid down, gentle Bakar lifted the little girl and sat her on his broad shoulder, where she looked around curiously at our rough group, who had begun to wander over. Two of them led the horses aside to where my own was grazing, while Hassan made the introductions.

"This is the Princess Meriam, Prince Ali." (For so he now called me, since our adventure into the city, mocking but uncertain.) I dropped to one knee before her as she sat above Bakar's great head.

"Welcome to our camp, Your Highness."

The chit carried herself well, as a Princess should, and looked down at me with a depth of expression and gravity that would have served an aged monarch proud, and said, with that clarity of tone common to true royalty and wandering actors, "I thank you, Prince Ali. It is good of you to assist me. Our country will honor your heroes."

Then she rubbed her eyes sleepily, for even Princesses of the blood are not immune to the effects of long journeys and short nights.

Hassan introduced the maid Saripah to me, and she acknowledged me with an appraising eye and a brief curtsy. A wench with a mind of her own, and not some servile servant, I decided. She reached up to lift the Princess down, and Bakar dropped to one knee to help her, and remained there as Saripah held her in her arms. I looked at Bakar, startled for a moment, then noticed a stillness in the camp, and turned to see that every man of them, old and young, rebel and bandit, rascal and zealot, was down on his knee, in honor of Meriam, their Princess and Queen-to-be. Every man except Achmed, that is, but he abruptly and obsequiously dropped as he caught my eye. I pointed out to Hassan the small hut of fresh branches we had built yesterday for the shelter of Meriam and her maid, and he took Saripah and her charge over to it, and nobody rose until they were out of sight, and then they burst into such a babble of sound that I had to turn on them and order them to be quiet lest they disturb the sleep of the little Princess.

I waited for Hassan to return and then strolled with him over to the fire, for the morning was still chill on my naked chest, but the shivers I felt were more for the joy of living than of cold, I swear. The green-wood smoke of the branches newly flung on the fire teased the nostrils, and the odors of bubbling, boiling, and spitting pots and pans added themselves like a profane incense. With my arm around Hassan's shoulder I congratulated him on the quick and successful outcome of his trip, and he assured me that he and Bakar had met with no untoward incident at all. I told him of the new recruits we had garnered while we waited for one of the men to prepare some food for us.

"Yes, we're going to need all the men we can get, my Prince. We may have enough for a quick skirmish, but even if the population as a whole is on our side, we need more trained fighters if we are to even hope to destroy Abdul the Red One and his men."

Bakar had followed the Princess to her shelter, and now he returned, accompanied by Saripah, who looked as fresh as a fancy despite the long journey, and who

124

now went over to lend a hand to the cook. I struck Bakar on the thigh as he squatted by me, a gesture which told him, I think, better than any thousand words I could have conjured up, how pleased I was with him.

Hassan continued in his pessimism. "Even with a larger force of trained men the city is too large and open for us to lay siege, and in spite of the ease with which you got us into the grounds that night, and last time, the Istana itself can be easily defended, and will be, now that the Red One is aware of our existence."

Needless to say I had been thinking about this very problem, and told him so. "We have to use minds where we lack men, Hassan. Now, I have a plan which I am certain will lead to success in the end; but to achieve it means that we must somehow make our way once again into the Istana secretly. Just this one time more. And, as you say, it will be heavily guarded now, and the guards will not easily be fooled as they were the last time. I think we outstayed our welcome then, but somehow we must think of a way to get in there."

Surprisingly it was Saripah who replied to this, the while handing us bowls of hot rice, meat and vegetables. "I'm sure I know of a way we can enter, Prince. But how many people will need to go inside—the least number possible?"

"Are you to be our master-planner, sister Saripah? Welcome to our council. If you indeed have a way, then I think only myself, Hassan, and Bakar need attempt it. And possibly not even Bakar, since he is so outstanding in any company."

"You will need to take me, as your guide. In fact, I will be indispensable."

Hassan (I noticed the rogue pressing her hand) broke in. "But, Ali, that means you will be leaving Achmed in charge here again. And with the Princess Meriam unguarded. Except by Bakar, of course."

I had worried about this myself, but wanted to know how the others felt, and received my answer, for there was doubt and dismay in my Captain's voice, and Bakar growled in his throat and shook his great head. I waited while Hassan explained the situation regarding

Achmed briefly to Saripah, and then spoke. "Yes, you are right, of course. Now that we have the Princess here it could be dangerous, and it would be unwise to tempt Achmed with the possible prize of reward by Abdul, even if he has decided to remain loyal to us so far. Supposing that on this trip we leave Bakar here alone to guard Meriam, while you, Hassan, appoint a deputy to run the camp routine in our absence. Achmed will come with us so that we can keep an eye on him."

The others agreed to this and we leaned forward to listen to Saripah's plan to take us inside the palace.

TWO:

Those coffee-drinkers, vendors and customers in the marketplace of 'Dak Betul who were not too dulled by eminent misery and despair might have noticed, had they raised their eyes on a certain afternoon some days later, four humble women making their way quietly across one corner of the square in the direction of the Istana gate. Had they been even more interested and taken the trouble to follow the four on their way they would have seen the four go past the main entrance at a slightly quickened pace, and continue along the outer wall, around the corner, and down toward the river bank, where a smaller side entrance served to handle the petty business of the palace. Closer observation would have revealed that while two of the women were a little over average height, and the fourth taller still, these three in particular walked, despite their sturdy build, in a clumsy, over-delicate way, mincing along beneath their bent and somewhat crooked backs. Only one, seemingly the youngest, moved with a normal and modest grace, and she it was whose face was less veiled, and whose head scarf was pushed back to disclose her fine hair and high brows in contrast to her companions, who were heavily shaded and covered against the sun.

It was as well that there was no such particular person that afternoon, for Hassan and Achmed and I could hardly have stood so subtle a study, though Saripah went boldly and unafraid. I cursed the cumbersome clothes that skirted my legs, even though they successfully curbed the length of my stride, and I gave thanks inwardly that the Malay costume of a wide-bottomed tunic disguised the lack of femininity and girlish parts of myself and my two companions. Saripah, to Hassan's ill-concealed annoyance, had chosen to costume herself in the other type of Malay dress, with the skintight, low-necked *baiju* that covered her from shoulder to hip, with a tight tube of brightly woven batik-designed sarong below.

Two guards secured the safety of the small arch which led to the back of the Istana grounds, and as we approached them Saripah let her own veil drop a little at one side to disclose her smooth cheek and gay eye. Apparently one guard was gossiping with his comrade on his master's time, for as we drew nearer he sauntered off toward the river as though on a beat. I was relieved mightily by this, for part of the success of our strategem would depend on having one guard fully taken up in observation of Saripah while we other three would cause no notice.

"Who comes?"

"I am Laila, and these are Fatimah and Hasnah and Isnani. We are washer-women and needle-women, and we were told that the Princess Latifah has need of us."

As Saripah spoke the guard rubbed his jaw, pondering, but then she put her finger on a tear in his tunic, under the arm.

"Perhaps tonight, when you are off duty, I might be able to repair your tunic . . . ?"

The fellow's face lighted up like a man who has lost a stone and finds a diamond in his search for it.

"Very well, then, enter. But make sure you seek me out tonight!"

He winked at her and touched his lips to her hair, and I heard Hassan growl in his throat, but I quietly stamped on his foot. It is remarkable how a sharp and sudden pain in one portion of the anatomy can cancel out a greater but duller one elsewhere.

We walked quickly in, with but scant notice taken of our rearguard three, moments before the fellow's companion returned from the river. As we walked across the back courtyard of the place, Hassan muttered: "If any needle-woman is to repair his clothes tonight, it will be this one. And he is likely to have a couple of extra holes here and there about him that will be beyond the skill of any seamstress I've met!"

Saripah, who was still a girl in spite of her brightness, could not forbear to giggle foolishly at this, and I had to laugh myself, until I trod on the hem of my confounded skirts, stumbled, and cursed, which made Saripah giggle again. Achmed had said practically nothing ever since we had started the adventure, still mutinous at his temporary emasculation, and with no liking for the chances we were taking, I guessed.

We fell silent as another soldier strolled from the direction of the side-door leading from the garden to the palace, by which we had intended to enter, but he headed us off by calling: "Hey, you women. If you want work, go around to the back where the kitchens and workrooms are!"

We didn't argue with him, we just went as he directed, holding our skirts daintily above the mud of the yard.

Saripah led us swiftly into a corridor which circumnavigated the busy work area, and hailed a maid whom she recognized as one of the Princess Latifah's, and instructed her to tell her mistress that four women were seeking work from her, requesting audience. As the maid moved away we followed at a slower pace, so that when she came out of Latifah's private rooms she was surprised to find us waiting there. With a toss of her head and a shrug of her shoulders she threw open the door, and would have followed us in, but that Hassan closed the door in her face.

Latifah, too, seemed somewhat surprised at this sudden invasion, for she looked up, startled, from some embroidery work she was engaged in. Her face was as beautiful as I had remembered it, though there were signs of strain whitening her soft brown cheeks, and

128

pulling at the corners of her large eyes. I advanced on her and swept off my headdress and veil.

"Prince Ali of Bohongistan at your service, Princess; though on this visit, it pains me that my robes lack a certain royalty."

"Prince Ali! Oh, I had not thought that you would have been able to return."

"Well, I have, happy to say. Here is Hassan, your Captain and mine, and this is Achmed, my deputy. This of course is Saripah, whom you already know."

I was glad to see that Latifah was truly noble, in that she took our fair companion's hand in friendship and pleasure, with no hint of patronage.

"So, Saripah, you have delivered the Princess Meriam over to our friends. Is she in good health?"

"Yes, Princess, and babbles on about you constantly."

I could see that this was likely to develop into a womanish gossip session of interminable length unless I took a firm hand so, endeavoring to avoid brusqueness, I interrupted.

"We have a lot to discuss, and little time in which to do it. I want Hassan and Saripah to sound out, if they can do it discreetly, the palace servants, and make out who is likely to be loyal to our cause."

"Right, my lord. Saripah, you had best take the Captain to the laundry. You know where it is."

The girl nodded, and she and Hassan adjusted their veils carefully before leaving. I followed them to the door, with Achmed.

"Achmed, you stay outside the door here, and warn us if anyone comes. Try to look humble, man, confound it! You're a poor old washer-woman hoping for a few drops from the royal washtub!" I set his veil up for him so that he looked a little less like a witch, and left him to it, closing the door firmly as I went back to the Princess.

"Latifah, we have to talk, and I wish first to apologize for being doubtful of you. I am thankful that I can trust you, and believe that you will be willing to do the same for me."

"I would be thankful if only to find a friend in this
129

benighted, iniquitous, greed-serving house of my family's shame."

Now that our band was split up, and while I was talking with Latifah, several things were happening, some of which I learned at a later time, and some which I had to reconstruct from the subsequent actions of others. I judge it to be more convenient for the sake of this tale if I recount them now as they occurred.

For instance, Achmed must have listened at the door, and, when he judged that the Princess and I were deep in conversation and likely to be so for some time, made off up the corridor leading to the inner part of the palace.

Meanwhile Latifah swore again to help us in every way, and it did me good to see the fresh blood of hope revivify her wan cheeks. But hope and earnest endeavor were not going to be good enough to help us defeat the Red One. As I said to her: "The only trouble is that I don't see yet how you can assist us. The guards at the gate must be distracted so that our men, fewer in number but better trained, can enter. It is impossible to either mount a siege or attack the walls. And it must be over quickly, else Abdul might hold you as hostage. On the other hand, but for similar reasons, it is impossible that you should come with us, for your absence from the Istana would leave no cards in the Red One's hand, and he would merely have to order all his men to hunt us all down and destroy us, finding all his course's obstacles neatly packaged in one group. And it seems to me that if we all exiled ourselves outside the country then Abdul would be free to travel to the utmost limits of tyranny, which would do no good to the citizens of this country. The only solution is that we attack, soon and sharply, and ensure that we are the victors."

"There must be a way. Let us think together."

I took to walking up and down the room, my skirts kilted above my knees, a very unromantic hero in appearance, I dare swear, and unsuited to play opposite the lovely heroine whose presence both inspired and distracted me. Which I told her in so many words, bringing color of another source to her cheeks. She seemed

130

disturbed at my boldness, but I flatter myself that my remark was not entirely unwelcome.

While we two were thinking both public and private thoughts, Saripah and Hassan were doing their bit to aid the Cause.

They came down the steps into the laundry area at the back of the palace, a crude lean-to occupied by two maids and a loafer, who had apparently nothing better to do than to sit on a trestle against the wall and chew grass, making no move to help the others as they struggled with the steaming washtubs and acres of wet clothes which had to be hung from the bamboo poles running across the ceiling and out over the yard. As Saripah stepped forward one of the maids looked up inquiringly.

"A very good day to you, sisters. Is this the laundry? Well, the Princess Latifah sent us down here to help, since we are in need of work and sustenance in these hard times."

The woman pointed to a heap of soiled sarongs and tunics on the ground in one corner and grumbled out a reply. "Well, we can always use some help. The lordly gentleman over there, lounging at his ease, is supposed to be helping us, but he is too occupied with his own thoughts, it seems, to be of much assistance."

This aroused absolutely no denial or comment even from the idler, but the woman's companion could not forbear to add her own share of lather to the tub. "Hmph! It's a wonder he takes the trouble to come here at all. Just a pure *nasi tambar*, that fellow, who eats out of other people's rice bowls!"

No interest whatsoever vouchsafed on the part of the *nasi tambar*.

Saripah and the disguised Hassan said nothing to this, but went over to the pile of clothes and started to sort them out. *Nasi tambar* pushed himself negligently away from the wall and sauntered over to them. "Don't believe what they say, my dears. I'm always willing to help *real* ladies."

So saying he put his arm casually around Saripah's

131

shoulders, but let out a sudden yelp as the weight of Hassan, transmitted through the latter's leg, descended on his toes. Our Captain was immediately apologetic, in a falsetto kind of way. "Oh, I'm *so* very sorry. Here, let me see your poor foot."

Before the fellow had put his foot to the floor, Hassan seized him by the ankle and lifted it as though for closer inspection, with the result that the fellow tottered off balance and then fell heavily into a pile of steaming hot linen fresh from the tub. The two maids paused in their work to laugh out loud, while Saripah merely looked properly solicitous, as Hassan, a human structure composed entirely of clumsy thumbs, succeeded in thoroughly damping the other's person and enthusiasm by swathing him, in a helpful manner, of course, in yards of cloth, damp, steamy, and frustrating. The while he continued to splutter and fight to unwind himself, the more his friendly helper clucked sympathy and attempted aid. Finally he managed to throw off the ministrations of his commiserating helper and disentangle himself, walking warily to his seat against the wall, subdued and diluted. Hassan and Saripah, exchanging satisfied looks, attended to their task of sorting.

Conjecture and induction. The Red One was lying asleep on his divan when there came a disturbance at the door. Irritably, as only a despot can be irritable, he opened his eyes and swung himself up into a sitting position as the door opened to disgorge the apologetic and fearful presence of a guard.

"Salaam, Sire. I would not have disturbed you, Sire, but . . ."

"But! But what? Is the jungle aflame? Is the town in ruins? Are the trumpets of the Day of Judgment sounded? What great event has given you the courage to disobey my order and to wake me?"

"None of these things, Sire, but . . . only . . . this washer-woman, this washer-woman who insisted on seeing you, Sire."

I am a man more of action than of words, but I wish I were the latter, that I might paint for your mind but a mere sketch, a small representation, a skeleton of the masterpiece of pure silence that must have existed for the next several seconds in that room.

"A washer-woman. A washer-woman! A washer-woman! The laundry, perhaps, is short of its weekly supply of soap? The river has dried up and there is no more water for washing? All the garments in the palace have miraculously been transmuted to gold? Well?"

The guard, no doubt wishing that praise should fall where it deserved, unceremoniously reached behind him and threw forward a veiled and clumsy female figure which promptly sank to its knees, salaamed in a bass voice, and ripped off its headdress.

"My lord! I pray forgiveness for the intrusion, but I believe you will pardon—nay, even welcome—the interruption, when you learn who I am, and the reason for my disguised visit."

"And who are you, that is so bold to make this claim?"

"I am known as Achmed the Bandit, Sire."

"Good news indeed! Guard, seize him and dispatch him forthwith. His capture and end will indeed be worth the price of his rude intrusion upon me, whatever brainless purpose caused it."

As the soldiers ran forward, called by the guard in the corridor, Achmed however looked up into the orange-browed eyes of Abdul, and spoke but five words. "Meriam, Prince Ali, the rebels."

"Stay, let the dog bark awhile."

"I have not come to attack you, nor yet to offer my life, but yet risking it in your behalf. The rebels plan to kill you, as they would me if they knew of my presence here. Hence my disguise. I have come to tell you the whole plan."

"Very well. Guards, stand outside the door and be ready for my call. You, Achmed, explain yourself, but come no closer."

The soldiers saluted, bowed, and withdrew, closing the doors behind them, sealing away the conspirators.

In the laundry work went on apace, though little enough of it was being produced by Hassan, who was

133

incompetent, or by the *nasi tambar*, who was uninterested. He had dried himself out and warmed up his daring, edging closer to Saripah, but not without a wary glance at her strange companion, who professed to ignore him.

"Your big friend is too rough for me. I like girls who are neat, and small, like yourself, dainty in their ways."

At this point Hassan (as he told me later) was about ready to throw aside all caution but a kick in the ankle from Saripah reminded him that we were all making sacrifices for the sake of the Cause, and this was to be his. His pert partner was well enough in charge of the situation, anyway.

"Oh, sir, you mustn't flatter me like that. I am unworthy of your attentions, a fine figure of a man like you, and handsome, too. You tempt me to break my promises."

The speech drew snorts of what were probably contempt from the two maids, and some mumbled benedictions from Hassan, but in his conceit the loafer probably took these signs as indications of agreement. But, a modest fellow at heart, he ventured nothing beyond: "You rate me too highly, my dear—though I must say that you are not alone in your opinion, and in the face of such agreement who am I not to say that you might have to go a long way indeed before meeting such another. But—who is this to whom you have rashly made promises, whom you seem to compare so ill favorably with myself?"

"Oh, and you are unpretentious, too. A girl *would* be lucky to be rewarded with even a small portion of your attention. And no doubt you are brave, also, and would brook no rival's interference. But best that I not disclose his name to you, for he is deserving of some small sympathy, and is, perhaps, though some might argue, too young to die."

"Oh well; you know a gentleman would do anything for his fair lady, as I would fight to the very death for your honor—*in* your honor, I should say. But if it comes to that, be assured that, in my magnanimity and for your sweet sake, I would spare his life. Come now, my blossom, reveal his name. Do I know him?"

Oh, what a pretty fluttering of eyelashes it must have been!

"You may indeed have heard of him, fine gentleman that you are, for he is well known throughout the countryside; and I thought then that I was lucky above all others in attracting his attention, if even for a space—but that was before I met you. Are you acquainted with Abdul the Red One?"

Like a pebble dropped into a pool, this innocent remark caused reactions far beyond its immediate point of impact, for while the *nasi tambar* walked slowly backward away from Saripah, gulping out: "Ab . . . dul . . . the . . . Red . . . One . . . ?" Hassan observed that the two maids spat surreptitiously and glanced uneasily at each other and at Saripah. In his shock the poor idler did not notice that he was but a few yards from, and rapidly moving toward, his late helper in times of trouble.

Saripah nodded brightly and clapped her hands. "You *do* know him! Then you must be aware of all his weaknesses, and can challenge him to a fight!"

"Ch-ch-ch-challenge! He'd kill me, poison me, execute me, stab me, beat me, strangle me, murder me—if he thought that I had even dared so much as to think of interfering with his plans."

He backed up against the disguised Hassan and, taking a startled look over his shoulder at that silent figure, the abject fool threw himself down on his knees, hands clasped in supplication toward Saripah. "Don't tell him, mistress, if you speak truth. Please, I implore you, don't torment me. He's so wicked he'd have me thrown into the river at a mere suggestion, a hint, a dreamed suspicion that I had dared . . . oh, what am I saying? If you tell him only that I said *that*, he would torture and kill me!"

Hassan noticed that the two maids were suddenly intensely absorbed in their work. Saripah was wide-eyed. "You don't *admire* Abdul the Red One, then?"

"No, of course not. He and his crew are hated by all

135

here in 'Dak Betul. Oh-oh-oh-oh, whatever am I saying to you, his mistress!"

At this point Hassan stepped forward and clamped his heavy hand on the other's shoulder. Eschewing his disguised voice he said, "No, not Abdul's, but mine."

Well, after they had thrown an ewer of water over the fellow's head, and revived him, and convinced him that Saripah was no houri in Paradise, he managed to sit up, still spluttering. Hassan dropped his veil. "Come on, you knave; if you are but an eighth part of the man you blow yourself up to be, you can be of assistance to us. We plan to destroy Abdul, and restore the Princess Meriam rightfully to power."

Saripah glanced over at the two thunderstruck maids. "Will you help us?"

"Why, yes; the poor child should have her rights."

"Aye, perhaps the likes of us will gain some rights of our own, and not be trodden underfoot by this orange-headed bastard, Abdul."

Hassan caught the *nasi tambar's* eye. "And you?"

"Ye-yes, if there are other than your two selves, and your words are not as empty of meaning as . . . as mine but recently were."

"Well spoken, indeed! There is more to you than I had thought! But, think you there are many of like mind in the palace?"

"All who have not newly been brought in by the tyrant to lord it like roosters over the rest of the barnyard here."

"It is well. First, then, let us finish washing this dirty linen before taking care of the greater stains upon this country's honor. We will talk of this later."

As they returned to the job, even the loafer taking a cautious hand in the supervision of the maids' work, Saripah, without turning her head, murmured to Hassan: "So, I am already your mistress, it seems, my bold Captain?"

The good Captain was not one whit abashed, but replied, "Well, I had hoped to lay the matter before you in a more reasonable way, and at a more appropriate time, but . . . ?"

He was rewarded by a toss of the hair, the shrug of a shoulder, and the sight of a raised eyebrow. Sighing deeply he applied himself to the task of wringing out some rather delicate-looking pieces of lace material, whose purpose seemed entirely feminine and the handling of which seemed a long way indeed from the normal tasks to be expected by a Captain of the Palace Guard.

At about this time Achmed must have been receiving from Abdul the first solid fruits of his treachery, I imagine. He took the bag of gold coins in his usual obsequious way, I suppose, while his paymaster smiled in anticipation. "This is welcome news indeed that you bring me, Achmed. This is for your present information, and there will be more, and of course a pardon, for your future assistance. Now I will go and give orders for the capture of this impudent false Prince and his helpers, and the immediate imprisonment of the honey-tongued Princess Latifah."

But as he started to go toward the door Achmed had the temerity to seize his gown. "No, my lord, do not do this. To do so would be but to capture the head, but to leave the tail of this serpent. And such a serpent may very well grow a new head, if you cannot force the capture of the Princess Meriam, even if I lead you to her. Give me a talisman that will admit me at all times to your presence, and be my protection from your men, and I will deliver not only this Prince Ali, but Princess Meriam and all the rebels, their followers!"

The Red One considered this for a moment.

"I trust you no further than you can throw that bag of gold, but my arm is long. Here, take this ring. It will keep you safe from danger on the part of my men, until such time as I may have cause to tell them to seek out its wearer and destroy him. Now, tell me of your plan."

Plans were afoot and even underfoot that day in the Istana, but I knew nothing at the time other than of those my Princess and I had concocted.

Achmed saved himself then by a fraction of chance, for he was returning to his post, moving stealthily down the corridor when I opened the door from the Princess' chamber and backed out, still talking. Which I admit was foolish of me, but then love has a way of prolonging farewells.

"So we shall follow your suggestion, Latifah. Look forward to my return, and pray that it will be quick and sure."

"I shall; and I will, my Prince."

I closed the door and turned to see where Achmed had gotten himself to, finding him at my elbow, which had been vacant a moment before. "Where have you been?"

"I was away for but a few seconds, Ali. I thought I heard a footfall around the corner, but I was mistaken, for the way is clear."

"Let us seize our chance, then. Let's collect the others and return to the camp. I have learned enough here, and have designed the move which will upset the heavy foot of the tyrant."

And so we went out of that place, all four of us.

THREE:

It was good to feel a horse between my legs again, becoming part of sheer animal strength and agility, combined with wits and skill, one great organism spinning the world around beneath our feet, my mount and I. The fresh morning air hummed in a scented breeze past my ears and against my breast, each hair on my body alive and tingling to the thrill of existing. I had galloped ahead of the others, too dull in the early day to urge their mounts past a mile-consuming steady trot. I also wanted to test the efficiency of our sentries, now that the possibility of active search by the Red One was no minor one. And sentries at this hour of breaking fast are notoriously lax.

But our men were well tutored, for I was challenged from the undergrowth beside the glade in which I rode, several yards before the camp would come to sight, and I congratulated the man. I told him to hold my horse while I went ahead on foot, intending to sneak through the brush and come upon the camp unobserved. I failed in this, however, and was all but speared by an over-zealous recruit who at first did not recognize me; but eventually I crept over the rise surrounding the camp, not suffering any other hindrances on the way.

I lay behind some rocks and surveyed the area, some men still asleep, and few of the others inclined to any strenuous activity. Immediately below me, though, the Princess Meriam was as full of vitality as a flea on a kitten, busy with the bedevilment of my faithful Bakar, who had perhaps been dragged from his bed untimely, but in no whit annoyed. The child had promoted herself in her regality, and was playing at being Queen, no less, with Bakar in the role of all her subjects, fulfilling this and that task of childish queenship for her. At last his loyalty was rewarded, for she summoned him before her, he advancing on his knees, grinning slavishly, until she held her hands above his head, which was much bowed to assist her.

"I name you my Chief Protector and Provider of Entertainment!"

She held the stiff pose of royalty as long as she could, while the giant, looking suitably awed and grateful, remained on his knees before her; then her mood changed, as she begged him to dance for her. Within my recollection I have seldom seem a sight more ludicrous than that which then presented itself, of the tall, barrel-chested, mighty-muscled, tree-legged Bakar, naked to the waist, his grizzled, seamed and rough-hewn face clenched all together in an apprehension of concentration, shuffling like some great Himalayan bear to the piping lilt of the young Princess, with his hips undulating to about the same degree as would those of a buffalo-surfeited python in like circumstances. Even his normally enraptured audience found something less than desired in his performance, for she put her hands on her hips and looked up at him, frowning, as he towered over her like some genie from the Thousand-and-One-Nights. "*That's* not the way, Uncle Bakar. Like this. Watch!"

And as the benevolently beaming and besotted Bakar

paused to observe her she broke into a little dance of her own, singing the while an innocent song of what she would do when she would be Queen, indeed. Falling into the pattern of the Malay *joget,* where the dancers must not touch, and where one sets the rhythm and the steps, while the other follows impromptu and instantaneous, Bakar placed his massive paws as did she her small ones, and the two turned and swayed as merry and sober as ants in sugar. By now some of my wastrels had bestirred themselves enough to catch sight of the display, and had gathered around in an admiring circle, clapping time with their hands, and even pairing off in partnership with the dance. They were interrupted by a shout from the forest—"Achmed and Hassan return!"

Bakar swept Meriam up into his arms, seated her on his broad shoulders, and strode off to the entrance, followed by the gang. I let myself down over the rocks onto the greensward and went over to where the ecstatic Princess was busily relating her prattle to Saripah. Ah, to see the world again through a child's eyes, and to find it as honest and stable, utterly true and sharply defined, existing only as the plaything and delight of the child who observes.

Later in the afternoon, when we had rested, I was taking my ease in the sun, letting the heat slip down between my muscles, my eyes closed. I overheard Saripah telling the Princess a story which she had learned at some time from a wandering Chinese trader, from that great and mysterious land to the north. It seems that there was once a merry and sage Emperor who delighted in evolving paradoxes for the confusion of his contemporaries. One day, or so he had told his courtiers, he was dozing in his pleasure-garden, watching a brightly painted butterfly undecided and unsure in the selection of equally colorful blossoms clamoring for its attention. As he watched, the Emperor dropped over the edge of sleep, and immediately began to dream; and in this dream, marvelous to behold, *h*e was become the butterfly, flitting uncertainly above the blossoms, and yonder, look . . . *there* sat the Emperor dozing in his chair. For some time he studied the garden through his insect eyes, drawing, in his flights across the sun-slashed scene, ever nearer to the figure lying in the chair, until at last, with a flutter of bravado, he dared to alight upon the topmost satin knob of the sleeper's cap.

Exhausted by the rigors of the flight, and by the sudden draining of energy incurred by his daring, the flitter-winged creature swooned and slept, to fall immediately into a dream. In which dream he seemed to become the Emperor beneath his sticky feet; and, as the Emperor, he dreamed he awoke. "And," quoth the Emperor to his courtiers, "ever since then I have been unsure as to whether I am an Emperor who has dreamed he was a butterfly, or whether in fact I am not a butterfly still dreaming that I am an Emperor!"

The Princess Meriam was delighted by the fantasy of the tale, but could not understand the Emperor's predicament. "Of course, everyone *knows* who he is!" she declared vehemently. "I am Meriam, I'm sure of that; and that is Uncle Bakar over there, and *he* is real, for he tickles me and I feel him; and that is Prince Ali lying here beside us, and I'm certain he knows who he is, and what is real. Don't you, Ali?"

"I think I'm as real as any of you," I laughed. "As real as this ground I stamp beneath my heels, and this air I breathe in, and the green trees and the blue sky and the golden sun swinging his way across the heavens there. And as real as the fact that I have work to do, and no time to waste on listening to foolish stories, my Princess! Come, Hassan, if you can tear yourself away from such an accomplished raconteur, whose lips seem to attract you as much as her tongue! Call the men to a meeting, leaving minimum guards on duty. Everyone must know his part in this."

When I had them gathered around me and above me, as I stood at the foot of the rocks, I began to draw a plan of the Istana in the earth at my feet, using my sword for instruction rather than destruction for a change, a role in which it was untutored yet proficient.

"Memorize this sketch. Remember it well, for you each may live or die according to your accurate remem-

141

brance. Now, this is the stockade which runs all around the Istana except on the river side, and here is the outer gate. These lines here represent the steps leading up to the main door of the palace proper—some of you have good and proud cause to remember them—and along this corridor to the right lies the entrance to the Grand Hall."

Achmed interrupted me at this point to say, surlily, that he well knew the layout of the palace, and would go to check our sentries while I described it for the others. Reluctantly I let him go, reluctant because I could not rid myself of a suspicion of his too easy acceptance of his secondary part in our new organization, but not willing at this time to further degrade him by ordering him to remain, in front of our men. Many things might have been different had I followed my first thought instead of letting myself be confused by the second, more reasoning, argument. Ah, 'tis always the way. The complete man needs no second thoughts, and the cautious man will never be complete.

So I droned on with my worthless plan of attack, and the rogue Achmed crept across to his sleeping quarters near Meriam's and Saripah's shelter. Looking around to see that he was unobserved, he began digging in the soft earth with his *keris* until he had a sizable hole, and then took from somewhere on his person, among his garments, the bag of gold and the seal ring, which must have been burning into his treacherous hide all the way on our journey back from 'Dak Betul, gloating over each item as it shone briefly in the dying sunlight, red as blood.

But however briefly—long enough to attract a watcher!

For unbeknownst to him, (and to anyone else for that matter, Allah's curse on it) there did happen to be a watcher. The little Princess had heard a clink, or some such trifling noise, and looked out of the hut through a crack conveniently low for her. She actually saw the glint of the ring before he buried it and covered the hole up, putting over the spot a sod of turf he had cut. Meriam was of course curious but being part magpie by nature was more interested in the pretties she had seen than in the mystery of Achmed's secretiveness.

She started to wander off, a picture of innocence, in the direction of the door but Saripah, jealous of her charge's well-being now that she too was returned from traveling, caught her up and laid her down on her straw sleeping mat. "No, my little Princess, no more roaming for you today. The night is drawing in and you must sleep. Goodness knows what hours your Uncle Bakar, foolish fellow, let you keep while I was away. I only hope that other Princess, your cousin, will sleep as comfortably tonight, all praise to her."

So there I was, tediously expounding my scheme, and parrying questions, when Achmed, after a hurried tour of the outposts, returned. So this, as I learned very soon, was one reason why my lecture was useless. The other, also resulting from the brute's simmering resentment over his lost position, and from his lust for gold, was possessed of more danger to our plans, but remained hidden from me for considerably longer.

For I had no way of knowing that Saripah's last hope was a futile one.

FOUR:

At the Istana, Abdul had bided his time, brooding over the problem presented to him by Achmed of my late presence in the palace, and the Princess Latifah's open participation in the plans of the rebels.

And now he had ordered her seized in her quarters, taken as she slept, bound, and brought before him as he sat on his divan with the wet-eyed Karim standing beside him. As she stood, still dazed with sleep, clad only in a flimsy night-sarong against the heat of the night, he gazed gloatingly at her in the light of the flickering wall-torches that set off gaudy sparks of color against the bright-sheened cloths that decorated the walls. Barefoot as she was, and but briefly covered from breast to knee, loose hair flowing down her back and over her bare arms as they, with the tightness of their binding behind her, drew her shoulders back and bosom up, she seemed diminutive and defenseless against the orange-headed tyrant and his lacky, who so coolly studied her face and figure. At last, with his ally the silence having had a chance to take effect on the girl, he leaned forward and spoke.

"So, my attractive and traitorous kinswoman, since you will not learn, you must be taught, it seems."

"If I am indeed a traitor, then in what else could you instruct me, my uncle? And against what true cause do you judge me to be treacherous?"

"You speak of causes, and of the truth of them, my dear. But it was not until the false Prince Ali, your lover, arrived here that you made any move against my rule and my power. Can it be that lechery has inspired your treachery?"

Despite herself, and knowing the unjustness of the charge, she could not prevent her blush, which spread from her face downward until hidden by the veiling folds of her sarong, knotted above her breast.

"Prince Ali is a true Prince . . . and a true man!"

"We shall see. . . . We shall certainly take time to test the truth of your *Prince* and your assertions when he is in our power. Now, let us hasten, for I am weary. What is the plan by which he hopes to overthrow us?"

"I do not know; and if I did know I should not tell you, even though I died to prevent the utterance."

The Red One sat back and considered her for a moment.

"You seem intent on delivering deliberate statements in pairs this evening. Now, I will tell you plainly, I will act upon your latter statement, caring not whether you do know his plans or not. If you do know, then 'twere wise to tell; if you do not . . . then death will, no doubt, eventually come to relieve you from a life which you will, I assure you, be most eager to escape from. You take my meaning?"

Her face now drained of color, Latifah yet had courage. She bowed her head before him as though in submission—then spat at his feet. "That is the only truth you will get from between my lips, my good Uncle!"

He was unperturbed. "Yes, it might just be that you could defy me."

Karim, his face oily with evil delight at the possibility of dishonoring and tormenting a woman, leaned forward to his master's ear. "Perhaps an overnight visit to the cavern beneath the river will help to make the Princess a little more . . . realistic . . . Sire?"

"Yes, an excellent suggestion, my dear Karim. I wonder how you thought of it. I was myself merely pondering which of our fine instruments will best serve us. I think that exquisite device we fashioned on the advice of that Chinese renegade we gave sanctuary to is worth considering. You didn't know, my dear Princess, did you, that since I have been living here in the Palace I have discovered a grotto beneath the river, to which I now have secret access, and which has become my private prison, and my chamber for scientific—to borrow a word from our Arab preceptors—scientific experimentation. Guards! Take the Princess below, and tell the executioner to make ready the water bed. Tell him to stand by, and I will presently come to supervise the lady's bedding."

At about this time Meriam, whose curiosity was stronger than the gentle tugs of sleep, was feigning sleep itself, and had been doing so for some little while. Saripah, whose glance told her that her charge was safely away, slipped out to meet with my carefree Captain, and as soon as she had left the shelter the little Princess threw back her blanket and went to the door. Assured by a sight of Saripah over by the distant firelight she went on her own small investigation of the treasure buried by Achmed.

Another cautious glance behind her assured her that all was well, with the men making merry around the blazing campfire, a hum of distant voices coming faintly to her ears. Her sharp young eyes soon detected the slice of cut turf, and without further ado she tore it up, placing it carefully to one side, and began to dig into the loose soil with her fingers. It was a matter of a few minutes to uncover the coins and the ring. The gold

145

meant nothing to her, but the ring held her fascinated as its many planes glinted and shone by the light of the distant fire and the rays of the moon which was just heaving itself above the treetops. Twisting and turning it in her hands she began to toddle away back to the hut, intending to hide the treasure where Saripah would not find it, but as she moved her sight was fixed upon a pair of legs directly in her path.

Shocked silent she looked up to see, looming over her, the burly figure of Achmed, a look of alarm and cunning on his own face. The two stood as they were, frozen by mutual discovery and fear, for slow-ticking seconds. Then suddenly Achmed bent and made a grab for her, but by this time her legs were unlocked from their fetters of fright and she dodged past him, managing to scream, "Saripah! Saripah!" before he lunged again and picked her up, his hairy hand hard across her mouth as she kicked and struggled.

As it was, perhaps because of some peculiarity in the wind's vagaries, we at the fireside did not hear her, loudly laughing as we were at some extravagant story of Hassan's, but Bakar, who was taking no part in the general festivity and was sitting away off from us, maybe already with some thought of his little Princess in his mind, and with his more acute hearing, picked up the cry and went loping off to see what the trouble was.

And we didn't notice his going, else we had prevented a tragedy.

Achmed must have first seen the giant as he lurched around the corner of the shelter, and the traitor barely had time to drop Meriam and reach for his *keris* before Bakar was upon him. To doubly compound the stupid situation which arose, preventing aid to Bakar, the valiant bodyguard was incapable of shouting and thus attracting attention, while of course Achmed had not the slightest wish to make a noise, thinking no doubt that if he could overcome Bakar he might still yet think of some story to save his own skin. Meanwhile, skilled as he was with his weapon, the unarmed dumb giant, incensed beyond his normal strength, evaded his thrusts and grappled with him. The two men rocked and

146

swayed like two silent shadows suddenly endowed with corporeal existence as each sought to break the other's hold and seize a fresh advantage.

Meriam had picked herself up and, after watching the two men in their mortal combat for a moment, ran off toward the safety and security of the fire. Hassan saw her first, and ran to her, closely followed by Saripah. At first the Princess could only sob and point behind her to the shelter, and our first thought was that some nightmare had disturbed her slumber, but in seconds we had grasped enough of her story for it to send us rushing stumbling to the hut.

Hassan arrived first, seconds too late however, for his first vision was of Achmed standing away as the great frame of Bakar, fatally stabbed behind the shoulder, toppled slowly to the ground like a felled tree. Without pause, without consideration, fired by an anguish that nearly paralleled my own, such was his friendship for the fallen giant, Hassan leaped forward, his own *keris* drawn, and the two began to duel. A quick glance told me that Hassan was in no immediate danger, and I ran and knelt at Bakar's side, raising his head in my arms. Though he had never been able to speak, and though he was now almost past words in any case, we two had no need of speech. I answered the unspoken query in his eyes and told him that Meriam was in no danger now. I asked him if I should call her, for we both knew that he was about to look upon this earth, this foreign earth, for the last time; but he shook his head, and I in my heart agreed with him, for death is a sorry thing to visit upon the soul of youth, at any time.

The rest of the men had come up, now, and were gathered in a grimly silent circle around the small patch of ground where I held Bakar, and where Hassan was executing vengeance on the miscreant Achmed. At least the cur asked for no quarter, which was somewhat in his favor and might save him from the very bottommost pits of Hell. I saw that Hassan had been wounded slightly in the arm, but though blood spouted from the cut, like water from a split bamboo pipe, he ignored it in his fury, and at last plunged his snake-waved dagger into

Achmed's heart, full to the hilt. The brute stood there grinning, I swear, for a half-minute before he staggered three weak steps toward us to fall like the dog he was across Bakar's legs. My erstwhile servant, new-freed friend, and lifetime companion managed to twitch a painful grin of congratulations and thanks upon his tight-drawn face as Hassan dropped to one knee beside us, and then turned to me, mouth open as though at the last he would say something.

And then he died.

As I laid him gently back upon the grass, Hassan, with a curse uttered, I swear, through a veil of tears, kicked the corpse of Achmed from our comrade's body, and so they lay there, trusty guardian and self-serving traitor, in the full light of the risen moon, the grass around them darkly green.

Something clutched at my heart and I rose, sickened, bereft, lonely.

Through the torrent of my grief I could dimly hear the voices of the others, but the pumping of my blood seemed to throb beside my ear, behind my eye, clotting my throat so that I stood as if struck senseless by the moon, whose light shone brightly into my eyes like a great lamp, round and silver-gold, above my head. The sight set off some phantasm in my brain, and faintly through my anguish I seemed to hear a voice, across a great distance, yet hovering in the aperture of my ear at the same time, telling me to guard against sentimentality, warning me that attachment to dream creatures would cause great harm to me. What devils these were that so crudely attempted to overturn the fine tunings of my mind I know not, and knew not then, and cared not to find out at any time. It felt as if the very blood of my heart welled up and overflowed through my eyes, and washed out the voice in a flux of healing unguent.

When I had recovered myself somewhat, and became as a man again, I turned back to the patch of sward to find that some of the men, who had grown to love Bakar as did I, had wrapped his body and were bearing it off for an honorable burial. Achmed's sorry corpse they would have thrown into the bush to rot had I not forbidden them. I cared nothing for the propriety of the thing, but we could not have our camp stunk up with his foulness, and I ordered them to take him some leagues hence and fetch him into some ditch and cover him.

Hassan, who had been near fainting, was now revived by the proximity of Saripah, who bore his head on her knees and bathed his wound. "Does it hurt still, my Captain?" she asked.

"The balm of your hands was enough to cure it, girl. But what is that in the Princess Meriam's hands that glitters so?" We turned to look where he pointed, and at Saripah's somewhat peremptory command the girl handed over what seemed to me to be a ring.

"By Allah, this is the seal of Abdul the Red One. This is his ring!" cried Saripah. I hastened over and examined the thing. It meant nothing to me, but Hassan confirmed the girl's statement.

"See here. Gold!" came a voice from behind, and we turned again to find that one of our men had come upon the hole in which Achmed had sought to hide his guilt. There was but one conclusion to be drawn from this evidence. "We have been betrayed, sold out by Achmed into the Red One's hands. He may be even now upon us here. And certainly whatever plans I have made are useless, since we depended upon the Princess Latifah to aid our subterfuge."

"And she is most certainly Abdul's prisoner and hostage by now," added Hassan, as a spur to the steed of my quick-rising fear.

"Double the sentries. The rest, sleep as best you may, but sleep armed. Tomorrow at sunup we leave for 'Dak Betul, while tonight I and the Captain here plan a new method of attack. Saripah, take Meriam here and quiet her. Soothe her into deep sleep, for she rides with us on the morrow!"

Lacking an Imam to do the duty, I said a few words and offered a prayer over the body of Bakar before we laid him to rest in the soft and pleasant glade, standing ready in the deep hole, facing Mecca, ready for the Last Day to call upon his poor, brave, dumb soul.

We slept ill, if at all, that night which was the blackest in my memory, despite the uncaring staring eye of the silver moon.

FIVE:

If we of the Cause slept ill, the Princess Latifah slept not at all.

When the Red One came to the cavern under the river he found her sitting on a bench against the wall, her arms still bound behind her, and her ankles hobbled. She didn't know what was about to happen to her, but the sights she saw around her did nothing to quiet her imagination. The whole vault stank of dampness, and one wall was covered almost entirely by a screen of water as it seeped through a fault in the rocks from the river immediately above this end wall. The corridor along which she had been brought was only just below ground level, so that the entrance to this cave was high on one wall, with rough-built wooden steps leading down to the floor level. Torches flared from wall-brackets and the roof, low as it was, could not be clearly made out for the smoke which piled up against it, with no other way out for it.

Against the wall opposite to the one which she leaned against, three men slumped to the rock floor in chains, fettered so that they could sit but not rest. Two were deep in sleep while the third muttered in his dreams, occasionally clattering the silence with screams. To her right, on the water-wall, a man hung spread-eagled facing the rock, so that he was pressed against it, hanging by the wrists, all but drowning in the steady veil of water which descended from above him. His continual gurglings and snorts sickened her soul, for she imagined that this was the water torture her captor had alluded to. In a dark corner a man hung senseless by his thumbs, the balls of his feet touching the ground, so that if conscious he might have been able to escape the fate which had now, however, fallen upon him. She could see that his thumbs were hideously elongated, the bones
150

parted, so that only his skin and tendons could be supporting him. A sixth man was bent back over a wheel, whose lower edge dipped out of sight into what was evidently a pit of water, the wheel arranged for turning so that when necessary its occupant could be swung backward or forward and plunged underwater for as long as the operator desired. Perhaps this was the water bed?

In the center of the floor was a large, crude framework of wood, some four feet off the ground, supported on legs at each corner, rectangular in shape, and with two pairs of grooves cut into the crosspieces at each narrow end. Resting on the floor below each groove was a leather bucket, attached to one end of a length of rope, to the other end of which was fixed an adjustable leather loop. This was a form of rack, in which the victim was stretched between the crosspieces unsupported from below, and with a rope and bucket tied to each ankle and wrist. Water could be added to the buckets in turn, so that all, or any single one, of the limbs could be slowly pulled from the socket. At the moment this instrument was unoccupied, as was the only other piece of "furniture" in the cave, a large stone trough whose purpose she could not divine. Metal clasps were at each corner of the trough, possibly to hold wrists and ankles.

Near the foot of the stairs, where the corridor could act as chimney, stood an iron framework in which was built a charcoal fire, and handily by it was a rack of iron instruments, pincers, pokers, branding irons. Toward the center of the grotto, placed so that the stair-landing could act as gallery for any interested audience, was a simple chopping block, a stained and scarred hunk of timber, with a heavy, broad-bladed scimitar leaning against it. The executioner had earlier retired to his nook below the stairs. Neither he nor the two guards, one at the stair foot and the other at its head, spoke a word, nor had done so, and Latifah was left to look and shudder. The damp struck a chill through her, for her thin night-sarong was no protection.

Shock had provided its own anesthesia, and she was

151

almost dulled to sleep, when hollow footsteps echoing along the corridor aroused her from apathy. Abdul swung into view at the end of the passage, came swiftly down the steps, and crossed to her. The executioner came to stand solicitously beside his master. The Red One stood before her until she at last looked up to meet his gaze.

"Well, Princess, have you changed your mind? Have you seen enough to persuade you to talk and tell me all you know? Or must I proceed to take a step which, believe me, will grieve me to carry out?"

"I have nothing to say."

"Perhaps, my dear, the threat of being made as dumb forever as that creature of your lover's will make you wish to talk while you are able. Executioner, fire me a pincers!"

"Yes, Sire. 'Twill take but a minute, Sire." And the grinning, squat, but brawny craftsman went to place an iron in the fire.

"Don't think, Latifah my dear, that the lack of a tongue will prevent you from answering the questions I ask. For you can still write . . . and you need only one hand to write with." With a smile almost of benevolence he glanced casually over to the block and the scimitar which rested against it. Latifah shivered again, but it had nothing to do with the chill of the underground vault this time. But still she kept her neck taut and her head steady as she faced him defiantly. "I will not talk. Or write. Ever."

The man came back with the glowing prongs held in a leather-gloved hand, slowly advancing the tool toward her, till the heat stank in her nostrils. Involuntarily she pressed her head back against the damp wall behind her, but still she met Abdul's eyes firmly, with a steady resolve.

A moment of this, as the instrument cooled, then the Red One laughed. "You've outfaced me, Princess. If you should live, when I have finished with you, then I would wish you to live in the sight of my subjects, unharmed, unspoiled, so that they will believe you when you tell them that you are with me, and that ours is the only true cause. No, I will not harm you physically, or at least, not in any way that can readily be discoverable or seen. It will be the water bed for you tonight. Prepare her!"

He turned away as the executioner came forward and picked her easily up, though she struggled within her bonds to resist. He threw her down into the stone trough, which she now saw was a shallow depression of about six inches worn into the stone, but long and broad enough to hold a human body. Without ceremony or any kind of consideration the man turned her onto her stomach and tore loose the bonds at elbow and ankle before rolling her to her back again. The damp rough stone bruised her shoulders, and her arms went dead as blood pumped into them again. Pulling her arms above her head the executioner clamped them into place, then did the same service for her ankles, adjusting the metal clasps so that she lay fully supported by the cold and clammy stone bottom of the trough, but taut between the two extremities, so that she could move her body neither to left nor right, nor twist it. As she lay there, turning her head frantically upon its pillow of hair, she noticed that above her, and a little forward of her vertical vision, a thin bamboo pole depended from a hole in the roof, with a small spigot in its lower end. The man stepped back deferentially as the Red One came to stand alongside.

Noticing the way her head turned on the soft wetness of her hair he put his hand under her neck and drew the hair back so that it hung down over the end of the trough, leaving no protection for the back of her skull against the sharp edge of the stone.

"You still defy me? You still would keep silent rather than betray the honor of your word? Ah, so; it pains me deeply to treat a kinswoman in this so uncourteous manner, but necessity prevails at this time. I shall sleep no more easily in my bed tonight than you in yours. But for you to rest easy you have only to speak, and for me . . . I need only to listen. Still no? Very well then, let me explain the mechanism here. Our Chinese guest explained that in his country they secure a victim in much the same manner as you are secured, except that the head is fixed rigidly in such a way that an intermittent series of drops of water fall upon the forehead. Several hours of this, he informed me, under pressure I hasten to add, will drive the most recalcitrant prisoner to such a state of desperation that he will confess to almost anything, such is the unbearableness of his situation.

"However, I have managed to refine this process even further. The forehead is not the most sensitive part of the human body. Now observe, please, the pipe above you."

He reached up and manipulated the spigot so that drops of water pattered on her belly.

"The small hole at the end here is so designed that the size and rate of the droplets can be randomly varied. For a few moments the drops may fall steadily upon you, and then they might cease for a time, and I can assure you that you will scream, at least to yourself, if you persist in your silence, until they start again. And as they fall they will collect in the basin in which you rest, until it overflows. Thus you will be chilled through your bones by the icy coldness, and will further be plagued by the alternating pattern of overflowing drops as they spatter on the floor beneath."

Latifah said nothing, still, but looked her scorn at him.

"You think you will be able to bear it. I know you will not. But you have not yet learned the acme, the peak of my ingenuity in this."

He reached up again and moved the pipe slightly so that now the drops fell into the little pit in her covering cloth that indicated her navel. Then, leaning his orange-haired head over her, he very gently loosened the knot that fastened her sarong above her breasts, and drew it down until she was naked to below her hips. The drops began to thunk, tink, tink, shonk, shonk, shak, thunk, tink, shak, shak, into the hollow of her naked navel, drumming against her tautened skin.

Shamed at last into utterance, a red creeping from her cheeks down, down, past her utterly exposed breasts, rising and falling in the rapid rhythm of shocked outrage and excited lungs, she gasped.

"You would treat a Princess of the blood, thus; expose her modesty to the gaze of such as these? What monster spawned you from my father's sister, for you were not born of human kin!"

"You speak?" His eyes wandered scorchingly over her body. "Many things are possible between neck and ankle, my dear, which will leave you with no hurt in afteryears. I am only concerned that the . . . merchandise I wish to display to my subjects shall not *appear* to be damaged. You wish to say more? Down here, you know, we dispense with formality. Only I own a title in this grotto. All else are my creatures. Still, you were a Princess, and may live to be one again. Here, let this suffice." And he picked up a damp and slimy rag from the floor and flung it across her breasts, making sure that it in no wise covered her chest and belly.

"You are silent again? Very well, sleep well, my dear. May your dreams be pleasant ones."

"If you are not in them, they may be."

"Executioner!"

"Sire?"

"You will see that no man nor creature goes nearer to the Princess than this line which I indicate around her. For any reason whatsoever. Understood?"

"Yes, Sire."

And wishing her again a good night's rest, the Red One ascended the stair and left. Grinning, the executioner followed him to the landing rail and leaned on it, looking across at Latifah where she lay silent. "Didn't say nothing about looking, did he?" he inquired of the guard.

The deep hollow of her navel was now filled, and a thin, irregular stream of water ran down each side of her naked stomach. As she breathed in, a larger stream ensued, running icily down her flanks, leaving a thinner shell of water in the pool to protect her against the shonk, shonk, shank, shak, shak, shak which tried to drill into her.

SIX:

I had ordered an early start for the morrow, and by the time the sun was up above the skyline we were well on our merry way. The prospect of at last taking part in an out-and-out fight against the enemy put heart into our men, although the odds against success were great, and we would be greatly outnumbered as well as being in the position of besiegers of the Istana, an unenviable situation since the defenders would have an easier time of it than we, who had to approach without cover; they being able to pick us off at their leisure from behind the ramparts. Unless I could think of some subterfuge which would give us easy entry.

Although Hassan and I had racked our brains during the night watches, we could think of no way in which we might make a secret or surprise entry, now that we had been betrayed. As I sat my horse, with the little Princess Meriam standing in my arms before me, I continued to ponder the problem. Beside me rode Saripah, ever more zealous in her guardianship of the Princess since last night's panic, for though both Hassan and I had argued with her that no real blame attached to her, she insisted on belaboring herself for the mischance. The good Captain rode in our rear, jollying the men along, though they little needed it. At this distance from the city we were safe unless we ran into troops of the Red One, and if we did . . . well, then, the fight would begin that much sooner.

Some half-dozen of Achmed's men had deserted in the morning, preferring to go their own way in the jungle now that their leader was dead. And I had let them go willingly, glad to be able to cut out the bad meat from our otherwise healthy group.

Meanwhile the rest of the men who had loyally decided to throw their lives into the Cause sang and marched, to a tune of their own, some rallying cry of rebellion that one of them had thought up. And it seemed to do us service, for along the way not a few recruits had slipped into our ranks from the forest, eager to know what was afoot, and even more eager to take part in the assault when they knew its purpose and our Cause. I had all but turned away one youngster —he could not have been more than fourteen—for he seemed too young to be of any real aid, but the men adopted him and forced me to take him along. And at least he was ready and willing to take part in the fighting when it commenced. And another volunteer likewise I was about to gently dissuade, on account of his age—a graybeard he was—but he stoutly maintained that as long as he could keep up with us we had no call to try to prevent his joining us for the Cause. And keep up he did, new life in his old legs, new hope in his heart, new spirit endowing his mind. Men need a cause for which to fight, and since they must fight, or relinquish the title "Man," they must search through life for a righteous cause.

We had decided to abandon the circuitous route we had hitherto used on our trips to the city and now, for the sake of time, we hastened along a broad main track, strung along which were several small *kampongs,* the villagers turning out at sound of us, and making honest and hearty obeisance at sight of the Princess, who played her role right royally, standing upright, firm and fair before me.

Early as we were, we scared the wits out of three drunkards who rolled up out of the ditch at roadside upon our coming, thinking perhaps that we were the legions of Shaitan come to fetch them for their sins. But as we harmed them not, they staggered alongside for a while until they learned our purpose, then, still drearydrunk, fell into our ranks. Their upraised voices lent a certain volume, if no additional charm, to our song of the Cause.

By late afternoon I had some seventy men behind me, of whom about three dozen were armed and trained by me, and who would have to bear the brunt of the fighting when it began. The others I planned to use as reinforcements and support, and perhaps to make a feint attack, if I could but think of a way which might give us some hope of success. My sword shone in the sunlight as I waved them all on.

Night had certainly passed, and perhaps day, though Latifah had no way of telling in that dank underground cavern, where no light found its way. The racking pain in her stretched arms and legs had vanished into a complete loss of sensation. Her body, from thigh to neck, was completely numb, iced through to her bones by the cold water in which she lay. Her neck and the back of her head throbbed with a red ache that gave her a semblance of warmth, but which did nothing to stay the shudders which pulsed snakelike along her body, though she hardly felt them any longer. The inside of her head was one great, empty, echoing chamber in which tolled the bell of dripping water: a fathomless lake into which dropped incessantly pebbles of ice, each fresh flock of ripples washing knife-edged against the cavity of her skull. A wire of red-hot pain circled her waist, gnawing into her vitals, spasmodically increasing in intensity as she breathed and let flow a new blade of fire. And as she breathed out again, leaving bare her newly voided navel, the ice-spears drove down into her once more, setting off sympathetic nerve twinges at nipple, armpit, and root of belly. As the shudders seized her throat, the rasping gasp of her breath formed with the orderless cacophony of belling droplets to make oddly mad music, orchestrated by a cunning lunatic.

Her eyes were wide open and red-rimmed, staring and lusterless, but yet with a gleam of sane self peering through the incipient insanity. The weight of her sodden hair pulled her smooth brow drum-tight, and to close her eyelids would have been like trying to lift a great stone with her little finger. So she was when Abdul the Red One came to visit.

He looked down at her, touched her forehead, ran his finger over her lips, drawn back tightly over her teeth with pain and stress. "You look as though you might be more reasonable now, my dear Princess. Though I doubt you can speak. Can you?"

158

She could do nothing but roll her eyes a little, as great spasms convulsed her stretched body.

"Executioner!"

"Sire?"

"Loose her. Lay her on that bench over there. Throw a blanket over her and let her get some warmth. Guard her well, for she has a woman's secret endurance and may try some trick. Though she will not have the strength for some time."

While he was talking the man unclasped the metal tongues that held her rigid, then put his arms underneath her and lifted her easily up. She could make not the slightest resistance, and her arms and legs hung lifeless down for lack of blood and numbness. He dropped her on the bench and snapped free the damp rag that covered her, going to his nook beneath the stairs for a blanket that he threw over her, doubled. She felt the agony of returning circulation, and clamped her teeth together, chattering as they were, to hold her screams while Abdul continued to talk.

"Hearken, niece. I am going, but will return within the hour or so, the space it will take me to consume my evening meal. When I return, prepare yourself to talk. Or, by Allah, I will give you a taste of heat first, and then return you to your bed for a week."

He ripped aside the blanket and placed his warm hand over her navel. "You feel this cold now, don't you? Well, if you do not talk when I come, I will have you branded and seared in that very same spot. And when you have recovered, I shall ask you again. And if still you defy me, I will put you under the dripping pipe again, while the wound is open."

While she stared up at him, wide-eyed from pain, unable to say a word, he dropped the blanket back upon her, swung on his heel, and climbed the stairs to the corridor.

Red ants consumed every inch of her flesh as blood sought anew the channels that had been closed to it for so long. Mercifully, she fainted then. But she told me, later, that she thought of me, at that last.

Just after dusk we arrived outside the city, and I halted the band. We had rested and fed some hours before, and now that the sight of the town was in their eyes, they were ready to plunge forward against any odds. I took Hassan aside. "Hassan, I have an idea. It will be a flimsy chance, but it is the only one I can think of. I am going on ahead. Tell Saripah to remain close by you with Meriam. Detail one of our men, and one of the recruits who knows the country hereabouts, in case we are defeated and they must flee, to guard them. You press on after me as fast as you can. I have some little business in the town first, then I will go directly to the main gate. If all goes well, you will arrive on foot, with all the men, within minutes of my own arrival there. Should I be delayed, and all is quiet at the gate when you come in sight of it, hold the men until I have passed through, then come after me as fast as you like."

I kicked my horse forward and galloped off toward the city of 'Dak Betul, where the tall top of the Istana was just visible in the starlight, above the roofs of its neighbors.

As I had anticipated, my work in the town was soon over, and I headed back up the road toward the main gate of the Palace grounds, where the fate of the Cause and all its human parts would be decided.

This time there were no guards outside the wall, but the great gates themselves were closed, and the heads and spear-points of six soldiers showed above the palisade. I had thrown dust on my face, streaking it with water to simulate sweat, and flung a face cloth loosely across my mouth. As I reached the gate I reared my horse up and called out, in a hoarse voice: "Open the gates! Open! Open!" The wicket gate opened a little way and a guard put his head out.

"Who comes?"

"A courier for His Highness. Open the gates immediately. Open, I say!"

The man hesitated, and I swung my horse around and impatiently beckoned him to me. He was cautious, but I reached down and seized his shoulder, then flashed my hand before him.

"Do you not recognize your master's seal ring, fool? Open the gates, or be prepared to answer to His Highness for your folly."

He ran back through the wicket, shouting to his fellows, and the gates began to creak open, ponderous against their counterweight. I gave inward thanks that my intuition regarding the purpose of Abdul's ring in Achmed's possession had led me correctly. From the corner of my eye I noticed Hassan's men breaking from cover to my left, and I prayed that my own activities would fully attract the attention of the guards. So soon as there was room I urged my mount forward through the gateway and galloped through the small group of men and reached the inside end of the alleyway. When I was clear I jumped down, slapped my horse off, and turned back toward the gate, shouting as I advanced: "Fools, I come to kill your master!"

As I had hoped it might be, they all without further ado turned to stare at me; then, awakening from their paralysis, they drew their *keris* and *parangs* and charged at me, not bothering to close the half-open gates. I drew my own sword and parried their unskillful blows. I played it cautiously, though, for I was more intent on keeping them occupied than attacking them. Nonetheless, I dispatched one to the death and another I wounded sorely in the arm, before, with a great roar, Hassan and his band poured through the gates to take them in the rear. Short work was soon made of them and Hassan looked to me for orders. On the walls I could see other guards now alerted by our cry, but they hesitated whether they should desert their posts to fight us, or remain at their stations to ward off any possible reinforcements we might have from outside the walls.

"Let a third of the men stay here and keep the way clear in case we have to retreat. Let them be sure to hold the gateway, at any cost. Send half of the rest to secure any other entrances to the Istana grounds. You follow me with the remainder, and make sure that Saripah and the Princess Meriam are with us and safe at all times. Come! For Meriam and the Cause!"

And side by side Hassan and I raced up the broad stairs to the Palace, my Captain's wounded left arm tucked into the top of his cummerbund, our picked men following us, the child and the woman in the center. It had seemed to me that our only chance for success in this venture was to capture or kill the Red One as soon as possible, seizing the serpent by the head, as it were, and letting the tail go where it might, for there would be no one person, or group, to replace the serpent's head of Abdul. And we could not withstand a steady and prolonged attack. Surprise was with us, so far, and we set off to scour the halls and corridors for the tyrant.

The alarm had reached those inside, though, and as we pushed against the tall doors of the entrance hall, two streams of guards poured in on us from left and right, through the corridor which surrounded the entire building within its exterior wall. Luckily they were too jammed together at their point of exit, and we managed to hold them off without great loss until we had the door open, and were inside, blocking the door behind us with the timber bars that were ready there for that use. Those guards outside would now have to retrace their tracks before they could come at us again inside, and so I took the chance and ran ahead of the others into the dim interior, bent upon finding Abdul before he could call a strong force around him.

In the corridors I came upon two separate men, who denied they knew where he was, before I sent them tumbling off to Paradise, or wherever their fortune took them.

My quarry was very far from Paradise at that moment, and in a place very like that other afterworld for which he was destined, being in fact in that grotto under the river, which few men, even those in his employ, knew of at all.

Latifah had come to know it very well, all too well, for it seemed to her that it might very well be the last

162

place in this world that she would ever know. She was determined above all things not to tell Abdul anything which would help him. She did not expect me to set my plans in motion for several days, and judged I would come far too late for rescue, for she did not see how she could last for long under the tortures which the Red One had laid out for her.

She had recovered consciousness some time since, and the warmth of the blanket did something to revive her, though, since she had pulled her sarong up and knotted it as before, above her breasts, the dampness of the cloth had proved to be the little she had needed to push her over the edge into fever. Her eyes ran, and her brow was hot, and her body was full of an unhealthy glow, pumping its heat to her head so that she had difficulty in collecting her thoughts, and of keeping them coherent when at last she had the facts arranged before her mind.

Over against the water wall the fettered wretch was silent, dead or sunk into merciful unconsciousness she did not know. One of the three across from her also appeared to be dead, and his companions were silent. On the wheel the fifth man also lay stark and still, while he who had been hung by his thumbs had been cut down some time during the night watches, to revived screams, and now lay in chains with the others. All were now silent, the one remaining guard leaning idly against the wall at the head of the stairs, while his cohort had gone for a meal, no doubt. The executioner dozed in his place below the steps, waiting for the return of the Red One.

He came in a hurry, impatient to press for her replies to his questions, and his swift approach shocked the sentry and the keeper of this dank and foul place out of their lethargy. He wasted no time but came immediately to her as she lay on the bench.

"Well?"

"Nothing!"

"When?"

"Never!"

"Easily said, but less easy to stand by. I warn you,

163

Latifah, much as I would hate to damage such a beautiful body, I will not be thwarted by what it contains and refuses to divulge, nor will I be patient any longer. And I have been patient, and somewhat gentle in my treatment of you so far."

"Have you any other virtues, Uncle?"

"Save your tongue for words of more importance, niece; and your wit for greater wisdom. Will you speak?"

"Not unless you welcome my curses, and accept my scorn with thankfulness!"

"We will see what you will offer me in a moment. Now your forehead is flushed and your body warm. See what brave phrases you can utter when you are truly hot. Executioner! Prepare the irons, and put the girl on the rack. Guard, help him!"

The gross brute saluted him and went to his charcoal grating, taking a large branding iron from its rack and putting its end well into the glow. Then, with the soldier, he carried the limp girl over to the framework in the floor's center. Lifting her to the middle, they quickly tied her wrists to the ends of the ropes leading to the leather buckets at the head of the crude machine. While Abdul impatiently ordered them to hurry, the executioner and his helper hurried off to the pool under the wheel and began to fill the buckets.

"You still will not change your mind?"

Her only reply was to reach clumsily for an iron tool on the rack and throw it at his head. He turned aside easily, and smiled down on her.

"So, you still have claws. Perhaps we will work on them later, if you should still prove recalcitrant."

A supply of water now close to his reach, the executioner dismissed the guard to his post at the stairhead, and secured Latifah's ankles in the same manner as her wrists. The buckets were not yet filled and so, by the time he had shortened the length of the ropes to his satisfaction, she was still just touching the floor, a situation he soon rectified by adding more water to the buckets until she was spread-eagled in the framework, with the weights not heavy enough to pull on her arms and legs unduly. He went to inspect his iron.

Again her orange-haired persecutor came to stand at the foot of the rack. As she strained her neck to look at him, visiting him with all the contempt she could muster in her weak and sickened state, she could see over his shoulder the sentry lounging against the rail, an interested spectator of the scene below him.

"You may kill me, but I give thanks that Prince Ali will visit his wrath on you, and bring you quickly to your own death. Quick to the time, but slow in the duration, monstrous beast that dares to masquerade in the guise of a man!"

He laughed out loud, the sound echoing strangely in that fearsome, flicker-lighted place of horror. "Prince Ali! Whatever his plans, he will find himself in the trap set by myself and my friend Achmed the Bandit."

His words dropped like leaden doom into her stomach, causing more disheartedness than all those drops of the previous night.

"Achmed?"

"Yes, my dear; my faithful, or at least, well-rewarded, Achmed."

He laughed again at her expression, as she let her head fall back in sudden and complete despair.

"You don't think that I would play this game with only one weapon at my command, do you?"

Footsteps came running, staggering along the corridor tunnel, and from her feverish, upside-down viewpoint she saw a man stumble to the rail.

"Sire! Sire; Prince Ali is even now attacking with his rebels, and they have . . . made entry . . . into the palace." Then he gulped, clutched at his throat, and rolled over the rail to fall in a broken heap on the stone floor, his dead, staring eyes fixed on hers.

She managed to summon a laugh to her lips, and painfully fought her head upright once more. "What of your trap, my dear Uncle?" She laughed again at the shock and surprise written large on his sallow features.

He stepped to her side and slapped her viciously across the face. "Even if your lover, the foreigner, is here, he will have to learn to love something other than you are now. Here, executioner; curse you, man, what is keeping you? Bring your tool here. Hurry!"

A moronic smirk on his greasy face, the squat man thrust a leather scrap in his palm, plucked the white iron from the flames, and approached his impatient master.

Above, in the Palace proper, I had advanced almost too far without support, for the approach of a large body of guards sent me hastening back the way I had come, my retreat almost cut off by a second group who had forced their way through my rebels surrounding the Palace and were now endeavoring to discover the whereabouts of my party. Their indecision saved me, for in the gloom of the corridor they let me approach too close, and I had felled two with swift thrusts of my blade and was past before they recovered. They were too bunched in their pursuit to gain on me, and I sped down the passages like a young leopard, breaking once again into the main hall to find a scene of confusion and chaos. Dozens of individual hand-to-hand fights were taking place all over the floor, and it was impossible to tell with whom was the advantage. I began to fight my way through to Hassan, who was the center of a large knot of men, wishing, not for the first time that day, that good Bakar, valiant Bakar, my trusty comrade-at-arms Bakar, was once again at my side.

The thought of him redoubled my anger and strength, and with a cry of "Meriam and the Cause!" I plunged into the melee, sword in one hand and dagger in the other, the latter doing the bulk of the bloody work at such close quarters. The party which had Saripah and a wide-eyed Meriam as its center was on the steps of the dais, and the fury of my attack from the rear soon allowed me to reach them. The one light moment in the whole affray, for me, was the sight, as I cut my way forward, step by step, of a stranger who could only be Hassan's *nasi tambar* flat on his face under one of the divans, busily inserting a broom handle between the legs of such of the enemy who were driven toward him.

As I reached Hassan's side I paused for a moment on the steps to survey the general situation. As I cast my eye around the great room I casually noted that our youngest recruit had found himself a *keris* and, though pale, was standing off an attacking soldier with vigor, while the old man who had so stubbornly insisted on joining us was laying about him with a long and heavy pole, using it as a flail at the legs of the enemy. My quick assessment showed me that the odds seemed numerically in favor of our band, but almost immediately the picture was reversed as through the corridor doors burst the two groups I had encountered on my way back. I gave a silent curse and touched my Captain's arm. He acknowledged me with a grim salute, and then we set to once again. For a minute it looked as though the two steps in my plan had failed beneath my feet, for I was no nearer finding the Red One than I had been on first entry into the Istana.

But then my heart lifted as a grand shout came from afar, a shout of: "For Meriam and the Cause!" Filling my lungs I bellowed out for someone to go unbar the tall doors to the hall. At the far end one of our fellows thrust home his *keris* with impatience into the heart of his opponent and made his way at a trot to the doors. He loosed the large timber bar, and was almost crushed underfoot as the huge wooden slabs burst open with a crash, and a hundred men charged into the hall. The townsmen! My plea had been answered, and the dwellers of the marketplace that I had called upon earlier had spread the word of rebellion and raised a force. Though they were armed mostly with wood billets and domestic knives and homemade clubs, their spirit won them through, and now our enemy was caught between the two groups.

Hassan nudged me with his useless shoulder, and drove down into the battle like a madman. I was about to follow when I noticed a strange movement in the curtains of the dais, a movement no wind had caused. I struck at them and elicited a cry of fear and pain.

Tearing aside the cloth I found none other than the wretched Karim, who would have fallen to his knees to whine for mercy had I not seized him by the throat and brought his face to mine.

"Where is the tyrant? Where is your master, the Red One, dog?"

The man's loose mouth chattered so much with fear that I could not make out his speech, and so I shook him again for the encouragement of a clearer tongue. He gasped, and I relaxed my hold, till he could speak again. "There! There, in the corner, behind the curtain."

I spun around to see where he pointed, and saw no man. I shook him again. "You lie, misborn of Shaitan's weakest angel. Where?"

"I swear it, Prince. Behind there is a door, which leads to a cavern beneath the river—where my master has his prison, and his torture place."

"Then where is the Princess Latifah?"

"She is there also, Prince; he has taken her to find out your plans."

I thrust him from me in disgust and rage, and thereby saved my life. Useless as he was in life, by his death he served a good cause, for even as I was about to turn from him, poor weak creature that he was, he staggered toward me and I saw a great rod sticking out from his back. A spear, aimed for me, had struck through the curtain, and he fell at my feet. Taking no chances for a similar spear throw being more certain in its aim and effect, I took Saripah roughly by the arm and pushed her down, with Meriam in her arms, behind Abdul's divan, where they would be safe for a time. And then I ran to the curtain behind which Karim had said there was a door.

Abdul stood again at the foot of the rack, tugging at his orange moustache, waiting with impatience while the cautious executioner made his way slowly to his side, the white-hot iron in his hand. He spat on the end and there was a quick flash of steam, no more.

"Hurry, fool, hurry. There's no time for niceties."

"Where shall I inflict the first burn, Sire?"

A last despairing glance around showed Latifah only

the sentry, leaning over the rail, licking his lips in excited anticipation. None of the other prisoners roused themselves. The figures of the Red One and the executioner blotted out all else. And then the squat brute moved to carry out his master's orders, and she tensed herself, neck rigid, head back, biting on her lower lip.

"Scar her navel. Burn out that pit!"

She felt the scorching heat descend toward her.

"No! Strip the cloth from her first. Let us see the flesh shrivel and scorch and sear!"

The heat receded and she sucked in a deep breath for the respite, momentary as she knew it to be. Looking beneath her shoulder as her head hung down she saw the executioner carefully lay his tool across the corner of the framework, the wood charring even though the heated end was away from it. Then, arms outstretched, the heavy figure reached toward her, touched the hem of her sarong, tugged it toward him, leaned forward still more to get a better purchase . . . and continued to lean forward, slowly tilting over the fulcrum of the crossbar until the whole of his weight fell on her, dragging her down to the ground beneath him, the pain at her ankles and wrists excruciating as the weighted buckets were pulled up by the unequal load. And as her head touched the floor and her body straightened, she saw the haft of a dagger projecting from his shoulder blades.

The Red One was frozen by amazement for the space of two seconds, and then he wheeled, and saw what Latifah now could thankfully see.

I pushed the guard from me with my foot, plucking my sword from between his ribs as he slithered over the edge of the landing to join his companion on the floor below, and stared across the space of the feebly lit cave at the orange-haired monster whose evil conception it had been. Still fixing his gaze I began to move slowly down the steps, red blade in my hand, wondering how to take him. It had been an accident that the executioner had laid down his iron, else I had not dared to throw my dagger at him, for fear of harming the Princess if the white-hot instrument had fallen with him upon her.

Abdul was weaponless, but before I could rush upon him he seized up the branding iron and held it close to Latifah's face, so that even where I was I could smell the sickening stench of scorched hair. By now I was opposite to him, and helpless. I dare not throw my sword at him, for in the instant that it would take me to raise it and change my grip he could drop the iron on the girl. We stared at each other. Latifah groaned a little with the pain of the weights, and I knew that I could not risk a wrong move. For in that tiny glance I recognized that, for all her wet, bedraggled, and singed hair, her red-rimmed eyes, her bleeding lip, her strained and twisted face, her hot and flushed cheeks and brow— this was the girl I loved, and the whole world suddenly began to revolve around the poles of her existence, and not my own.

Abdul, wily to the end, broke the deadlock first, by motioning me to go slowly to the foot of the machine, while he began to move around its head, the instrument inches from her head, cooling now to redness, but none-theless searing hot. Gradually we circled the rack, I cursing myself for my helplessness, he cautiously placing his feet firmly, moving step by slow step. Then he had his back to the stairs and the width of the frame was between us. Slowly he reached back with his left hand, feeling the air until he touched the great broad-bladed headsman's scimitar that still rested upright against the block. He grasped it, and backed away toward the stairs. As I made a move to turn past the end of the rack he made a gesture as if to throw the iron over on Latifah's body, where she had managed to heave the corpse of the executioner off her, and once more I was perforce still. Her action was unlucky, for as the weight of her former torturer decreased the buckets came into action once more and silently raised her up level with the top of the framework, forestalling the wild plan I had of vaulting across the timbers to get between the Red One and his victim.

He reached the stairs at last and began to climb them, one careful step at a time, still within throwing range of the girl. In a sudden movement he changed his weapons in his hands, till he had the scimitar firmly in his right, handle to his grip, and ready to be used. I still stood there, chained by his craftiness, but ready for the trick I knew he must play.

And he made that move! As he reached the top of the stairway he flung out from him the iron, whirling in red circles toward the helpless Princess. Clenching my teeth, I leaned over her and, using all the skill I could command, parried the flying metal as I would have the furious attack of a swordsman. With a great shudder of relief I felt the shock, heard the dull clang, and saw the now-impotent bar go sliding off my blade to land with a jet of steam below the waterwheel.

I heard Abdul's feet go flying along the corridor. I jumped over the side of the framework, put one arm around Latifah's waist, kissed her gently but quickly on the bruised and chapped lips, made four great sweeps with my sword, and laid her gently on the floor, before leaping the other beam, jumping to the stair rail, and loping after the Red One with great strides that filled my heart again with happy strength. By the time I was in the tunnel he had vanished around a corner, and when I came up to that same corner he had gone through the door, a hundred feet from me. Sudden joy at impending duel put eagle's wings to my feet and I fairly flew down that little length.

But I was to be disappointed in my duel.

As soon as he was through the door and past the covering curtain, Abdul saw that he was lost, his men either prisoner in the great hall or still fighting on vainly in small knots. But his eye lighted on another prey, and wild and insane violence and revenge for the loss of his plans must have swept through him.

There, but a few feet from him, cowered Saripah and the little Princess whose rule he had attempted to usurp. Taking two monstrous strides toward them, he raised his scimitar above his head, using both hands to lift the mighty weapon. And as the great blade swept up on its preliminary arc Saripah threw herself across the body of her charge, exposing her back to the blade wheeling above her. And at that moment my sword took him in the heart through the rib cage at the back.

It was the third man I had butchered from the rear that day, but in each case no honorable alternative had been left to me. The force of the Red One's upward swing carried his body up and over in a backward circle, so that he landed on the hilt of my sword and drove it quite through so that he was completely transfixed. He died an instantaneous death, and a clean one; the only two matters with which I had argument in the case.

Because Saripah had turned away and hugged Meriam to her breast, so that the expected blow would take herself rather than her ward, she did not see me as I took the broad-bladed scimitar and with one blow severed the orange-haired head of Abdul the Red One. I left my sword in his body and, taking the head by its sick-hued hair, strode to the edge of the dais, calling out as I stood there: "So die all tyrants. Put up your swords, men of Abdul, and you will receive honorable treatment hereafter, to depart from this country as you please. Abdul the Red One, the tyrant of 'Dak Betul, is dead. Long live the Princess Meriam."

In the flush of personal victory I had half-forgotten that one battle won does not necessarily mean the end of the war, and though an almost complete hush settled on the milling throng below, there were still those who would resist to the bitter end, and one of these it was who fetched me a blow on the head that laid me low and took my senses from me. Hassan later informed me that the fellow had indeed met with a bitter end, for which I was sorry. He must have been a brave and loyal man by his own lights, to continue the fight against the odds.

It was soon over, then, they tell me, but I knew nothing of it for I lay swathed in the curtains which I had brought down in my fall.

SEVEN

I slept a deep sleep; I dreamed, and slept again; woke, to see for a moment the beautiful Latifah, restored to all her dark glory, watching over me; smiled; slept again, dreamed again, and woke to a sunny morning two days later.

It is simple to write this, now, and it is a short writing of a simple sequence of events. And yet . . . and yet, there were lifetimes in those incidents, in each one of them.

I was asleep, at first, and yet, although I did not truly dream, still I was *aware;* aware of forces that pushed and shrugged against me, tilting me this way and that, as though I were a blind fish deep down in a black-blue sea. The forces gently squeezed me, with a slow, restful pulse, so that I drifted contentedly, for eons. And then I seemed cast upon a shore of staring white sand, with a white sun staring down on me like an enormous eye, a dead, sterile eye. And I turned, and the sea had receded, leaving me in this awful bleached, parched, parchment of a desert. And a feeling of quiet terror came over me, as if I were about to be left in this place for eternity, alone, lonely, with no person and no thing to care for or about me; and I could not sustain this lack of pity or compassion and so I screamed (I thought) for something that *would* care, or for which I *could* care, and my scream lasted another eon; until two great words struck me like a blow—*"Beware compassion"*— and I was knocked to the ground. And I rolled over and gazed into that awful white light that searched through me like a silver probe, and I could not move my hands to shield my eyes and so I closed them. And again words beat at me, from north and from the south; from the east and from the west: *"Beware: love! Forswear: feeling!"*

And the words buffeted me like huge winds and carried me up, and again I found myself in a dark-blue sea, warmed and cooled; and moved and stilled; and rested and nudged. Until I was at one with the forces and (I suppose) slept a true sleep from which I wafted up to see my love at my side.

And I smiled to show her my love, and fell back again slowly into the blue-blackness which now, of a terrible suddenness, was no longer peaceful but which, instead, roiled and boiled, and crushed me, and hurled me, and tore at me with great spongy fingers which sheathed bones of hard horn. And they seized me and set me up so that I could do no else but stare ahead. And again there was the awesome white blankness of the sand, but this time I seemed to be above it, or looking at it from a perpendicular angle. Wonderful to behold, flashes of my life were starkly represented on it, but I could see myself. Yes, there I was in the grotto, circling around the stretched figure of Latifah, and Abdul, orange hair glinting in the flickering flames, circling with me as though we danced a duet of death. And it was gone. And now Karim falling at my feet, with the spear protruding through the curtain. Gone. Now Bakar, dying in my arms . . . and I wanted to cry out to him, and tell him I was there and near him . . . but they would not let me, but showed me the rally in the marketplace as I leaped the barricade on my horse. Ah, what a brave sight I was! But no, now I spied upon myself spying upon the Princess Latifah as I first saw her, all prisoned like her fish. And the flashes moved faster now, flick, flick, flick, flick, as fast as the cut and thrust of a good swordsman's arm.

The fight with Achmed at the campfire. A red glint on swords.

The fight at the rocks with Hassan.

A long green blur.

The river.

Another splash of green.

The beach.

The sea.

And then.

Nothing.

Nothing.

Nothing. I had never seen nothingness before, and

cannot describe it. I can only tell you that it is . . . horrible. The place beyond insanity. The time past the end of eternity. As if one had been running along a dark corridor and suddenly stepped out and over the edge of the highest cliff one can imagine. I wanted to scream, but could not scream, for I had no voice, no throat to scream with, I was become that terrible Nothing.

I fell into that Nothing, being Nothing myself, and Nothing happened to me.

But I know that time elapsed, that I existed through that long period of Nothing. And was told something, and learned something, and knew something.

For when *I* became a Something again, lapped by the restful blue-black forces I plummeted into, I knew that I must leave the Princess Latifah, my beauty, my other self, my love; and leave Hassan and those others I called my men; and Meriam; and the city of 'Dak Betul. I must leave all this behind, and go I knew not whither; certainly not to Bohongistan or India. And though I tried to fight this command, I could not find a way around it, though its reason I knew not.

And I knew that I must not meet One Other. Some Other Person, who could do me irreparable harm if I but chanced to observe him from afar, even.

These things I knew, and then the gentle forces took me with them and plunged me into a healthful sleep from which I woke to a sunny morning, two days after my injury had been received.

EIGHT:

I drifted down the river toward the sea in a daze, worn out by the internal struggle between what I knew I *had* to do and what I *wanted* to do. The sun beat down on the sluggish brown stream, and the days were hot, sticky, humid, wholly uncomfortable. My meager provisions were as tasteless as my life, and even the sight of my true blade and the recollections of heady days of spirit and valiant times of honor it had brought me cast me only into further gloom.

While I had lain senseless in the great hall, Hassan had produced the Princess Meriam, and the whole host, well and wounded, bent the knee and acclaimed her as rightful ruler of 'Dak Betul.

Then Hassan and Saripah themselves had gone down to that cavern beneath the river, and brought Latifah up, setting free the other prisoners that lived. Latifah had seemed shocked and out of her wits when they found her, and no wonder at that! But when they came back into the hall, with Hassan's tunic around her shoulders, and she saw me lying where I had fallen, her own distress was banished, and she knelt, crying, by my side.

Well, without awaiting my orders (which in any case would have matched his) Hassan caused the corridor to the grotto sealed off, and then let the river in from above, so that no remnant of that sorry place would survive. Taking complete charge, the good Captain had the dead taken out and given burial, the Istana cleaned up and restored, and all traces of Abdul the Red One's tyrannic rule removed and obliterated. In Meriam's name he revoked all bad laws, and set up a tribunal to judge on cases of complaints against the orange-haired monster's false justice.

Latifah refused to let anyone nurse me other than herself, and in the process became restored to her own self most wonderfully. As soon as I was fit, a matter of hours after I awoke, and had fed, I called a council of myself, Latifah, Hassan, the loyal Saripah, who had proved herself a person of some wit and no little ingenuity, and who deserved to be recognized for more than the maid she was; and, of course, Meriam. Young as the child was, she had seen enough to make her wise beyond her years. I only wished that poor Bakar could have been there, for if he could not have added words to the council, his solid presence and stolid matter-of-factness would have been a great asset to us. Surprisingly, with an innocent seriousness that startled us all, it was Meriam who mentioned his name, requesting that dear Uncle Bakar be brought to lie in the Palace grounds, so that she could always feel him near her. I was not the only one to turn my head away, and agree, gruffly.

Hassan and Saripah were of course hot to be married, and it was I who suggested that Latifah act as Regent for Meriam until she reached majority, with these two as perpetual guardians and councillors for both Princesses. I noticed that Hassan was about to question my own status, and looked in surprise at Latifah, but he caught my eye and was silent. Latifah, too, gave me a quick glance before she modestly lowered her large black eyes. In the short while since I had recovered we had had no opportunity to talk of love and such things, even if I had not been prepared to deliberately avoid such speech.

Meriam agreed to our proposals, which we explained very carefully to her, and we sketched out the form of a Proclamation. I pleaded weariness, feigning a lassitude I did not possess, and hinted, rather strongly, to Latifah, that she should go and take some rest herself now that her long vigil was over. I also told Saripah to take Meriam away and to see to it that the child was fit and ready to take part in the Proclamation ceremonies on the morrow. Hassan, the lovesick oaf, hastened out with them but as they reached the doorway I called him back, letting the others go on. I told him dryly that he had all the time in the world, and a whole palace full of rooms in which to make love to Saripah, which raised an abashed grin on his crestfallen face.

Then I got down to the serious side of my business with him.

"How long will it take you to fit out a small boat for me, one which I can take downriver without a crew?"

"What? A boat?"

"Yes, something that I can manage by myself, and with enough food and water to get me to the coast."

"You're leaving us then, Ali?"

"Yes, I'm afraid it's so."

"And the Princess Latifah? What of her?"

"Well, what of her?"

"Only . . . that I had thought . . ."

"That I loved her as do you Saripah?"

177

"Something like that."

I smiled, a trifle sadly I confess, and turned to stare out the window, over that same garden where I had first seen, and lost my heart to, my lovely Princess.

"Well, as you say, it is something like that, except . . ."

"Except what, Ali? You are a man of mystery indeed. No merchant, you, and surely Prince in truth. Is it perhaps that you already have a wife, back there in that strange land from whence you came here?"

"No! No woman, no girl, no houri that I have met or have yet to meet can stand in the way; or can compare with her! But . . ."

He came to me and took my arm with his unwounded one, looking me straight in the eye.

"These pauses in your speech are unlike you, friend Ali. No quick decisions? No firm resolves? I am sure you have an honorable reason. And by virtue of that same honor I swear that if you lack the title of Prince, and think yourself low in degree, then you are wrong, and your Princess will say you are wrong, and will care nothing of the matter. Why, friend, if that's all it is, we'll have Meriam make you a Prince on the morrow by royal decree, to ease your conscience!"

In spite of my sorrow I could not but laugh aloud at his words of cheer and comradeship. With such friends, what can the world not offer, be it palace or poverty, horn of plenty or hard rations, that will make it a bad place to be in?

I clapped him on the shoulder, making him wince.

"No, Hassan, none of these things which you fear are the cause of my departure, or the root of my decision. Come, we have been friends, comrades-in-arms, brothers of the sword. Trust me, ask no questions, and do as I ask. Fit me out with a boat, as I say, and let me be off before the sun goes down this night, so that I may be well on my way before nightfall overtakes me. And say not one word to Latifah. With luck she sleeps deeply now, and will not awaken until tomorrow. I rely on you to keep her away from this chamber. That will be your most difficult task, but stand guard and defy her if necessary. Tell her that I am still weak and need to
178

sleep; tell her that I have requested, nay, commanded that no one disturb me. Man, tell her that I have a woman, one of Abdul's little pets, in here with me, if you think that will keep her away! Do this for me. Not because I have been your leader, but because you are my companion and my friend."

True to the unfair code of friendship I had forced upon him, my young Captain did not press me further, and did me excellent service, for within the hour I was seated in the light boat at the Istana wharf, ready to leave. Three days journey would take me to the sea, I was told. Well enough, three days might give me a chance to change this mind that seemed to have been lodged within my own skull like a pebble in a coconut. The more I rattled it about, the more it wore away my brain, and the more unchanged it remained.

I stood and reached up, taking his hands in mine. I gave him a firm grip, and he returned the pressure; then I pushed off and paddled out into the slow current. As I turned to look back for the last time he was still standing there, his scimitar out and upraised in a soldier's salute. Solemnly I drew my own blade, kissed it, and held it out and aloft in his direction. And so we parted, and I drifted down through the quiet afternoon city of 'Dak Betul, until at last it was hidden behind me by a bend in the river, and the jungle began to close in on me.

And two days later I was still drifting, though I had spent the previous day paddling furiously, hoping to drive out the devil in my brain by sheer effort and fatigue, but to no avail.

I passed the spot where Bakar and I had crossed the river on our first trip inland, and knew that I could not be far from the coast now. Lazy crocodiles, indolent in the heat of the day, eyed me from the sandbars, and I roused myself to activity to manage the tricky currents set up by the winding path of the stream.

Two hours more and I was floating gently, rocked by the small waves that came into the narrow estuary. Why I had come here, what rendezvous I was to make, I still did not know, but I ran the boat up on the left shore, to a little beach, and, taking the remaining food and water from it, made my meal in the shade of a fan-shaped Traveler's Palm. I rested awhile, then walked slowly along the beach, idly staring out over the waves. *It must have been the other side of that headland that we were washed ashore on,* I thought as I strolled. *Perhaps I shall find other wreckage washed up there.* I quickened my steps, with a purpose now in mind, and trod the hard, firm sand left bare by the outgoing tide, pure white and glaring to my eyes. To relieve them I looked either at the cool green jungle to my left, or out over the sea, blue as a peacock's feather-fancied eyes. And as I turned my lackluster gaze seaward for perhaps the tenth time I saw a ship come bellying around the point ahead, a ship such as I had never seen before. It was quite close inshore, obviously following the line of the coast, and I could make it out quite clearly.

She was a large ship, evidently built for ocean-going, broad in the beam, with a high castle aft, but only a gentle rise at the bow. The bow itself was flat, rising up out of the water at a steep angle, and the sides came forward to form almost a double prow, with a wide, flat, angled surface between them. Three masts were stepped in her, each with peculiar sets of sails that were jointed for raising, transversely, rather than constructed to roll up to the yards like those of the ships I knew.

As it began gradually to draw abreast of me, or abeam, if I considered myself as another drifting vessel, I found myself shouting, shouting as if my very life depended upon the crew hearing me. I tore off my white shirt and began waving it like a madman, and soon I perceived that they had seen me, for they reefed their sails and hove to. Presently a boat was lowered and a crew began to row it across the space between us. As it drew closer my interest mounted, for these were not men such as I had seen elsewhere. They were of my color, or perhaps a little paler, with some of a sickly saffron hue, mostly naked to the waist, with bandanas around their heads, and short-legged garments on their lower limbs.

One or two of them wore earrings as I did, but the cast of their features was narrower, and their bones were somehow different. There was more likeness between myself and my Malay friends than between either of us and these strangers. They did not run the boat up to the shore but stood off from it a little way, beckoning me, and calling in some foreign language whose roots I could not reckon, to come forward.

Impelled by I knew not what, the heavy burden of regrets in my heart not quite counterbalanced by the stir of fresh adventure, I ran forward with a will, and vaulted over the side of the boat, which promptly turned and made away to the strange ship. They asked me many questions, which I could not answer, and one, whom I took to be an officer, from his robes and cap (which he must have found cursed uncomfortable in this heat) spoke slowly to me, fingering my sword and my clothes, before giving up in disgust and settling to silence. I in my turn gazed with interest around me, but could make nothing of them. When we were about half-way to the ship I happened to glance back along the shore to where my own boat lay. And with a leaping heart saw a great, narrow-prowed barge shoot out of the estuary, hesitate near my beached boat, then continue to make its way toward us.

I saw that it was manned by at least two dozen oars-men and that, by its ornamentation, it was a royal craft. As it gained on us, I could see the royal pennant of 'Dak Betul streaming from its high, dragon-carved prow.

The officer in our boat had seen it too, and drew his sword, but though I tried to reassure him with gestures, he only urged his own men on to greater speed, and suddenly drew my sword from out my cummerbund. I made no protest, leaning instead over the gunwale to observe the other boat, which now drew parallel.

"Is Prince Ali there?" called a voice across the narrowing stretch of water that separated us.

I waved in reply, and called in turn: "Yes; who would know?"

A new voice spoke and I saw the Princess Latifah,

my Latifah, standing in the center of the boat, her long black hair flowing in the wind. "I would know, Prince. Wither goest thou? What dost thou seek to escape?"

The officer in my boat tried to pull me down, perhaps thinking we were some group of warring natives in league to plunder his vessel, but I pulled free.

"I seek to escape from nothing, but I must pursue I know not what. I am driven to this strange ship, and where I go is a black mystery to me."

"Why did you not take me?"

"I had not thought to. I had not thought to separate you from your country and your people."

"You force me to declare myself, unmaidenly as it may be. But I have but one country, and no people. I am some other person's subject."

Our cries must have sounded oddly to both crews, those who understood us and those who did not. Standing straddle-legged now, with the sea breeze filling my shirt, and running cool and fine against my face and through my hair, I called again: "You shame me, Princess, in your declaration. I would have told you of my love at first meeting, but although I had enough heart for you, I had not enough to cause you pain, and something told me that I must leave your country."

"No matter now. I love you too, and will go with you, wherever the winds of the sea take this ship, if our fortune or your fate should be to travel in it."

Our boat came to the ship's side, where a short ladder hung over, and the officer motioned me to ascend, following after me. As I reached the deck, the planks warm beneath my bare feet, I noticed a small fleet of similar ships lying out on the horizon, barely perceptible. The officer turned back to shout down below and, looking, I saw the boat stand off while the royal barge came alongside. The oarsmen saluted with their blades as I leaned down to help Latifah up, then, evidently to her previous command, turned and made off, while the ship's boat in turn drew in close.

I took Latifah's hand and pressed it, too proud to make further indication of my love before the small crowd of seamen who now had gathered around us, talking their strange lingo the while. The officer motioned us to remain where we were, and bowed slightly to Latifah, whose royal rank he may have guessed from her bearing and rich clothing, which contrasted greatly with my own sorry wardrobe. With a quizzical glance at me he turned on his heel and went aft, to where I could see other oddly clothed men of rank standing, near to an upright timber on which was engraved the name of the ship, which I could not read, and what I took to be a date, in Arabic numerals—1292.

Suddenly I had the feeling of something great impending, some momentous news to be told me. It was somehow as if I had lived through this precise experience before, and wanted only a little more searching in my mind to be able to predict the events and speech to take place in the next few seconds. But yet my emotions were mixed, for compounded with the feeling of excitement and the desire for this fulfillment was another of an ineffable sadness. . . . A memory growing dim seemed to relate to a certain man. . . . A man . . .

But my reveries were interrupted as the officer returned, bringing with him another, older, man, of devout and serious mien, who looked as though he might have seen all the secrets under the heavens, with the far-reaching light blue eyes of the sailor, the traveler, the one who cannot rest but must always look for further horizons, who would venture past the edge of the earth itself. The officer was making some kind of introduction, for such were his tone and gesture, but of course I caught nothing of it, nor Latifah, and we smiled and nodded in reply, holding hands like children about to embark on some special treat, some picnic.

I tried to make out the name of the personage, tried to remember it, for the officer was taking great pains to pronounce it slowly: "Mes. Ser. Mar. Co. Po. Lo." A strange name, in a strange tongue.

NINE:

"Has he . . . gone over, Doctor?"

"I'm sure he has, Teri."

"No returning?"

"I think not."

"Like the other?"

"Yes, exactly like the other. But not as we, my dear."

"No, we were lucky."

"Lucky? A word needing definition. As my scientific helper you should make precise statements only!"

"Still, even if he has found a happiness . . . over there . . . then there is still . . . this, remaining here. Will we put it with the other?"

"Naturally. I am surprised that you asked. You know I think there will be a use for it, when other ones come back from time ahead to "dream" in this world of ours. Yes, we had best move it now, before it is beyond use."

"Yes, Doctor Mordant."

"So formal, Teri?"

Take an inimitable style, in-depth creativity, and insight mixed with irony —Put them together and you have Jack Vance, a tradition that needs no introduction to science-fiction readers.

Have him weave his delicate artistry around castles and turrets, filling them with the strong personalities of a super-cultured culture, their irascible Birds and gauze insect-girl Phanes, all threatened by an invasion force of uni-cognitive Meks and crumbling ideology.

The result is *The Last Castle*—well-deserved winner of the Nebula Award, a story well worth reading.

Turn this book over for
second complete novel

THE LAST CASTLE

by

JACK VANCE

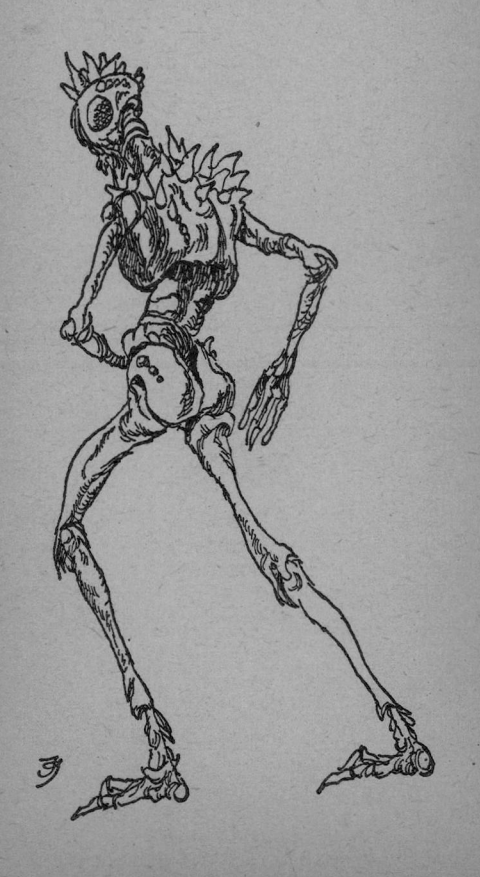

ACE BOOKS, INC.
1120 Avenue of the Americas
New York, N.Y. 10036

Chapter I

1

Toward the end of a stormy summer afternoon, with the sun finally breaking out under ragged black rain-clouds, Castle Janeil was overwhelmed and its population destroyed. Until almost the last moment factions among the castle clans contended as to how Destiny properly should be met. The gentlemen of most prestige and account elected to ignore the entire undignified circumstance and went about their normal pursuits, with neither more nor less punctilio than usual. A few cadets, desperate to the point of hysteria, took up weapons and prepared to resist the final assault. Still others, perhaps a quarter of the total population, waited passively, ready— almost happy—to expiate the sins of the human race. In the end, death came uniformly to all, and all extracted as much satisfaction from their dying as this essentially graceless process could afford. The proud sat turning the pages of their beautiful books, discussing the qualities of a century-old essence, or fondling a favorite Phane, and died without deigning to heed the fact. The hotheads raced up the muddy slope which, outraging all normal rationality, loomed above the parapets of Janeil. Most were buried under sliding rubble, but a few gained the ridge to gun, hack and stab, until they themselves were

shot, crushed by the half-alive power-wagons, hacked or stabbed. The contrite waited in the classic posture of expiation—on their knees, heads bowed—and perished, so they believed, by a process in which the Meks were symbols and human sin the reality. In the end all were dead: gentlemen, ladies, Phanes in the pavilions; Peasants in the stables. Of all those who had inhabited Janeil, only the Birds survived, creatures awkward, gauche and raucous, oblivious to pride and faith, more concerned with the wholeness of their hides than the dignity of their castle. As the Meks swarmed down over the parapets, the Birds departed their cotes and, screaming strident insults, flapped east toward Hagedorn, now the last castle of Earth.

2

Four months before, the Meks had appeared in the park before Janeil, fresh from the Sea Island massacre. Climbing to the turrets and balconies, sauntering the Sunset Promenade, from ramparts and parapets, the gentlemen and ladies of Janeil, some two thousand in all, looked down at the brown-gold warriors. Their mood was complex: amused indifference, flippant disdain, and a substratum of doubt and foreboding: all the product of three basic circumstances: their own exquisitely subtle civilization, the security provided by Janeil's walls, and the fact that they could conceive no recourse, no means for altering circumstances.

The Janeil Meks had long since departed to join the revolt; there only remained Phanes, Peasants and Birds from which to fashion what would have been the travesty of a punitive force. At the moment there seemed no need for such a force. Janeil was deemed impregnable. The walls, two hundred feet tall, were black rock-melt contained in the meshes of a silver-blue steel alloy. Solar cells provided energy for all the needs of the castle, and in the event of emergency, food could be synthesized from carbon dioxide and water vapor, as well as syrup for Phanes, Peasants and Birds. Such a need was not en-

visaged. Janeil was self-sufficient and secure, though inconveniences might arise when machinery broke down and there were no Meks to repair it. The situation then was disturbing but hardly desperate. During the day the gentlemen so inclined brought forth energy-guns and sport-rifles and killed as many Meks as the extreme range allowed.

After dark the Meks brought forward power-wagons and earth-movers, and began to raise a dike around Janeil. The folk of the castle watched without comprehension until the dike reached a height of fifty feet and dirt began to spill down against the walls. Then the dire purpose of the Meks became apparent, and insouciance gave way to dismal foreboding. All the gentlemen of Janeil were erudite in at least one realm of knowledge; certain were mathematical theoreticians, while others had made a profound study of the physical sciences. Some of these, with a detail of Peasants to perform the sheerly physical exertion, attempted to restore the energy-cannon to functioning condition. Unluckily, the cannon had not been maintained in good order. Various components were obviously corroded or damaged. Conceivably these components might have been replaced from the Mek shops on the second sub-level, but none of the group had any knowledge of the Mek nomenclature or warehousing system. Warrick Madency Arban* suggested that a workforce of Peasants search the warehouse, but in view of the limited mental capacity of the Peasants, nothing was done and the whole plan to restore the energy-cannon came to naught.

The gentlefolk of Janeil watched in fascination as the dirt piled higher and higher around them, in a circular mound like a crater. Summer neared its end, and on one stormy day dirt and rubble rose above the parapets, and began to spill over into the courts and piazzas: Janeil must soon be buried and all within suffocated. It was then that a group of impulsive young cadets, with more elán than dignity, took up weapons and charged up the slope. The Meks dumped dirt and stone upon them, but a hand-

---

*Arban of the Madency family in the Warrick clan.

ful gained the ridge where they fought in a kind of dreadful exaltation.

Fifteen minutes the fight raged and the earth became sodden with rain and blood. For one glorious moment the cadets swept the ridge clear and had not most of their fellows been lost under the rubble anything might have occurred. But the Meks regrouped and thrust forward. Ten men were left, then six, then four, then one, then none. The Meks marched down the slope, swarmed over the battlements, and with somber intensity killed all within. Janeil, for seven hundred years the abode of gallant gentlemen, and gracious ladies, had become a lifeless hulk.

3

The Mek, standing as if a specimen in a museum case, was a man-like creature native, in his original version, to a planet of Etamin. His tough rusty-bronze hide glistened metallically as if oiled or waxed; the spines thrusting back from scalp and neck shone like gold, and indeed were coated with a conductive copper-chrome film. His sense organs were gathered in clusters at the site of a man's ears; his visage—it was often a shock, walking the lower corridors, to come suddenly upon a Mek—was corrugated muscle, not dissimiliar to the look of an uncovered human brain. His maw, a vertical irregular cleft at the base of this "face," was an obsolete organ by reason of the syrup sac which had been introduced under the skin of the shoulders; the digestive organs, originally used to extract nutrition from decayed swamp vegetation and coelenterates, had atrophied. The Mek typically wore no garment except possibly a work-apron or a tool-belt, and in the sunlight his rust-bronze skin made a handsome display. This was the Mek solitary, a creature intrinsically as effective as man—perhaps more by virtue of his superb brain which also functioned as a radio transceiver. Working in the mass, by the teeming thousands, he seemed less admirable, less competent: a hybrid of sub-man and cockroach.

Certain savants, notably Morninglight's D.R. Jardine and Salonson of Tuang, considered the Mek bland and phlegmatic, but the profound Claghorn of Castle Hagedorn asserted otherwise. The emotions of the Mek, said Claghorn, were different from human emotions, and only vaguely comprehensible to man. After diligent research Claghorn isolated over a dozen Mek emotions.

In spite of such research, the Mek revolt came as an utter surprise, no less to Claghorn, D.R. Jardine and Salonson than to anyone else. Why? asked everyone. How could a group so long submissive have contrived so murderous a plot?

The most reasonable conjecture was also the simplest: the Mek resented servitude and hated the Earthmen who had removed him from his natural environment. Those who argued against this theory claimed that it projected human emotions and attitudes into a non-human organism, that the Mek had every reason to feel gratitude toward the gentlemen who had liberated him from the conditions of Etamin Nine. To this, the first group would inquire, "Who projects human attitudes now?" And the retort of their opponents was often: "Since no one knows for certain, one projection is no more absurd than another."

CHAPTER II

1

CASTLE HAGEDORN occupied the crest of a black diorite crag overlooking a wide valley to the south. Larger, more majestic than Janeil, Hagedorn was protected by walls a mile in circumference, and three hundred feet tall. The parapets stood a full nine hundred feet above the valley, with towers, turrets and observation eyries raising even higher. Two sides of the crag, at east and west, dropped sheer to the valley. The north and south slopes, a trifle less steep, were terraced and planted with vines, artichokes, pears and pomegranates. An avenue rising from the valley circled the crag and passed through a portal

The clans of Hagedorn, their colors and associated families:

CLANS	COLORS	FAMILIES
Xanten	yellow; black piping	Haude, Quay, Idelsea, Esledune, Salonson, Roseth.
Beaudry	dark blue; white piping	Onwane, Zadig, Prine, Fer, Sesune.
Overwhele	gray, green; red rosettes	Claghorn, Abreu, Woss, Hinken, Zumbeld.
Aure	brown, black	Zadhause, Fotergil, Marune, Baudune, Godalming, Lesmanic
Isseth	purple, dark red	Mazeth, Floy, Luder-Hepman, Uegus, Kerrithew, Bethune.

The first gentleman of the castle, elected for life, is known as "Hagedorn."

The clan chief, selected by the family elders, bears the name of his clan, thus: "Xanten," "Beaudry," "Overwhele," "Aure," "Isseth"—both clans and clan chiefs.

The family elder, selected by household heads, bears the name of his family. Thus "Idelsea," "Zadhause," "Bethune," and "Claghorn," are both families and family elders.

The remaining gentlemen and ladies bear first the clan, then the family, then the personal name. Thus: Aure Zadhause Ludwick, abbreviated to A.Z. Ludwick, and Beaudry Fer Dariane, abbreviated to B.F. Dariane.

into the central plaza. Opposite stood the great Rotunda, with at either side the tall Houses of the twenty-eight families.

The original castle, constructed immediately after the return of men to Earth, stood on the site now occupied by the plaza. The tenth Hagedorn, assembling an enormous force of Peasants and Meks, had built the new walls, after which he demolished the old castle. The twenty-eight Houses dated from this time, five hundred years before.

Below the plaza were three service levels: the stables and garages at the bottom, next the Mek shops and Mek living quarters, then the various storerooms, warehouses and special shops: bakery, brewery, lapidary, arsenal, repository, and the like.

The current Hagedorn, twenty-sixth of the line, was a Claghorn of the Overwheles. His selection had occasioned general surprise, because O.C. Charle, as he had been before his elevation, was a gentleman of no remarkable presence. His elegance, flair, and erudition were only ordinary; he had never been notable for any significant originality of thought. His physical proportions were good; his face was square and bony, with a short straight nose, a benign brow, and narrow gray eyes. His expression, normally a trifle abstracted—his detractors used the word "vacant"—by a simple lowering of the eyelids, a downward twitch of the coarse blond eyebrows, at once became stubborn and surly, a fact of which O.C. Charle, or Hagedorn, was unaware.

The office, while exerting little or no formal authority, exerted a pervasive influence, and the style of the gentleman who was Hagedorn affected everyone. For this reason the selection of Hagedorn was a matter of no small importance, subject to hundreds of considerations, and it was the rare candidate who failed to have some old solecism or gaucherie discussed with embarrassing candor. While the candidate might never take overt umbrage, friendships were inevitably sundered, rancors augmented, reputations blasted. O.C. Charle's elevation represented a compromise between two factions among

11

the Overwheles, to which clan the privilege of selection had fallen.

The gentlemen between whom O.C. Charle represented a compromise were both highly respected, but distinguished by basically different attitudes toward existence. The first was the talented Garr of the Zumbeld family. He exemplified the traditional virtues of Castle Hagedorn: he was a notable connoisseur of essences, and he dressed with absolute savoir, with never so much as a pleat nor a twist of the characteristic Overwhele rosette awry. He combined insouciance and flair with dignity; his repartee coruscated with brilliant allusions and turns of phrase; when aroused his wit was utterly mordant. He could quote every literary work of consequence; he performed expertly upon the nine-stringed lute, and was thus in constant demand at the Viewing of Antique Tabards. He was an antiquarian of unchallenged erudition and knew the locale of every major city of Old Earth, and could discourse for hours upon the history of the ancient times. His military expertise was unparalleled at Hagedorn, and challenged only by D.K. Magdah of Castle Delora and perhaps Brusham of Tuang. Faults? Flaws? Few could be cited: over-punctilio which might be construed as waspishness; an intrepid pertinacity which could be considered ruthlessness. O.Z. Garr could never be dismissed as insipid or indecisive, and his personal courage was beyond dispute. Two years before, a stray band of Nomads had ventured into Lucerne Valley, slaughtering Peasants, stealing cattle, and going so far as to fire an arrow into the chest of an Isseth cadet. O.Z. Garr instantly assembled a punitive company of Meks, loaded them aboard a dozen power-wagons, and set forth in pursuit of the Nomads, finally overtaking them near Drene River, by the ruins of Worster Cathedral. The Nomads were unexpectedly strong, unexpectedly crafty, and were not content to turn tail and flee. During the fighting, O.Z. Garr displayed the most exemplary demeanor, directing the attack from the seat of his power-wagon, a pair of Meks standing by with shields to ward away arrows. The conflict ended in a rout of the Nomads; they

left twenty-seven lean black-cloaked corpses strewn on the field, while only twenty Meks lost their lives.

O.Z. Garr's opponent in the election was Claghorn, elder of the Claghorn family. As with O.Z. Garr, the exquisite discriminations of Hagedorn society came to Claghorn as easily as swimming to a fish. He was no less erudite than O.Z. Garr, though hardly so versatile, his principal field of study being the Meks, their physiology, linguistic modes, and social patterns. Claghorn's conversation was more profound, but less entertaining and not so trenchant as that of O.Z. Garr; he seldom employed the extravagant tropes and allusions which characterized Garr's discussions, preferring a style of speech which was unadorned. Claghorn kept no Phanes; O.Z. Garr's four matched Gossamer Dainties were marvels of delight, and at the viewing of Antique Tabards Garr's presentations were seldom outshone. The important contrast between the two men lay in their philosophic outlook. O.Z. Garr, a traditionalist, a fervent exemplar of his society, subscribed to its tenets without reservation. He was beset by neither doubt nor guilt; he felt no desire to alter the conditions which afforded more than two thousand gentlemen and ladies lives of great richness. Claghorn, while by no means an Expiationist, was known to feel dissatisfaction with the general tenor of life at Castle Hagedorn, and argued so plausibly that many folk refused to listen to him, on the grounds that they became uncomfortable. But an indefinable malaise ran deep, and Claghorn had many influential supporters.

When the time came for ballots to be cast, neither O.Z. Garr nor Claghorn could muster sufficient support. The office finally was conferred upon a gentleman who never in his most optimistic reckonings had expected it: a gentleman of decorum and dignity but no great depth; without flippancy, but likewise without vivacity; affable but disinclined to force an issue to a disagreeable conclusion: O.C. Charle, the new Hagedorn.

Six months later, during the dark hours before dawn, the Hagedorn Meks evacuated their quarters and departed, taking with them power-wagons, tools, weapons and electrical equipment. The act had clearly been long

in the planning, for simultaneously the Meks at each of the eight other castles made a similar departure.

The initial reaction at Castle Hagedorn, as elsewhere, was incredulity, then shocked anger, then—when the implications of the act were pondered—a sense of foreboding and calamity.

The new Hagedorn, the clan chiefs, and certain other notables appointed by Hagedorn met in the formal council chamber to consider the matter. They sat around a great table covered with red velvet: Hagedorn at the head; Xanten and Isseth at his left; Overwhele, Aure and Beaudry at his right; then the others, including O.Z. Garr, I.K. Linus, A.G. Bernal, a mathematical theoretician of great ability, and B.F. Wyas, an equally sagacious antiquarian who had identified the sites of many ancient cities: Palmyra, Lübeck, Eridu, Zanesville, Burton-on-Trent, and Massilia among others. Certain family elders filled out the council: Marune and Baudune of Aure; Quay, Roseth and Idelsea of Xanten; Uegus of Isseth, Claghorn of Overwhele.

All sat silent for a period of ten minutes, arranging their minds and performing the silent act of psychic accommodation known as "intression."

At last Hagedorn spoke. "The castle is suddenly bereft of its Meks. Needless to say, this is an inconvenient condition to be adjusted as swiftly as possible. Here, I am sure, we find ourselves of one mind."

He looked around the table. All thrust forward carved ivory tablets to signify assent—all save Claghorn, who however did not stand it on end to signify dissent.

Isseth, a stern white-haired gentleman magnificently handsome in spite of his seventy years, spoke in a grim voice. "I see no point in cogitation or delay. What we must do is clear. Admittedly the Peasants are poor material from which to recruit an armed force. Nonetheless, we must assemble them, equip them with sandals, smocks and weapons so that they do not discredit us, and put them under good leadership: O.Z. Garr or Xanten. Birds can locate the vagrants, whereupon we will track them down, order the Peasants to give them a good drubbing, and herd them home on the double."

Xanten, thirty-five years old—extraordinarily young to be a clan chief—and a notorious firebrand, shook his head. "The idea is appealing but impractical. Peasants simply could not stand up to the Meks, no matter how we trained them."

The statement was manifestly accurate. The Peasants, small andromorphs originally of Spica Ten, were not so much timid as incapable of performing a vicious act.

A dour silence held the table. O.Z. Garr finally spoke. "The dogs have stolen our power-wagons, otherwise I'd be tempted to ride out and chivy the rascals home with a whip."*

"A matter of perplexity," said Hagedorn, "is syrup. Naturally they carried away what they could. When this is exhausted—what then? Will they starve? Impossible for them to return to their original diet. What was it? Swamp mud? Eh, Claghorn, you're the expert in these matters. Can the Meks return to a diet of mud?"

"No," said Claghorn. "The organs of the adult are atrophied. If a cub were started on the diet, he'd probably survive."

"Just as I assumed." Hagedorn scowled portentously

---

*This, only an approximate translation, fails to capture the pungency of the language. Several words have no contemporary equivalents. "Skirkling," as in "to send skirkling," denotes a frantic pell-mell flight in all directions, accompanied by a vibration or twinkling or jerking motion. To "volith" is to toy idly with a matter, the implication being that the person involved is of such Jovian potency that all difficulties dwindle to contemptible triviality. "Raudlebogs" are the semi-intelligent beings of Etamin Four, who were brought to Earth, trained first as gardeners, then construction laborers, then sent home in disgrace because of certain repulsive habits they refused to forgo.

The statement of O.Z. Garr, therefore, becomes something like this: "Were power-wagons at hand, I'd volith riding forth with a whip to send the raudlebogs skirkling home."

down at his clasped hands to conceal his total lack of any constructive proposal.

A gentleman in the dark blue of the Beaudrys appeared in the doorway: he poised himself, held high his right arm, and bowed so that the fingers swept the floor.

Hagedorn rose to his feet. "Come forward, B.F. Robarth; what is your news?" For this was the significance of the newcomer's genuflection.

"The news is a message broadcast from Halcyon. The Meks have attacked; they have fired the structure and are slaughtering all. The radio went dead one minute ago."

All swung around, some jumped to their feet. "Slaughter?" croaked Claghorn.

"I am certain that by now Halcyon is no more."

Claghorn sat staring with eyes unfocused. The others discussed the dire news in voices heavy with horror.

Hagedorn once more brought the council back to order. "This is clearly an extreme situation—the gravest, perhaps, of our entire history. I am frank to state that I can suggest no decisive counter-act."

Overwhele inquired, "What of the other castles? Are they secure?"

Hagedorn turned to B.F. Robarth. "Will you be good enough to make general radio contact with all other castles, and inquire as to their condition?"

Xanten said, "Others are as vulnerable as Halcyon: Sea Island and Delora, in particular, and Maraval as well."

Claghorn emerged from his reverie. "The gentlemen and ladies of these places, in my opinion, should consider taking refuge at Janeil or here, until the uprising is quelled."

Others around the table looked at him in surprise and puzzlement. O.Z. Garr inquired in the silkiest of voices: "You envision the gentlefolk of these castles scampering to refuge at the cock-a-hoop swaggering of the lower orders?"

"Indeed, should they wish to survive," responded Claghorn politely. A gentleman of late middle age, Claghorn was stocky and strong, with black-gray hair, magnificent green eyes, and a manner which suggested great internal

16

force under stern control. "Flight by definition entails a certain diminution of dignity," he went on to say. "If O.Z. Garr can propound an elegant manner of taking to one's heels, I will be glad to learn it, and everyone else should likewise heed, because in the days to come the capability may be of comfort to all."

Hagedorn interposed before O.Z. Garr could reply. "Let us keep to the issues. I confess I cannot see to the end of all this. The Meks have demonstrated themselves to be murderers; how can we take them back into our service? But if we don't—well, to say the least, conditions will be austere until we can locate and train a new force of technicians. We must consider along these lines."

"The spaceships!" exclaimed Xanten. "We must see to them at once!"

"What's this?" inquired Beaudry, a gentleman of rock-hard face. "How do you mean, 'see to them'?"

"They must be protected from damage! What else? They are our link to the Home Worlds. The maintenance Meks probably have not deserted the hangars, since, if they propose to exterminate us, they will want to deny us the spaceships."

"Perhaps you care to march with a levy of Peasants to take the hangars under firm control?" suggested O.Z. Garr in a somewhat supercilious voice. A long history of rivalry and mutual detestation existed between himself and Xanten.

"It may be our only hope," said Xanten. "Still—how does one fight with a levy of Peasants? Better that I fly to the hangars and reconnoiter. Meanwhile, perhaps you, and others with military expertise, will take in hand the recruitment and training of a Peasant militia."

"In this regard," stated O.Z. Garr, "I await the outcome of our current deliberations. If it develops that there lies the optimum course, I naturally will apply my competences to the fullest degree. If your own capabilities are best fulfilled by spying out the activities of the Meks, I hope that you will be largehearted enough to do the same."

The two gentlemen glared at each other. A year previously their enmity had almost culminated in a duel.

Xanten, a gentleman tall, clean-limbed, and nervously active, was gifted with great natural flair, but likewise evinced a disposition too easy for absolute elegance. The traditionalists considered him "sthross," indicating a manner flawed by an almost imperceptible slackness and lack of punctilio: not the best possible choice for clan chief.

Xanten's response to O.Z. Garr was blandly polite. "I shall be glad to take this task upon myself. Since haste is of the essence I will risk the accusation of precipitousness and leave at once. Hopefully I return to report tomorrow." He rose, performed a ceremonious bow to Hagedorn, another all-inclusive salute to the council, and departed.

He crossed to Esledune House where he maintained an apartment on the thirteenth level: four rooms furnished in the style known as Fifth Dynasty, after an epoch in the history of the Altair Home Planets, from which the human race had returned to Earth. His current consort, Araminta, a lady of the Onwane family, was absent on affairs of her own, which suited Xanten well enough. After plying him with questions she would have discredited his simple explanation, preferring to suspect an assignation at his country place. Truth to tell, he had become bored with Araminta and had reason to believe that she felt similarly—or perhaps his exalted rank had provided her less opportunity to preside at glittering social functions than she had expected. They had bred no children. Araminta's daughter by a previous connection had been tallied to her. Her second child must then be tallied to Xanten, preventing him from siring another child.*

Xanten doffed his yellow council vestments, and, assisted by a young Peasant buck, donned dark yellow

---

*The population of Castle Hagedorn was fixed; each gentleman and each lady was permitted a single child. If by chance another were born the parent must either find someone who had not yet sired to sponsor it, or dispose of it another way. The usual procedure was to give the child into the care of the Expiationists.

hunting-breeches with black trim, a black jacket, black boots. He drew a cap of soft black leather over his head, and slung a pouch over his shoulder, into which he loaded weapons: a coiled blade, an energy gun.

Leaving the apartment, he summoned the lift and descended to the first level armory, where normally a Mek clerk would have served him. Now Xanten, to his vast disgust, was forced to take himself behind the counter, and rummage here and there. The Meks had removed most of the sporting rifles, all the pellet ejectors and heavy energy-guns: an ominous circumstance, thought Xanten. At last he found a steel sling-whip, spare power slugs for his gun, a brace of fire grenades and a high-powered monocular.

He returned to the lift and rode to the top level, ruefully considering the long climb when eventually the mechanism broke down, with no Meks at hand to make repairs. He thought of the apoplectic furies of rigid traditionalists such as Beaudry and chuckled: eventful days lay ahead!

Stopping at the top level, he crossed to the parapets and proceeded around to the radio room. Customarily three Mek specialists connected into the apparatus by wires clipped to their quills sat typing messages as they arrived; now B.F. Robarth stood before the mechanism, uncertainly twisting the dials, his mouth wry with deprecation and distaste for the job.

"Any further news?" Xanten asked.

B.F. Robarth gave him a sour grin. "The folk at the other end seem no more familiar with this cursed tangle than I. I hear occasional voices. I believe that the Meks are attacking Castle Delora."

Claghorn had entered the room behind Xanten. "Did I hear you correctly? Delora Castle is gone?"

"Not gone yet, Claghorn. But as good as gone. The Delora walls are little better than a picturesque crumble."

"Sickening situation!" muttered Xanten. "How can sentient creatures perform such evil? After all these centuries, how little we actually knew of them!" As he spoke he recognized the tactlessness of his remark; Claghorn had devoted much time to a study of the Meks.

"The act itself is not astounding," said Claghorn shortly. "It has occurred a thousand times in human history."

Mildly surprised that Claghorn should use human history in reference to a case involving the sub-orders, Xanten asked, "You were never aware of this vicious aspect to the Mek nature?"

"No. Never. Never indeed."

Claghorn seemed unduly sensitive, thought Xanten. Understandable, all in all. Claghorn's basic doctrine as set forth during the Hagedorn selection was by no means simple, and Xanten neither understood it nor completely endorsed what he conceived to be its goals; but it was plain that the revolt of the Meks had cut the ground out from under Claghorn's feet. Probably to the somewhat bitter satisfaction of O.Z. Garr, who must feel vindicated in his traditionalist doctrines.

Claghorn said tersely, "The life we've been leading couldn't last forever. It's a wonder it lasted as long as it did."

"Perhaps so," said Xanten in a soothing voice. "Well, no matter. All things change. Who knows? The Peasants may be planning to poison our food. . . . I must go." He bowed to Claghorn, who returned him a crisp nod, and to B.F. Robarth, then departed the room.

He climbed the spiral staircase—almost a ladder—to the cotes, where the Birds lived in an invincible disorder, occupying themselves with gambling, quarrels, and a version of chess, with rules incomprehensible to every gentleman who had tried to understand it.

Castle Hagedorn maintained a hundred Birds, tended by a gang of long-suffering Peasants, whom the Birds held in vast disesteem. The Birds were garish garrulous creatures, pigmented red, yellow or blue, with long necks, jerking inquisitive heads and an inherent irreverence which no amount of discipline or tutelage could overcome. Spying Xanten, they emitted a chorus of rude jeers: "Somebody wants a ride! Heavy thing!" "Why don't the self-anointed two-footers grow wings for themselves?" "My friend, never trust a Bird! We'll sky you, then fling you down on your fundament!"

20

"Quiet!" called Xanten. "I need six fast silent Birds for an important mission. Are any capable of such a task?"

"Are any capable, he asks!" "*A ros ros ros!* When none of us have flown for a week!" "Silence? We'll give you silence, yellow and black!"

"Come then. You. You. You of the wise eye. You there. You with the cocked shoulder. You with the green pompon. To the basket."

The Birds designated, jeering, grumbling, reviling the Peasants, allowed their syrup sacs to be filled, then flapped to the wicker seat where Xanten waited. "To the space depot at Vincenne," he told them. "Fly high and silently. Enemies are abroad. We must learn what harm if any has been done to the spaceships."

"To the depot, then!" Each Bird seized a length of rope tied to an overhead framework; the chair was yanked up with a jerk calculated to rattle Xanten's teeth, and off they flew, laughing, cursing each other for not supporting more of the load, but eventually all accommodating themselves to the task and flying with a coordinated flapping of the thirty-six sets of wings. To Xanten's relief, their garrulity lessened; silently they flew south, at a speed of fifty or sixty miles per hour.

The afternoon was already waning. The ancient countryside, scene to so many comings and goings, so much triumph and so much disaster, was laced with long black shadows. Looking down, Xanten reflected that though the human stock was native to this soil, and though his immediate ancestors had maintained their holdings for seven hundred years, Earth still seemed an alien world. The reason of course was by no means mysterious or rooted in paradox. After the Six-Star War, Earth had lain fallow for three thousand years, unpopulated save for a handful of anguished wretches who somehow had survived the cataclysm and who had become semi-barbaric Nomads. Then seven hundred years ago certain rich lords of Altair, motivated to some extent by political disaffection, but no less by caprice, had decided to return to Earth. Such was the origin of the nine great strongholds, the resident gentlefolk and the staffs of specialized andromorphs. . . . Xanten flew over an area where an

21

antiquarian had directed excavations, revealing a plaza flagged with white stone, a broken obelisk, a tumbled statue. . . . The sight, by some trick of association, stimulated Xanten's mind to an astonishing vision, so simple and yet so grand that he looked around, in all directions, with new eyes. The vision was Earth re-populated with men, the land cultivated, Nomads driven back into the wilderness.

At the moment the image was farfetched. And Xanten, watching the soft contours of Old Earth slide below, pondered the Mek revolt which had altered his life with such startling abruptness.

Claghorn had long insisted that no human condition endured forever, with the corollary that the more complicated such a condition, the greater its susceptibility to change. In which case the seven hundred year continuity at Castle Hagedorn—as artificial, extravagant and intricate as life could be—became an astonishing circumstance in itself. Claghorn had pushed his thesis further. Since change was inevitable, he argued that the gentlefolk should soften the impact by anticipating and controlling the changes—a doctrine which had been attacked with great fervor. The traditionalists labeled all of Claghorn's ideas demonstrable fallacy, and cited the very stability of castle life as proof of its viability. Xanten had inclined first one way, then the other, emotionally involved with neither cause. If anything, the fact of O.Z. Garr's traditionalism had nudged him toward Claghorn's views, and now it seemed as if events had vindicated Claghorn. Change had come, with an impact of the maximum harshness and violence.

There were still questions to be answered, of course. Why had the Meks chosen this particular time to revolt? Conditions had not altered appreciably for five hundred years, and the Meks had never previously hinted dissatisfaction. In fact they had revealed nothing of their feelings, though no one had ever troubled to ask them—save Claghorn.

The Birds were veering east to avoid the Ballarat Mountains, to the west of which were the ruins of a great city, never satisfactorily identified. Below lay the Lu-

22

cerne Valley, at one time a fertile farm land. If one looked with great concentration, the outline of the various holdings could sometimes be distinguished. Ahead, the spaceship hangars were visible, where Mek technicians maintained four spaceships jointly the property of Hagedorn, Janeil, Tuang, Morninglight and Maraval, though, for a variety of reasons, the ships were never used.

The sun was setting. Orange light twinkled and flickered on the metal walls. Xanten called instructions up to the Birds: "Circle down. Alight behind that line of trees, but fly low so that none will see."

Down on stiff wings curved the Birds, six ungainly necks stretched toward the ground. Xanten was ready for the impact; the Birds never seemed able to alight easily when they carried a gentleman. When the cargo was something in which they felt a personal concern, dandelion fluff would never have been disturbed by the jar.

Xanten expertly kept his balance, instead of tumbling and rolling in the manner preferred by the Birds. "You all have syrup," he told them. "Rest; make no noise; do not quarrel. By tomorrow's sunset, if I am not here, return to Castle Hagedorn and say that Xanten was killed."

"Never fear!" cried the Birds. "We will wait forever!" "At any rate till tomorrow's sunset!" "If danger threatens, if you are pressed—*a ros ros ros!* Call for the Birds" "*A ros!* We are ferocious when aroused!"

"I wish it were true," said Xanten. "The Birds are arrant cowards; this is well-known. Still I value the sentiment. Remember my instructions, and quiet above all! I do not wish to be set upon and stabbed because of your clamor."

The Birds made indignant sounds. "Injustice, injustice! We are quiet as the dew!"

"Good." Xanten hurriedly moved away lest they should bellow new advice or reassurances after him.

Passing through the forest, he came to an open meadow at the far edge of which, perhaps a hundred yards distant, was the rear of the first hangar. He stopped to consider. Several factors were involved. First: the main-

tenance Meks, with the metal structure shielding them from radio contact, might still be unaware of the revolt. Hardly likely, he decided, in view of the otherwise careful planning. Second: the Meks, in continuous communication with their fellows, acted as a collective organism. The aggregate functioned more competently than its parts, and the individual was not prone to initiative. Hence, vigilance was likely to be extreme. Third: if they expected anyone to attempt a discreet approach, they would necessarily scrutinize most closely the route which he proposed to take.

Xanten decided to wait in the shadows another ten minutes, until the setting sun shining over his shoulder should most effectively blind any who might watch.

Ten minutes passed. The hangars, burnished by the dying sunlight, bulked long, tall, completely quiet. In the intervening meadow long golden grass waved and rippled in a cool breeze. . . . Xanten took a deep breath, hefted his pouch, arranged his weapons, and strode forth. It did not occur to him to crawl through the grass.

He reached the back of the nearest hangar without challenge. Pressing his ear to the metal he heard nothing. He walked to the corner, looked down the side: no sign of life. Xanten shrugged: very well, then; to the door.

He walked beside the hangar, the setting sun casting a long black shadow ahead of him. He came to a door opening into the hangar administrative office. Since there was nothing to be gained by trepidation, Xanten thrust the door aside and entered.

The offices were empty. The desks, where centuries before underlings had sat, calculating invoices and bills of lading, were bare, polished free of dust. The computers and information banks, black enamel, glass, white and red switches, looked as if they had been installed only the day before.

Xanten crossed to the glass pane overlooking the hangar floor, shadowed under the bulk of the ship.

He saw no Meks. But on the floor of the hangar, arranged in neat rows and heaps, were elements and assemblies of the ship's control mechanism. Service panels

24

gaped wide into the hull to show where the devices had been detached.

Xanten stepped from the office out into the hangar. The spaceship had been disabled, put out of commission. Xanten looked along the neat rows of parts. Certain savants of various castles were expert in the theory of space-time transfer; S.X. Rosenbox of Maraval had even derived a set of equations which, if translated into machinery, eliminated the troublesome Hamus effect. But not one gentleman, even were he so oblivious to personal honor as to touch a hand to a tool, would know how to replace, connect and tune the mechanisms heaped upon the hangar floor.

The malicious work had been done—when? Impossible to say.

Xanten returned to the office, stepped back out into the twilight, and walked to the next hangar. Again no Meks; again the spaceship had been gutted of its control mechanisms. Xanten proceeded to the third hangar, where conditions were the same.

At the fourth hangar he discerned the faint sounds of activity. Stepping into the office, looking through the glass wall into the hangar, he found Meks working with their usual economy of motion, in a near silence which was uncanny.

Xanten, already uncomfortable from skulking through the forest, became enraged by the cool destruction of his property. He strode forth into the hangar. Slapping his thigh to attract attention he called in a harsh voice, "Return the components to place! How dare you vermin act in such a manner?

The Meks turned about their blank countenances to study him through black beaded lens-clusters at each side of their heads.

"What?" bellowed Xanten. "You hesitate?" He brought forth his steel whip, usually more of a symbolic adjunct than a punitive instrument, and slashed it against the ground. "Obey! This ridiculous revolt is at its end!"

The Meks still hesitated, and events wavered in the balance. None made a sound, though messages were passing among them, appraising the circumstances, es-

tablishing a consensus. Xanten could allow them no such leisure. He marched forward, wielding the whip, striking at the only area where the Meks felt pain: the ropy face. "To your duties," he roared. "A fine maintenance crew are you! A destruction crew is more like it!"

The Meks made the soft blowing sound which might mean anything. They fell back, and now Xanten noted one standing at the head of the companionway leading into the ship: a Mek larger than any he had seen before and one in some fashion different. This Mek was aiming a pellet gun at his head. With an unhurried flourish, Xanten whipped away a Mek who had leaped forward with a knife, and without deigning to aim, fired at and destroyed the Mek who stood on the companionway, even as the slug sang past his head.

The other Meks were nevertheless committed to an attack. All surged forward. Lounging disdainfully against the hull, Xanten shot them as they came, moving his head once to avoid a chunk of metal, again reaching to catch a throw-knife and hurl it into the face of him who had thrown it.

The Meks drew back, and Xanten guessed that they had agreed on a new tactic: either to withdraw for weapons or perhaps to confine him within the hangar. In any event no more could be accomplished here. He made play with the whip and cleared an avenue to the office. With tools, metal bars and forgings striking the glass behind him, he sauntered through the office and out into the night.

The full moon was rising: a great yellow globe casting a smoky saffron glow, like an antique lamp. Mek eyes were not well-adapted for night-seeing, and Xanten waited by the door. Presently Meks began to pour forth, and Xanten hacked at their necks as they came.

The Meks drew back inside the hangar. Wiping his blade, Xanten strode off the way he had come, looking neither right nor left. He stopped short. The night was young. Something tickled his mind: the recollection of the Mek who had fired the pellet gun. He had been larger, possibly a darker bronze, but, more significantly,

26

he had displayed an indefinable poise, almost authority—though such a word, when used in connection with the Meks, was anomalous. On the other hand, someone must have planned the revolt, or at least originated the concept. It might be worthwhile to extend the reconnaissance, though his primary information had been secured.

Xanten turned back and crossed the landing area to the barracks and garages. Once more, frowning in discomfort, he felt the need for discretion. What times these were! when a gentleman must skulk to avoid such as the Meks! He stole up behind the garages, where a half-dozen power-wagons* lay dozing.

Xanten looked them over. All were of the same sort, a metal frame with four wheels, an earth-moving blade at the front. Nearby must be the syrup stock. Xanten presently found a bin containing a number of containers. He loaded a dozen on a nearby wagon, slashed the rest with his knife, so that the syrup gushed across the ground. The Meks used a somewhat different formulation; their syrup would be stocked at a different locale, presumably inside the barracks.

Xanten mounted a power-wagon, twisted the *awake* key, tapped the *go* button, and pulled a lever which set the wheels into reverse motion. The power-wagon lurched back. Xanted halted it, turned it so that it faced the barracks. He did likewise with three others, then set them all into motion, one after the other. They trundled forward; the blades cut open the metal wall of the barracks, the roof sagged. The power-wagons continued,

---

*Power-wagons, like the Meks, originally swamp-creatures from Etamin 9, were great rectangular slabs of muscle, slung into a rectangular frame and protected from sunlight, insects and rodents by a synthetic pelt. Syrup sacs communicated with their digestive apparatus, wires led to motor nodes in the rudimentary brain. The muscles were clamped to rocker arms which actuated rotors and drive-wheels. The power-wagons, economical, long-lived, and docile, were principally used for heavy cartage, earth-moving, heavy-tillage, and other arduous jobs.

pushing the length of the interior, crushing all in their way.

Xanten nodded in profound satisfaction and returned to the power-wagon he had reserved for his own use. Mounting to the seat, he waited. No Meks issued from the barracks. Apparently they were deserted, with the entire crew busy at the hangars. Still, hopefully, the syrup stocks had been destroyed, and many might perish by starvation.

From the direction of the hangars came a single Mek, evidently attracted by the sounds of destruction. Xanten crouched on the seat and as it passed, coiled his whip around the stock neck. He heaved; the Mek spun to the ground.

Xanten leaped down, seized its pellet-gun. Here was another of the larger Meks, and now Xanten saw it to be without a syrup sac, a Mek in the original state. Astounding! How did the creature survive? Suddenly there were many new questions to be asked—hopefully a few to be answered. Standing on the creature's head, Xanten hacked away the long antenna quills which protruded from the back of the Mek's scalp. It was now insulated, alone, on its own resources—a situation to reduce the most stalwart Mek to apathy.

"Up!" ordered Xanten. "Into the back of the wagon!" He cracked the whip for emphasis.

The Mek at first seemed disposed to defy him, but after a blow or two obeyed. Xanten climbed into the seat and started the power-wagon, directed it to the north. The Birds would be unable to carry both himself and the Mek—or in any event they would cry and complain so raucously that they might as well be believed at first. They might or might not wait until the specified hour of tomorrow's sunset; as likely as not they would sleep the night in a tree, awake in a surly mood and return at once to Castle Hagedorn.

All through the night the power-wagon trundled, with Xanten on the seat and his captive huddled in the rear.

CHAPTER III

1

THE GENTLEFOLK of the castles, for all their assurance, disliked to wander the countryside by night, by reason of what some derided as superstitious fear. Others cited travelers benighted beside moldering ruins and their subsequent visions: the eldritch music they had heard, or the whimper of moon-mirkins, or the far horns of spectral huntsmen. Others had seen pale lavender and green lights, and wraiths which ran with long strides through the forest; and Hode Abbey, now a dank tumble, was notorious for the White Hag and the alarming toll she exacted.

A hundred such cases were known, and while the hardheaded scoffed, none needlessly traveled the countryside by night. Indeed, if ghosts truly haunt the scenes of tragedy and heartbreak, then the landscape of Old Earth must be home to ghosts and specters beyond all numbering—especially that region across which Xanten rolled in the power-wagon, where every rock, every meadow, every vale and swale was crusted thick with human experience.

The moon rose high; the wagon trundled north along an ancient road, the cracked concrete slabs shining pale in the moonlight. Twice Xanten saw flickering orange lights off to the side, and once, standing in the shade of a cypress tree, he thought he saw a tall, quiet shape, silently watching him pass. The captive Mek sat plotting mischief, Xanten well knew. Without its quills it must feel depersonified, bewildered, but Xanten told himself that it would not do to doze.

The road led through a town, certain structures of which still stood. Not even the Nomads took refuge in these old towns, fearing either miasma or perhaps the redolence of grief.

The moon reached the zenith. The landscape spread

away in a hundred tones of silver, black and gray. Looking about, Xanten thought that for all the notable pleasures of civilized life, there was yet something to be said for the spaciousness and simplicity of Nomadland. The Mek made a stealthy movement. Xanten did not so much as turn his head. He cracked his whip in the air. The Mek became quiet.

All through the night the power-wagon rolled along the old road, with the moon sinking into the west. The eastern horizon glowed green and lemon-yellow, and presently, as the pallid moon disappeared, the sun rose over the distant line of the mountains. At this moment, off to the right, Xanten spied a drift of smoke.

He halted the wagon. Standing up on the seat, he craned his neck to spy a Nomad encampment about a quarter-mile distant. He could distinguish three or four dozen tents of various sizes and a dozen dilapidated power-wagons. On the hetman's tall tent he thought he saw a black ideogram that he recognized. If so, this would be the tribe which not long before had trespassed on the Hagedorn domain, and which O.Z. Garr had repulsed.

Xanten settled himself upon the seat, composed his garments, set the power-wagon in motion, and guided it toward the camp.

A hundred black-cloaked men, tall and lean as ferrets, watched his approach. A dozen sprang forward and whipping arrows to bows, aimed them at his heart. Xanten turned them a glance of supercilious inquiry, drove the wagon up to the hetman's tent, halted. He rose to his feet. "Hetman," he called. "Are you awake?"

The hetman parted the canvas which closed off his tent, peered out, and after a moment came forth. Like the others he wore a garment of limp black cloth, swathing head and body alike. His face thrust through a square opening: narrow blue eyes, a grotesquely long nose, a chin long, skewed and sharp.

Xanten gave him a curt nod. "Observe this." He jerked his thumb toward the Mek in the back of the wagon. The hetman flicked aside his eyes, studied the Mek a tenth-second, and returned to a scrutiny of Xanten. "His

kind have revolted against the gentlemen," said Xanten. "In fact they massacre all the men of Earth. Hence we of Castle Hagedorn make this offer to the Nomads. Come to Castle Hagedorn. We will feed, clothe and arm you. We will train you to discipline and the arts of formal warfare. We will provide the most expert leadership within our power. We will then annihilate the Meks, expunge them from Earth. After the campaign, we will train you to technical skills, and you may pursue profitable and interesting careers in the service of the castles."

The hetman made no reply for a moment. Then his weathered face split into a ferocious grin. He spoke in a voice which Xanten found surprisingly well-modulated. "So your beasts have finally risen up to rend you! A pity they forebore so long! Well, it is all one to us. You are both alien folk and sooner or later your bones must bleach together."

Xanten pretended incomprehension. "If I understand you aright, you assert that in the face of alien assault, all men must fight a common battle; and then, after the victory, cooperate still to their mutual advantage. Am I correct?"

The hetman's grin never wavered. "You are not men. Only we of Earth soil and Earth water are men. You and your weird slaves are strangers together. We wish you success in your mutual slaughter."

"Well, then," declared Xanten, "I heard you aright after all. Appeals to your loyalty are ineffectual, so much is clear. What of self-interest, then? The Meks, failing to expunge the gentlefolk of the castles, will turn upon the Nomads and kill them as if they were so many ants."

"If they attack us, we will war on them," said the hetman. "Otherwise let them do as they will."

Xanten glanced thoughtfully at the sky. "We might be willing, even now, to accept a contingent of Nomads into the service of Castle Hagedorn, this to form a cadre from which a larger, more versatile, group may be formed."

From the side, another Nomad called in an offensively

jeering voice, "You will sew a sac on our backs where you can pour your syrup, hey?"

Xanten replied in an even voice, "The syrup is highly nutritious and supplies all bodily needs."

"Why then do you not consume it yourself?"

Xanten disdained reply.

The hetman spoke. "If you wish to supply us weapons, we will take them, and use them against whomever threatens us. But do not expect us to defend you. If you fear for your lives, desert your castles and become Nomads."

"Fear for our lives?" exclaimed Xanten. "What nonsense! Never! Castle Hagedorn is impregnable, as is Janeil, and most of the other castles as well."

The hetman shook his head. "Any time we choose we could take Hagedorn, and kill all you popinjays in your sleep."

"What?" cried Xanten in outrage. "Are you serious?"

"Certainly. On a black night we would send a man aloft on a great kite and drop him down on the parapets. He would lower a line, haul up ladders and in fifteen minutes the castle is taken."

Xanten pulled at his chin. "Ingenious, but impractical. The Birds would detect such a kite. Or the wind would fail at a critical moment. . . . All this is beside the point. The Meks fly no kites. They plan to make a display against Janeil and Hagedorn, then, in their frustration, go forth and hunt Nomads."

The hetman moved back a step. "What then? We have survived similar attempts by the men of Hagedorn. Cowards all. Hand to hand, with equal weapons, we would make you eat the dirt like the dogs you are."

Xanten raised his eyebrows in elegant disdain. "I fear that you forget yourself. You address a clan chief of Castle Hagedorn. Only fatigue and boredom restrain me from punishing you with this whip."

"Bah," said the hetman. He crooked a finger to one of his archers. "Spit this insolent lordling."

The archer discharged his arrow, but Xanten, who had been expecting some such act, fired his energy gun, destroying arrow, bow, and the archer's hands. He said, "I

see I must teach you common respect for your betters; so it means the whip after all." Seizing the hetman by the scalp, he coiled the whip smartly once, twice, thrice around the narrow shoulders. "Let this suffice. I cannot compel you to fight, but at least I can demand decent respect." He leaped to the ground, and seizing the hetman, pitched him into the back of the wagon alongside the Mek. Then, backing the power-wagon around, he departed the camp without so much as a glance over his shoulder, the thwart of the seat protecting his back from arrows.

The hetman scrambled erect, drew his dagger. Xanten turned his head slightly. "Take care! Or I will tie you to the wagon and you shall run behind in the dust."

The hetman hesitated, made a spitting sound between his teeth, drew back. He looked down at his blade, turned it over, and sheathed it with a grunt. "Where do you take me?"

Xanten halted the wagon. "No farther. I merely wished to leave your camp with dignity, without dodging and ducking a hail of arrows. You may alight. I take it you still refuse to bring your men into the service of Castle Hagedorn?"

The hetman once more made the spitting sound between his teeth. "When the Meks have destroyed the castles, we shall destroy the Meks, and Earth will be cleared of star-things."

"You are a gang of intractable savages. Very well, alight, return to your encampment. Reflect well before you again show disrespect to a Castle Hagedorn clan chief."

"Bah," muttered the hetman. Leaping down from the wagon, he stalked back down the track toward his camp.

2

About noon Xanten came to Far Valley, at the edge of the Hagedorn lands. Nearby was a village of Expiationists: malcontents and neurasthenics in the opinion of

castle gentlefolk, and a curious group by any standards. A few had held enviable rank; certain others were savants of recognized erudition; but others yet were persons of neither dignity nor reputation, subscribing to the most bizarre and extreme of philosophies. All now performed toil no different from that relegated to the Peasants, and all seemed to take a perverse satisfaction in what—by castle standards—was filth, poverty and degradation.

As might be expected, their creed was by no means homogeneous. Some might better have been described as "nonconformists" or "disassociationists"; another group were "passive expiationists," and others still, a minority, argued for a dynamic program.

Between castle and village was little intercourse. Occasionally the Expiationists bartered fruit or polished wood for tools, nails, medicaments; or the gentlefolk might make up a party to watch the Expiationists at their dancing and singing. Xanten had visited the village on many such occasions and had been attracted by the artless charm and informality of the folk at their play. Now, passing near the village, Xanten turned aside to follow a lane which wound between tall blackberry hedges and out upon a little common where goats and cattle grazed. Xanten halted the wagon in the shade and saw that the syrup sac was full. He looked back at his captive. "What of you? If you need syrup, pour yourself full. But no, you have no sac. What then do you feed upon? Mud? Unsavory fare. I fear none here is rank enough for your taste. Ingest syrup or munch grass, as you will; only do not stray overfar from the wagon, for I watch with an intent eye."

The Mek, sitting hunched in a corner, gave no signal that it comprehended, nor did it move to take advantage of Xanten's offer.

Xanten went to a watering trough and holding his hands under the trickle which issued from a lead pipe, rinsed his face, then drank a swallow or two from his cupped hand.

Turning, he found that a dozen folk of the village had approached. One he knew well, a man who might have

34

become Godalming, or even Aure, had he not become infected with expiationism.

Xanten performed a polite salute. "A.G. Philidor: it is I, Xanten."

"Xanten, of course. But here I am A.G. Philidor no longer, merely Philidor."

Xanten bowed. "My apologies; I have neglected the full rigor of your informality."

"Spare me your wit," said Philidor. "Why do you bring us a shorn Mek? For adoption, perhaps?" This last alluded to the gentlefolk practice of bringing over-tally babies to the village.

"Now who flaunts his wit? But you have not heard the news?"

"News arrives here last of all. The Nomads are better informed."

"Prepare yourself for surprise. The Meks have revolted against the castles. Halcyon and Delora are demolished, and all killed; perhaps others by this time."

Philidor shook his head. "I am not surprised."

"Well then, are you not concerned?"

Philidor considered. "To this extent. Our own plans, never very feasible, become more farfetched than ever."

"It appears to me," said Xanten, "that you face grave and immediate danger. The Meks surely intend to wipe out every vestige of humanity. You will not escape."

Philidor shrugged. "Conceivably the danger exists. . . . We will take counsel and decide what to do."

"I can put forward a proposal which you may find attractive," said Xanten. "Our first concern, of course, is to supress the revolt. There are at least a dozen Expiationist communities, with an aggregate population of two or three thousand—perhaps more. I propose that we recruit and train a corps of highly disciplined troops, supplied from the Castle Hagedorn armory, led by Hagedorn's most expert military theoreticians."

Philidor stared at him incredulously. "You expect us, the Expiationists, to become your soldiers?"

"Why not?" asked Xanten ingenuously. "Your life is at stake no less than ours."

"No one dies more than once."

Xanten in his turn evinced shock. "What? Can this be a former gentleman of Hagedorn speaking? Is this the face a man of pride and courage turns to danger? Is this the lesson of history? Of course not! I need not instruct you in this; you are as knowledgeable as I."

Philidor nodded. "I know that the history of man is not his technical triumphs, his kills, his victories. It is a composite, a mosaic of a trillion pieces, the account of each man's accommodation with his conscience. This is the true history of the race."

Xanten made an airy gesture. "A.G. Philidor, you over-simplify grievously. Do you consider me obtuse? There are many kinds of history. They interact. You emphasize morality. But the ultimate basis of morality is survival. What promotes survival is good, what induces mortifaction is bad."

"Well spoken!" declared Philidor. "But let me propound a parable. May a nation of a million beings destroy a creature who otherwise will infect all with a fatal disease? Yes, you will say. Once more: ten starving beasts hunt you, that they may eat. Will you kill them to save your life? Yes, you will say again, though here you destroy more than you save. Once more: a man inhabits a hut in a lonely valley. A hundred spaceships descend from the sky, and attempt to destroy him. May he destroy these ships in self-defense, even though he is one and they are a hundred thousand? Perhaps you say yes. What then if a whole world, a whole race of beings, pits itself against this single man? May he kill all? What if the attackers are as human as himself? What if he were the creature of the first instance, who otherwise will infect a world with disease? You see, there is no area where a simple touchstone avails. We have searched and found none. Hence, at the risk of sinning against Survival, we—I, at least; I can only speak for myself—have chosen a morality which at least allows me calm. I kill—nothing. I destroy—nothing."

"Bah," said Xanten contemptuously. "If a Mek platoon entered this valley and began to kill your children, you would not defend them?"

Philidor compressed his lips, turned away. Another

36

man spoke. "Philidor has defined morality. But who is absolutely moral? Philidor, or I, or you, might desert his morality in such a case."

Philidor said, "Look about you. Is there anyone here you recognize?"

Xanten scanned the group. Nearby stood a girl of extraordinary beauty. She wore a white smock and in the dark hair curling to her shoulders she wore a red flower. Xanten nodded. "I see the maiden O.Z. Garr wished to introduce into his ménage at the castle."

"Exactly," said Philidor. "Do you recall the circumstances?"

"Very well indeed," said Xanten. "There was vigorous objection from the Council of Notables—if for no other reason than the threat to our laws of population control. O.Z. Garr attempted to sidestep the law in this fashion. 'I keep Phanes,' he said. 'At times I maintain as many as six, or even eight, and no one utters a word of protest. I will call this girl Phane and keep her among the rest.' I and others protested. There was almost a duel over this matter. O.Z. Garr was forced to relinquish the girl. She was given into my custody and I conveyed her to Far Valley."

Philidor nodded. "All this is correct. Well—we attempted to dissuade Garr. He refused to be dissuaded, and threatened us with his hunting force of perhaps thirty Meks. We stood aside. Are we moral? Are we strong or weak?"

"Sometimes it is better," said Xanten, "to ignore morality. Even though O.Z. Garr is a gentleman and you are but Expiationists. . . . Likewise in the case of the Meks. They are destroying the castles, and all the men of Earth. If morality means supine acceptance, then morality must be abandoned!"

Philidor gave a sour chuckle. "What a remarkable situation! The Meks are here, likewise Peasants and Birds and Phanes, all altered, transported and enslaved for human pleasure. Indeed, it is this fact that occasions our guilt, for which we must expiate, and now you want us to compound this guilt!"

"It is a mistake to brood overmuch about the past,"

said Xanten. "Still, if you wish to preserve your option to brood, I suggest that you fight Meks now, or at the very least take refuge in the castle."

"Not I," said Philidor. "Perhaps others may choose to do so."

"You will wait to be killed?"

"No. I and no doubt others will take refuge in the remote mountains."

Xanten clambered back aboard the power-wagon. "If you change your mind, come to Castle Hagedorn."

He departed.

The road continued along the valley, wound up a hillside, crossed a ridge. Far ahead, silhouetted against the sky, stood Castle Hagedorn.

Chapter IV

1

XANTEN REPORTED TO THE COUNCIL.

"The spaceships cannot be used. The Meks have rendered them inoperative. Any plan to solicit assistance from the Home Worlds is pointless."

"This is sorry news," said Hagedorn with a grimace. "Well, then—so much for that."

Xanten continued. "Returning by power-wagon I encountered a tribe of Nomads. I summoned the hetman and explained to him the advantages of serving Castle Hagedorn. The Nomads, I fear, lack both grace and docility. The hetman gave so surly a response that I departed in disgust.

"At Far Valley I visited the Expiationist village, and made a similar proposal, but with no great success. They are as idealistic as the Nomads are churlish. Both are of a fugitive tendency. The Expiationists spoke of taking refuge in the mountains. The Nomads presumably will retreat into the steppes."

Beaudry snorted. "How will flight help them? Perhaps they gain a few years—but eventually the Meks

will find every last one of them; such is their methodicity."

"In the meantime," O.Z. Garr declared peevishly, "we might have organized them into an efficient combat corps, to the benefit of all. Well, then, let them perish; we are secure."

"Secure, yes," said Hagedorn gloomily. "But what when the power fails? When the lifts break down? When air circulation cuts off so that we either stifle or freeze? What then?"

O.Z. Garr gave his head a grim shake. "We must steel ourselves to undignified expedients, with as good grace as possible. But the machinery of the castle is sound, and I expect small deterioration or failure for conceivably five or ten years. By that time anything may occur."

Claghorn, who had been leaning indolently back in his seat, spoke at last: "This essentially is a passive program. Like the defection of the Nomads and Expiationists, it looks very little beyond the immediate moment."

O.Z. Garr spoke in a voice carefully polite. "Claghorn is well aware that I yield to none in courteous candor, as well as optimism and directness: in short the reverse of passivity. But I refuse to dignify a stupid little inconvenience by extending it serious attention. How can he label this procedure passivity? Does the worthy and honorable head of the Claghorns have a proposal which more effectively maintains our status, our standards, our self-respect?"

Claghorn nodded slowly, with a faint half-smile which O.Z. Garr found odiously complacent. "There is a simple and effective method by which the Meks might be defeated."

"Well, then!" cried Hagedorn. "Why hesitate? Let us hear it!"

Claghorn looked around the red velvet-covered table, considering the faces of all: the dispassionate Xanten; Beaudry, burly, rigid, face muscles clenched in an habitual expression unpleasantly like a sneer; old Isseth, as handsome, erect and vital as the most dashing cadet;

39

Hagedorn, troubled, glum, his inward perplexity all too evident; the elegant Garr; Overwhele, thinking savagely of the inconveniences of the future; Aure, toying with his ivory tablet, either bored, morose or defeated; the others displaying various aspects of doubt, foreboding, hauteur, dark resentment, impatience; and in the case of Floy, a quiet smile—or as Isseth later characterized it, an imbecilic smirk—intended to convey his total disassociation from the entire irksome matter.

Claghorn took stock of the faces, and shook his head. "I will not at the moment broach this plan, as I fear it is unworkable. But I must point out that under no circumstances can Castle Hagedorn be as before, even should we survive the Mek attack."

"Bah!" exclaimed Beaudry. "We lose dignity, we become ridiculous, by even so much as discussing the beasts."

Xanten stirred himself. "A distasteful subject, but remember! Halcyon is destroyed, and Delora, and who knows what others? Let us not thrust our heads in the sand! The Meks will not waft away merely because we ignore them."

"In any event," said O.Z. Garr, "Janeil is secure and we are secure. The other folk, unless they are already slaughtered, might do well to visit us during the inconvenience, if they can justify the humiliation of flight to themselves. I myself believe that the Meks will soon come to heel, anxious to return to their posts."

Hagedorn shook his head gloomily. "I find this hard to believe. But very well then, we shall adjourn."

2

The radio communication system was the first of the castle's vast array of electrical and mechanical devices to break down. The failure occurred so soon and so decisively that certain of the theoreticians, notably I.K. Harde and Uegus, postulated sabotage by the departing Meks. Others remarked that the system had never been absolutely dependable, that the Meks themselves

had been forced to tinker continuously with the circuits, that the failure was simply a result of faulty engineering. I.K. Harde and Uegus inspected the unwieldy apparatus, but the cause of failure was not obvious. After a half-hour of consultation they agreed that any attempt to restore the system would necessitate complete re-design and re-engineering, with consequent construction of testing and calibration devices, and the fabrication of a complete new family of components. "This is manifestly impossible," stated Uegus in his report to the council. "Even the simplest useful system would require several technician-years. There is not even one single technician to hand. We must therefore await the availability of trained and willing labor."

"In retrospect," stated Isseth, the oldest of the clan chiefs, "it is clear that in many ways we have been less than provident. No matter that the men of the Home Worlds are vulgarians! Men of shrewder calculation than our own would have maintained inter-world connection."

"Lack of shrewdness and providence were not the deterring factors," stated Claghorn. "Communication was discouraged simply because the early lords were unwilling that Earth should be overrun with Home-World parvenus. It is as simple as that."

Isseth grunted, and started to make a rejoinder, but Hagedorn said hastily, "Unluckily, as Xanten tells us, the spaceships have been rendered useless, and while certain of our number have a profound knowledge of the theoretical considerations, again who is there to perform the toil? Even were the hangars and spaceships themselves under our control."

O.Z. Garr declared, "Give me six platoons of Peasants and six power-wagons equipped with high-energy cannon, and I'll regain the hangars; no difficulties there!"

Beaudry said, "Well, here's a start, at least. I'll assist in the training of the Peasants, and though I know nothing of cannon operation, rely on me for any advice I can give."

Hagedorn looked around the group, frowned, pulled at his chin. "There are difficulties to this program. First,

we have at hand only the single power-wagon in which Xanten returned from his reconnaissance. Then, what of our energy cannons? Has anyone inspected them? The Meks were entrusted with maintenance, but it is possible, even likely, that they wrought mischief here as well. O.Z. Garr, you are reckoned an expert military theoretician; what can you tell us in this regard?"

"I have made no inspection to date," stated O.Z. Garr. "Today the Display of Antique Tabards will occupy us all until the Hour of Sundown Appraisal*." He looked at his watch. "Perhaps now is as good a time as any to adjourn, until I am able to provide detailed information in regard to the cannons."

Hagedorn nodded his heavy head. "The time indeed grows late. Your Phanes appear today?"

"Only two," replied O.Z. Garr. "The Lazule and the Eleventh Mystery. I can find nothing suitable for the Gossamer Delights nor my little Blue Fay, and the Gloriana still requires tutelage. Today B.Z. Maxelwane's Variflors should repay the most attention."

"Yes," said Hagedorn. "I have heard other remarks to this effect. Very well, then, until tomorrow. Eh, Claghorn, you have something to say?"

"Yes, indeed," said Claghorn mildly. "We have all too little time at our disposal. Best that we make the most of it. I seriously doubt the efficacy of Peasant troops; to pit Peasants against Meks is like sending rabbits against wolves. What we need, rather than rabbits, are panthers."

"Ah, yes," said Hagedorn vaguely. "Yes, indeed."

"Where, then, are panthers to be found?" Claghorn looked inquiringly around the table. "Can no one sug-

---

*Display of Antique Tabards; Hour of Sundown Appraisal: the literal sense of the first term was yet relevant; that of the second had become lost and the phrase was a mere formalism, connoting that hour of late afternoon when visits were exchanged, and wines, liqueurs and essences tasted: in short, a time of relaxation and small talk before the more formal convivialities of dining.

42

gest a source? A pity. Well then, if panthers fail to appear, I suppose rabbits must do. Let us go about the business of converting rabbits into panthers, and instantly. I suggest that we postpone all fetes and spectacles until the shape of our future is more certain."

Hagedorn raised his eyebrows, opened his mouth to speak, closed it again. He looked intently at Claghorn to ascertain whether or not he joked. Then he looked dubiously around the table.

Beaudry gave a rather brassy laugh. "It seems that erudite Claghorn cries panic."

O.Z. Garr stated: "Surely, in all dignity, we cannot allow the impertinence of our servants to cause us such eye-rolling alarm. I am embarrassed even to bring the matter forward."

"I am not embarrassed," said Claghorn, with the full-faced complacence which so exasperated O.Z. Garr. "I see no reason why you should be. Our lives are threatened, in which case a trifle of embarrassment, or anything else, becomes of secondary importance."

O.Z. Garr rose to his feet, performed a brusque salute in Claghorn's direction, of such a nature as to constitute a calculated affront. Claghorn, rising, performed a similar salute, so grave and overly complicated as to invest Garr's insult with burlesque overtones. Xanten, who detested O.Z. Garr, laughed aloud.

O.Z. Garr hesitated, then, sensing that under the circumstances taking the matter further would be regarded as poor form, strode from the chamber.

3

The Viewing of Antique Tabards, an annual pageant of Phanes wearing sumptuous garments, took place in the Great Rotunda to the north of the central plaza. Possibly half of the gentlemen, but less than a quarter of the ladies, kept Phanes. These were creatures native to the caverns of Albireo Seven's moon: a docile race, both playful and affectionate, which after several thousand years of selective breeding had become sylphs of piquant

beauty. Clad in a delicate gauze which issued from pores behind their ears, along their upper arms and down their backs, they were the most inoffensive of creatures, anxious always to please, innocently vain. Most gentlemen regarded them with affection, but rumors sometimes told of ladies drenching an especially hated Phane in tincture of ammonia, which matted her pelt and destroyed her gauze forever.

A gentleman besotted by a Phane was considered a figure of fun. The Phane, though so carefully bred as to seem a delicate girl, if used sexually became crumpled and haggard, with gauzes drooping and discolored, and everyone would know that such and such a gentleman had misused his Phane. In this regard, at least, the women of the castles might exert their superiority, and did so by conducting themselves with such extravagant provocation that the Phanes in contrast seemed the most ingenious and fragile of nature sprites. Their life span was perhaps thirty years, during the last ten of which, after they had lost their beauty, they encased themselves in mantles of gray gauze and performed menial tasks in boudoirs, kitchens, pantries, nurseries and dressing rooms.

The Viewing of Antique Tabards was an occasion more for the viewing of Phanes than the tabards, though these, woven of Phane-gauze, were of great intrinsic beauty in themselves.

The Phane owners sat in a lower tier, tense with hope and pride, exulting when one made an especially splendid display, plunging into black depths when the ritual postures were performed with other than grace and elegance. During each display, highly formal music was plucked from a lute by a gentleman from a clan different to that of the Phane owner, the owner never playing the lute to the performance of his own Phane. The display was never overtly a competition and no formal acclamation was allowed, but all watching made up their minds as to which was the most entrancing and graceful of the Phanes, and the repute of the owner was thereby exalted.

The current Viewing was delayed almost half an hour

by reason of the defection of the Meks, and certain hasty improvisations had been necessary. But the gentlefolk of Castle Hagedorn were in no mood to be critical and took no heed of the occasional lapses as a dozen young Peasant bucks struggled to perform unfamiliar tasks. The Phanes were as entrancing as ever, bending, twisting, swaying to plangent chords of the lute, fluttering their fingers as if feeling for raindrops, crouching suddenly and gliding, then springing upright as straight as wands, finally bowing and skipping from the platform.

Halfway through the program a Peasant sidled awkwardly into the Rotunda, and mumbled in an urgent manner to the cadet who came to inquire his business. The cadet at once made his way to Hagedorn's polished jet booth. Hagedorn listened, nodded, spoke a few terse words and settled calmly back in his seat as if the message had been of no consequence, and the gentlefolk of the audience were reassured.

The entertainment proceeded. O.Z. Garr's delectable pair made a fine show, but it was generally felt that Lirlin, a young Phane belonging to Isseth Floy Gazuneth, for the first time at a formal showing, made the most captivating display.

The Phanes appeared for a last time, moving all together through a half-improvised minuet, then performing a final half-gay, half-regretful salute, departed the rotunda. For a few moments more the gentlemen and ladies would remain in their booths, sipping essences, discussing the display, arranging affairs and assignations. Hagedorn sat frowning, twisting his hands. Suddenly he rose to his feet. The rotunda instantly became silent.

"I dislike intruding an unhappy note at so pleasant an occasion," said Hagedorn. "But the news has just been given to me, and it is fitting that all should know. Janeil Castle is under attack. The Meks are there in great force, with hundreds of power-wagons. They have circled the castle with a dike which prevents any effective use of the Janeil energy-cannon.

"There is no immediate danger to Janeil, and it is

45

difficult to comprehend what the Meks hope to achieve, the Janeil walls being all of two hundred feet high.

"The news, nevertheless, is somber, and it means that eventually we must expect a similar investment—though it is even more difficult to comprehend how Meks could hope to inconvenience us. Our water derives from four wells sunk deep into the earth. We have great stocks of food. Our energy is derived from the sun. If necessary, we could condense water and synthesize food from the the air—at least I have been so assured by our great biochemical theoretician, X.B. Ladisname. Still—this is the news. Make of it what you will. Tomorrow the Council of Notables will meet."

CHAPTER V

1

"WELL, THEN," said Hagedorn to the council, "for once let us dispense with formality. O.Z. Garr: what of our cannon?"

O.Z. Garr, wearing the magnificent gray and green uniform of the Overwhele Dragoons, carefully placed his morion on the table, so that the panache stood erect. "Of twelve cannon, four appear to be functioning correctly. Four have been sabotaged by excision of the power-leads. Four have been sabotaged by some means undetectable to careful investigation. I have commandeered a half-dozen Peasants who demonstrate a modicum of mechanical ability, and have instructed them in detail. They are currently engaged in splicing the leads. This is the extent of my current information in regard to the cannon."

"Moderately good news," said Hagedorn. "What of the proposed corps of armed Peasants?"

"The project is under way. A.F. Mull and I.A. Berzelius are now inspecting Peasants with a view to recruitment and training. I can make no sanguine projection as to the military effectiveness of such a corps, even if trained and led by such as A.F. Mull, I.A. Berzelius

46

and myself. The Peasants are a mild, ineffectual race, admirably suited to the grubbing of weeds, but with no stomach whatever for fighting."

Hagedorn glanced around the council. "Are there any other suggestions?"

Beaudry spoke in a harsh, angry voice. "Had the villains but left us our power-wagons, we might have mounted the cannon aboard—the Peasants are equal to this, at least. Then we could roll to Janeil and blast the dogs from the rear."

"These Meks seem utter fiends!" declared Aure. "What conceivably do they have in mind? Why, after all these centuries, must they suddenly go mad?"

"We all ask ourselves the same questions," said Hagedorn. "Xanten, you returned from reconnaissance with a captive. Have you attempted to question him?"

"No," said Xanten. "Truth to tell, I haven't thought of him since."

"Why not attempt to question him? Perhaps he can provide a clue or two."

Xanten nodded assent. "I can try. Candidly, I expect to learn nothing."

"Claghorn, you are the Mek expert," said Beaudry. "Would you have thought the creatures capable of so intricate a plot? What do they hope to gain? Our castles?"

"They are certainly capable of precise and meticulous planning," said Claghorn. "Their ruthlessness surprises me—more, possibly, than it should. I have never known them to covet our material possessions, and they show no tendency toward what we consider the concomitants of civilization: fine discriminations of sensation and the like. I have often speculated—I won't dignify the conceit with the status of a theory—that the structural logic of a brain is of rather more consequence than we reckon with. Our own brains are remarkable for their utter lack of rational structure. Considering the haphazard manner in which our thoughts are formed, registered, indexed and recalled, any single rational act becomes a miracle. Perhaps we are incapable of rationality; perhaps all thought is a set of impulses generated by one emo-

tion, monitored by another, ratified by a third. In contrast, the Mek brain is a marvel of what seems to be careful engineering. It is roughly cubical and consists of microscopic cells interconnected by organic fibrils, each a monofilament molecule of negligible electrical resistance. Within each cell is a film of silica, a fluid of variable conductivity and dielectric properties, a cusp of a complex mixture of metallic oxides. The brain is capable of storing great quantities of information in an orderly pattern. No fact is lost, unless it is purposely forgotten, a capacity which the Meks possess. The brain also functions as a radio transceiver, possibly as a radar transmitter and detector, though this again is speculation.

"Where the Mek brain falls short is in its lack of emotional color. One Mek is precisely like another, without any personality differentiation perceptible to us. This, clearly, is a function of their communicative system: unthinkable for a unique personality to develop under these conditions. They served us efficiently and—so we thought—loyally, because they felt nothing about their condition, neither pride in achievement, nor resentment, nor shame. Nothing whatever. They neither loved us nor hated us, nor do they now. It is hard for us to conceive this emotional vacuum, when each of us feels something about everything. We live in a welter of emotions. They are as devoid of emotion as an icecube. They were fed, housed, and maintained in a manner they found satisfactory. Why did they revolt? I have speculated at length, but the single reason which I can formulate seems so grotesque and unreasonable that I refuse to take it seriously. If this after all is the correct explanation . . ." His voice drifted away.

"Well?" demanded O.Z. Garr peremptorily. "What, then?"

"Then—it is all the same. They are committed to the destruction of the human race. My speculation alters nothing."

Hagedorn turned to Xanten. "All this should assist you in your inquiries."

"I was about to suggest that Claghorn assist me, if he is so inclined," said Xanten.

"As you like," said Claghorn, "though in my opinion the information, no matter what, is irrelevant. Our single concern should be a means to repel them and to save our lives."

"And—except the force of 'panthers' you mentioned at our previous session—you can conceive of no subtle weapon?" asked Hagedorn wistfully. "A device to set up electrical resonances in their brains, or something similar?"

"Not feasible," said Claghorn. "Certain organs in the creatures' brains function as overload switches. Though it is true that during this time they might not be able to communicate." After a moment's reflection he added thoughtfully, "Who knows? A.G. Bernal and Uegus are theoreticians with a profound knowledge of such projections. Perhaps they might construct such a device, or several, against a possible need."

Hagedorn nodded dubiously, and looked toward Uegus. "Is this possible?"

Uegus frowned. " 'Construct'? I can certainly design such an instrument. But the components—where? Scattered through the storerooms helter-skelter, some functioning, others not. To achieve anything meaningful I must become no better than an apprentice, a Mek." He became incensed, and his voice hardened. "I find it hard to believe that I should be forced to point out this fact. Do you hold me and my talents then of such small worth?"

Hagedorn hastened to reassure him. "Of course not! I for one would never think of impugning your dignity."

"Never!" agreed Claghorn. "Nevertheless, during this present emergency, we will find indignities imposed upon us by events, unless now we impose them upon ourselves."

"Very well," said Uegus, a humorless smile trembling at his lips. "You shall come with me to the storeroom. I will point out the components to be brought forth and assembled, you shall perform the toil. What do you say to that?"

"I say yes, gladly, if it will be of real utility. However,

I can hardly perform the labor for a dozen different theoreticians. Will any others serve beside myself?"

No one responded. Silence was absolute, as if every gentleman present held his breath.

Hagedorn started to speak, but Claghorn interrupted. "Pardon, Hagedorn, but here, finally, we are stuck upon a basic principle, and it must be settled now."

Hagedorn looked desperately around the council. "Has anyone relevant comment?"

"Claghorn must do as his innate nature compels," declared O.Z. Garr in the silkiest of voices. "I cannot dictate to him. As for myself, I can never demean my status as a gentleman of Hagedorn. This creed is as natural to me as drawing breath; if ever it is compromised I become a travesty of a gentleman, a grotesque mask of myself. This is Castle Hagedorn, and we represent the culmination of human civilization. Any compromise therefore becomes degradation; any expedient diminution of our standards becomes dishonor. I have heard the word 'emergency' used. What a deplorable sentiment! To dignify the rat-like snappings and gnashings of such as the Meks with the word 'emergency' is to my mind unworthy of a gentleman of Hagedorn!"

A murmur of approval went around the council table.

Claghorn leaned far back in his seat, chin on his chest, as if in relaxation. His clear blue eyes went from face to face, then returned to O.Z. Garr whom he studied with dispassionate interest. "Obviously you direct your words to me," he said, "and I appreciate their malice. But this is a small matter." He looked away from O.Z. Garr, to stare up at the massive diamond and emerald chandelier. "More important is the fact that the council as a whole, in spite of my earnest persuasion, seems to endorse your viewpoint. I can urge, expostulate, insinuate no longer, and I will now leave Castle Hagedorn. I find the atmosphere stifling. I trust that you survive the attack of the Meks, though I doubt that you will. They are a clever, resourceful race, untroubled by qualms or preconceptions, and we have long underestimated their quality."

Claghorn rose from his seat, inserted the ivory tablet into its socket. "I bid you all farewell."

Hagedorn hastily jumped to his feet and held forth his arms imploringly. "Do not depart in anger, Claghorn! Reconsider! We need your wisdom, your expertise!"

"Assuredly you do," said Claghorn. "But even more, you need to act upon the advice I have already extended. Until then, we have no common ground, and any further interchange is futile and tiresome." He made a brief, all-inclusive salute and departed the chamber.

Hagedorn slowly resumed his seat. The others made uneasy motions, coughed, looked up at the chandelier, studied their ivory tablets. O.Z. Garr muttered something to B.F. Wyas who sat beside him, who nodded solemnly. Hagedorn spoke in a subdued voice: "We will miss the presence of Claghorn, his penetrating if unorthodox insights . . . We have accomplished little. Uegus, perhaps you will give thought to the projector under discussion. Xanten, you were to question the captive Mek. O.Z. Garr, you undoubtedly will see to the repair of the energy cannon. . . . Aside from these small matters, it appears that we have evolved no general plan of action, to help either ourselves or Janeil."

Marune spoke. "What of the other castles? Are they still extant? We have had no news. I suggest that we send Birds to each castle, to learn their condition."

Hagedorn nodded. "Yes, this is a wise motion. Perhaps you will see to this, Marune?"

"I will do so."

"Good. We will now adjourn."

2

The Birds dispatched by Marune of Aure, one by one returned. Their reports were similar:

"Sea Island is deserted. Marble columns are tumbled along the beach. Pearl Dome is collapsed. Corpses float in the Water Garden."

"Maraval reeks of death. Gentlemen, Peasants, Phane—all dead. Alas! Even the Birds have departed!"

"Delora: *a ros ros ros!* A dismal scene! No sign of life!"

"Alume is desolate. The great wooden door is smashed. The Green Flame is extinguished."

"There is nothing at Halcyon. The Peasants were driven into a pit."

"Tuang: silence."

"Morninglight: death."

Chapter VI

1

THREE DAYS LATER, Xanten constrained six Birds to a lift chair, directed them first on a wide sweep around the castle, then south to Far Valley.

The Birds aired their usual complaints, then bounded down the deck in great ungainly hops which threatened to throw Xanten immediately to the pavement. At last gaining the air, they flew up in a spiral; Castle Hagedorn became an intricate miniature far below, each House marked by its unique cluster of turrets and eyries, its own eccentric roof line, its long streaming pennon.

The Birds performed the prescribed circle, skimming the crags and pines of North Ridge; then, setting wings aslant the upstream, they coasted away toward Far Valley.

Over the pleasant Hagedorn domain flew the Birds and Xanten: over orchards, fields, vineyards, Peasant villages. They crossed Lake Maude with its pavilions and docks, the meadows beyond where the Hagedorn cattle and sheep grazed, and presently came to Far Valley, at the limit of Hagedorn lands.

Xanten indicated where he wished to alight; the Birds, who would have preferred a site closer to the village where they could have watched all that transpired, grumbled and cried out in wrath and set Xanten down so roughly that had he not been alert the shock would have pitched him head over heels.

Xanten alighted without elegance but at least remained on his feet. "Await me here!" he ordered. "Do not stray; attempt no flamboyant tricks among the lift-straps. When I return I wish to see six quiet Birds, in

52

neat formation, lift-straps untwisted and untangled. No bickering, mind you! No loud caterwauling, to attract unfavorable comment! Let all be as I have ordered!"

The Birds sulked, stamped their feet, ducked aside their necks, made insulting comments just under the level of Xanten's hearing. Xanten, turning them a final glare of admonition, walked down the lane which led to the village.

The vines were heavy with ripe blackberries and a number of the girls of the village filled baskets. Among them was the girl O.Z. Garr had thought to preempt for his personal use. As Xanten passed, he halted and performed a courteous salute. "We have met before, if my recollection is correct."

The girl smiled, a half-rueful, half-whimsical smile. "Your recollection serves you well. We met at Hagedorn, where I was taken a captive. And later, when you conveyed me here, after dark, though I could not see your face." She extended her basket. "Are you hungry? Will you eat?"

Xanten took several berries. In the course of the conversation he learned that the girl's name was Glys Meadowsweet, that her parents were not known to her, but were presumably gentlefolk of Castle Hagedorn who had exceeded their birth tally. Xanten examined her even more carefully than before but could see resemblance to none of the Hagedorn families. "You might derive from Castle Delora. If there is any family resemblance I can detect, it is to the Cosanzas of Delora—a family noted for the beauty of its ladies."

"You are not married?" she asked artlessly.

"No," said Xanten, and indeed he had dissolved his relationship with Araminta only the day before. "What of you?"

She shook her head. "I would never be gathering blackberries otherwise; it is work reserved for maidens. . . . Why do you come to Far Valley?"

"For two reasons. The first to see you." Xanten heard himself say this with surprise. But it was true, he realized with another small shock of surprise. "I have never

53

spoken with you properly and I have always wondered if you were as charming and gay as you are beautiful."

The girl shrugged and Xanten could not be sure whether she were pleased or not, compliments from gentlemen sometimes setting the stage for a sorry aftermath. "Well, no matter. I came also to speak to Claghorn."

"He is yonder," she said in a voice toneless, even cool, and pointed. "He occupies that cottage." She returned to her blackberry picking. Xanten bowed and proceeded to the cottage the girl had indicated.

Claghorn, wearing loose knee-length breeches of gray homespun, worked with an axe chopping faggots into stove-lengths. At the sight of Xanten he halted his toil, leaned on the axe and mopped his forehead. "Ah, Xanten. I am pleased to see you. How are the folk of Castle Hagedorn?"

"As before. There is little to report, even had I come to bring you news."

"Indeed, indeed?" Claghorn leaned on the axe handle, surveying Xanten with a bright blue gaze.

"At our last meeting," went on Xanten, "I agreed to question the captive Mek. After doing so I am distressed that you were not at hand to assist, so that you might have resolved certain ambiguities in the responses."

"Speak on," said Claghorn. "Perhaps I shall be able to do so now."

"After the council meeting I descended immediately to the storeroom where the Mek was confined. It lacked nutriment; I gave it syrup and a pail of water, which it sipped sparingly, then evinced a desire for minced clams. I summoned kitchen help and sent them for this commodity and the Mek ingested several pints. As I have indicated, it was an unusual Mek, standing as tall as myself and lacking a syrup sac. I conveyed it to a different chamber, a storeroom for brown plush furniture, and ordered it to a seat.

"I looked at the Mek and it looked at me. The quills which I removed were growing back; probably it could at least receive from Meks elsewhere. It seemed a super-

54

ior beast, showing neither obsequiousness nor respect, and answered my questions without hesitation.

"First I remarked: 'The gentlefolk of the castles are astounded by the revolt of the Meks. We had assumed that your life was satisfactory. Were we wrong?'

" 'Evidently.' I am sure that this was the word signaled, though never had I suspected the Meks of dryness or wit of any sort.

" 'Very well then,' I said. 'In what manner?'

" 'Surely it is obvious,' he said. 'We no longer wished to toil at your behest. We wished to conduct our lives by our own traditional standards.'

"The response surprised me. I was unaware that the Meks possessed standards of any kind, much less traditional standards."

Claghorn nodded. "I have been similarly surprised by the scope of the Mek mentality."

"I reproached the Mek: 'Why kill? Why destroy our lives in order to augment your own?' As soon as I had put the question I realized that it had been unhappily phrased. The Mek, I believe, realized the same; however, in reply he signaled something very rapidly which I believe was: 'We knew we must act with decisiveness. Your own protocol made this necessary. We might have returned to Etamin Nine, but we prefer this world Earth, and will make it our own, with our own great slipways, tubs and basking ramps.'

"This seemed clear enough, but I sensed an adumbration extending yet beyond. I said, 'Comprehensible. But why kill, why destroy? You might have taken yourself to a different region. We could not have molested you.'

" 'Infeasible, by your own thinking. A world is too small for two competing races. You intended to send us back to dismal Etamin Nine.'

" 'Ridiculous!' I said. 'Fantasy, absurdity. Do you take me for a mooncalf?'

" 'No,' the creature insisted. 'Two of Castle Hagedorn's notables were seeking the highest post. One assured us that, if elected, this would become his life's aim.'

" 'A grotesque misunderstanding,' I told him. 'One man, a lunatic, can not speak for all men!'

" 'No? One Mek speaks for all Meks. We think with one mind. Are not men of a like sort?'

" 'Each thinks for himself. The lunatic who assured you of this tomfoolery is an evil man. But at least matters are clear. We do not propose to send you to Etamin Nine. Will you withdraw from Janeil, take yourselves to a far land and leave us in peace?'

" 'No,' he said. 'Affairs have proceeded too far. We will now destroy all men. The truth of the statement is clear: one world is too small for two races.'

" 'Unluckily, then, I must kill you,' I told him. 'Such acts are not to my liking, but, with opportunity, you would kill as many gentlemen as possible.' At this the creature sprang upon me, and I killed it with an easier mind than had it sat staring.

"Now, you know all. It seems that either you or O.Z. Garr stimulated the cataclysm. O.Z. Garr? Unlikely. Impossible. Hence, you, Claghorn, you! have this weight upon your soul!"

Claghorn frowned down at the axe. "Weight, yes. Guilt, no. Ingenuousness, yes; wickedness, no."

Xanten stood back. "Claghorn, your coolness astounds me! Before, when rancorous folk like O.Z. Garr conceived you a lunatic—"

"Peace, Xanten!" exclaimed Claghorn. "This extravagant breast-beating becomes maladroit. What have I done wrong? My fault is that I tried too much. Failure is tragic, but a phthisic face hanging over the cup of the future is worse. I meant to become Hagedorn, I would have sent the slaves home. I failed, the slaves revolted. So do not speak another word. I am bored with the subject. You can not imagine how your bulging eyes and your concave spine oppress me."

"Bored you may be," cried Xanten. "You decry my eyes, my spine—but what of the thousands dead?"

"How long would they live in any event? Lives as cheap as fish in the sea. I suggest that you put by your reproaches and devote a similar energy to saving yourself. Do you realize that a means exists? You stare at me

56

blankly. I assure you that what I say is true, but you will never learn the means from me."

"Claghorn," said Xanten, "I flew to this spot intending to blow your arrogant head from your body—" Claghorn, no longer heeding, had returned to his wood-chopping.

"Claghorn!" cried Xanten. "Attend me!"

"Xanten, take your outcries elsewhere, if you please. Remonstrate with your Birds."

Xanten swung on his heel and marched back down the lane. The girls picking berries looked at him questioningly and moved aside. Xanten halted to look up and down the lane. Glys Meadowsweet was nowhere to be seen. In a new fury he continued. He stopped short. On a fallen tree a hundred feet from the Birds sat Glys Meadowsweet, examining a blade of grass as if it had been an astonishing artifact of the past. The Birds, for a marvel, had actually obeyed him and waited in a fair semblance of order.

Xanten looked up toward the heavens, kicked at the turf. He drew a deep breath and approached to Glys Meadowsweet. He noted that she had tucked a flower into her long loose hair.

After a second or two she looked up and searched his face. "Why are you so angry?"

Xanten slapped his thigh, then seated himself beside her. " 'Angry'? No. I am out of my mind with frustration. Claghorn is as obstreperous as a sharp rock. He knows how Castle Hagedorn can be saved but he will not divulge his secret."

Glys Meadowsweet laughed—an easy, merry sound, like nothing Xanten had ever heard at Castle Hagedorn. "Secret? When even I know it?"

"It must be a secret," said Xanten. "He will not tell me."

"Listen. If you fear the Birds will hear, I will whisper." She spoke a few words into his ear.

Perhaps the sweet breath befuddled Xanten's mind. But the explicit essence of the revelation failed to strike home into his consciousness. He made a sound of sour amusement. "No secret there. Only what the prehistoric Scythians termed *bathos*. Dishonor to the gentlemen! Do

57

we dance with the Peasants? Do we serve the Birds essences and discuss with them the sheen of our Phanes?"

" 'Dishonor,' then?" She jumped to her feet. "Then it is also dishonor for you to talk to me, to sit here with me, to make ridiculous suggestions—"

"I made no suggestions!" protested Xanten. "I sit here in all decorum—"

"Too much decorum, too much honor!" With a display of passion which astounded Xanten, Glys Meadowsweet tore the flower from her hair and hurled it at the ground. "There. Hence!"

"No," said Xanten in sudden humility. He bent, picked up the flower, kissed it, replaced it in her hair. "I am not over-honorable. I will try my best." He put his arms on her shoulders, but she held him away.

"Tell me," she inquired with a very mature severity, "do you own any of those peculiar insect-women?"

"I? Phanes? I own no Phanes."

With this Glys Meadowsweet relaxed and allowed Xanten to embrace her, while the Birds clucked, guffawed and made vulgar scratching sounds with their wings.

CHAPTER VII

1

THE SUMMER WANED. On June 30 Janeil and Hagedorn celebrated the Fete of Flowers, even though the dike was rising high around Janeil. Shortly after, Xanten flew six select Birds into Castle Janeil by night, and proposed to the council that the population be evacuated by Bird-lift—as many as possible, as many who wished to leave. The council listened with stony faces and without comment passed on to a consideration of other affairs.

Xanten returned to Castle Hagedorn. Using the most careful methods, speaking only to trusted comrades, Xanten enlisted thirty or forty cadets and gentlemen to

his persuasion, though inevitably he could not keep the doctrinal thesis of his program secret.

The first reaction of the traditionalists was mockery and charges of poltroonery. At Xanten's insistence, challenges were neither issued nor accepted by his hot-blooded associates.

On the evening of September 9 Castle Janeil fell. The news was brought to Castle Hagedorn by excited Birds who told the grim tale again and again in voices ever more hysterical.

Hagedorn, now gaunt and weary, automatically called a council meeting; it took note of the gloomy circumstances. "We, then, are the last castle! The Meks cannot conceivably do us harm; they can build dikes around our castle walls for twenty years and only work themselves to distraction. We are secure; but yet it is a strange and portentous thought to realize that at last, here at Castle Hagedorn, live the last gentlemen of the race!"

Xanten spoke in a voice strained with earnest conviction: "Twenty years—fifty years—what difference to the Meks? Once they surround us, once they deploy, we are trapped. Do you comprehend that now is our last opportunity to escape the great cage that Castle Hagedorn is to become?"

" 'Escape,' Xanten? What a word! For shame!" hooted O.Z. Garr. "Take your wretched band, escape! To steppe or swamp or tundra! Go as you like, with your poltroons, but be good enough to give over these incessant alarms!"

"Garr, I have found conviction since I become a 'poltroon.' Survival is good morality. I have this from the mouth of a noted savant."

"Bah! Such as whom?"

"A.G. Philidor, if you must be informed of every detail."

O.Z. Garr clapped his hand to his forehand. "Do you refer to Philidor, the Expiationist? He is of the most extreme stripe, an Expiationist to out-expiate all the rest! Xanten, be sensible, if you please!"

"There are years ahead for all of us," said Xanten in a wooden voice, "if we free ourselves from the castle."

"But the castle is our life!" declared Hagedorn. "In essence, Xanten, what would we be without the castle? Wild animals? Nomads?"

"We would be alive."

O.Z. Garr gave a snort of disgust and turned away to inspect a wall-hanging.

Hagedorn shook his head in doubt and perplexity. Beaudry threw his hands up into the air. "Xanten, you have the effect of unnerving us all. You come in here and inflict this dreadful sense of urgency—but why? In Castle Hagedorn we are as safe as in our mothers' arms. What do we gain by throwing aside all—honor, dignity, comfort, civilized niceties—for no other reason than to slink through the wilderness?"

"Janeil was safe," said Xanten. "Today where is Janeil? Death, mildewed cloth, sour wine. What we gain by *slinking* is the assurance of survival. And I plan much more than simple *slinking*."

"I can conceive of a hundred occasions when death is better than life!" snapped Isseth. "Must I die in dishonor and disgrace? Why may my last years not be passed in dignity?"

Into the room came B.F. Robarth. "Councilmen, the Meks approach Castle Hagedorn."

Hagedorn cast a wild look around the chamber. "Is there a consensus? What must we do?"

Xanten threw up his hands. "Everyone must do as he thinks best! I argue no more: I am done. Hagedorn, will you adjourn the council so that we may be about our affairs? I to my *slinking?*"

"Council is adjourned," said Hagedorn, and all went to stand on the ramparts.

Up the avenue into the castle trooped Peasants from the surrounding countryside, packets slung over their shoulders. Across the valley, at the edge of Bartholomew Forest, was a clot of power-wagons and an amorphous brown-gold mass: Meks.

Aure pointed west. "Look—there they come, up the Long Swale." He turned, peered east. "And look, there at Bambridge: Meks!"

By common consent, all swung about to scan North

Ridge. O.Z. Garr pointed to a quiet line of brown-gold shapes. "There they wait, the vermin! They have penned us in! Well, then, let them wait!" He swung away, rode the lift down to the plaza, and crossed swiftly to Zumbeld House, where he worked the rest of the afternoon with his Gloriana, of whom he expected great things.

2

The following day the Meks formalized the investment. Around Castle Hagedorn a great circle of Mek activity made itself apparent: sheds, warehouses, barracks. Within this periphery, just beyond the range of the energy cannon, power-wagons thrust up mounds of dirt.

During the night these mounds lengthened toward the castle, similarly the night after. At last the purpose of the mounds became clear: they were a protective cover above passages or tunnels leading toward the crag on which Castle Hagedorn rested.

The following day several of the mounds reached the base of the crag. Presently a succession of power-wagons loaded with rubble began to flow from the far end. They issued, dumped their loads, and once again entered the tunnels.

Eight of these above-ground tunnels had been established. From each trundled endless loads of dirt and rock, gnawed from the crag on which Castle Hagedorn sat. To the gentlefolk who crowded the parapets the meaning of the work at last became clear.

"They make no attempt to bury us," said Hagedorn. "They merely mine out the crag from below us!"

On the sixth day of the siege, a great segment of the hillside shuddered, slumped, and a tall pinnacle of rock reaching almost up to the base of the walls collapsed.

"If this continues," muttered Beaudry, "our time will be less than that of Janeil."

"Come then," called O.Z. Garr, suddenly active. "Let us try our energy cannon. We'll blast open their wretched tunnels, and then what will the rascals do?" He went to

61

the nearest emplacement and shouted down for Peasants to remove the tarpaulin.

Xanten, who happened to be standing nearby, said, "Allow me to assist you." He jerked away the tarpaulin. "Shoot now, if you will."

O.Z. Garr stared at him uncomprehendingly, then leaped forward and swiveled the great projector about so that it aimed at a mound. He pulled the switch; the air crackled in front of the ringed snout, rippled, flickered with purple sparks. The target area steamed, became black, then dark red, then slumped into an incandescent crater. But the underlying earth, twenty feet in thickness, afforded too much insulation; the molten puddle became white-hot but failed to spread or deepen. The energy cannon gave a sudden chatter, as electricity short-circuited through corroded insulation. The cannon went dead. O.Z. Garr inspected the mechanism in anger and disappointment; then, with a gesture of repugnance, he turned away. The cannons were clearly of limited effectiveness.

Two hours later, on the east side of the crag, another great sheet of rock collapsed, and just before sunset a similar mass sheared from the western face, where the wall of the castle rose almost in an uninterrupted line from the cliff below.

At midnight Xanten and those of his persuasion, with their children and consorts, departed Castle Hagedorn. Six teams of Birds shuttled from the flight deck to a meadow near Far Valley, and long before dawn had transported the entire group. There were none to bid them farewell.

3

A week later another section of the east cliff fell away, taking a length of rock-melt buttress with it. At the tunnel mouths the piles of excavated rubble had become alarmingly large.

The terraced south face of the crag was the least dis-

turbed, the most spectacular damage having occurred to east and west. Suddenly, a month after the initial assault, a great section of the terrace slumped forward, leaving an irregular crevasse which interrupted the avenue and hurled down the statues of former notables emplaced at intervals along the avenue's balustrade.

Hagedorn called a council meeting. "Circumstances," he said in a wan attempt at facetiousness, "have not bettered themselves. Our most pessimistic expectations have been exceeded: a dismal situation. I confess that I do not relish the prospect of toppling to my death among all my smashed belongings."

Aure made a desperate gesture. "A similar thought haunts me! Death—what of that? All must die! But when I think of my precious belongings I become sick. My books trampled! my fragile vases smashed! my tabards ripped! my rugs buried! my Phanes strangled! my heirloom chandeliers flung aside! These are my nightmares."

"Your possessions are no less precious than any others," said Beaudry shortly. "Still, they have no life of their own; when we are gone, who cares what happens to them?"

Marune winced. "A year ago I put down eighteen dozen flasks of prime essence; twelve dozen Green Rain; three each of Balthazar and Faidor. Think of these, if you would contemplate tragedy!"

"Had we only known!" groaned Aure. "I would have—I would have . . ." His voice trailed away.

O.Z. Garr stamped his foot in impatience. "Let us avoid lamentation at all costs! We had a choice, remember? Xanten beseeched us to flee; now he and his like go skulking and foraging through the north mountains with the Expiationists. We chose to remain, for better or worse, and unluckily the worse is occurring. We must accept the fact like gentlemen."

To this the council gave melancholy assent. Hagedorn brought forth a flask of priceless Rhadamanth, and poured with a prodigality which previously would have been unthinkable. "Since we have no future—to our glorious past!"

That night disturbances were noted here and there

around the ring of Mek investment: flames at four separate points, a faint sound of hoarse shouting. On the following day it seemed that the tempo of activity had lessened a trifle.

During the afternoon, however, a vast segment of the east cliff fell away. A moment later, as if after majestic deliberation, the tall east wall split off and toppled, leaving the backs of six great houses exposed to the open sky.

An hour after sunset a team of Birds settled to the flight-deck. Xanten jumped from the seat. He ran down the circular staircase to the ramparts and came down to the plaza by Hagedorn's palace.

Hagedorn, summoned by a kinsman, came forth to stare at Xanten in surprise. "What do you do here? We expected you to be safely north with the Expiationists!"

"The Expiationists are not safely north," said Xanten. "They have joined the rest of us. We are fighting."

Hagedorn's jaw dropped. "Fighting? The gentlemen are fighting Meks?"

"As vigorously as possible."

Hagedorn shook his head in wonder. "The Expiationists too? I understood that they had planned to flee north."

"Some have done so, including A.G. Philidor. There are factions among the Expiationists just as here. Most are not ten miles distant. The same with the Nomads. Some have taken their power-wagons and fled. The rest kill Meks with fanatic fervor. Last night you saw our work. We fired four storage warehouses, destroyed syrup tanks, killed a hundred or more Meks, as well as a dozen power-wagons. We suffered losses, which hurt us because there are few of us and many Meks. This is why I am here. We need more men. Come fight beside us!"

Hagedorn turned, motioning to the great central plaza. "I will call forth the folk from their Houses. Talk to everyone."

The Birds, complaining bitterly at the unprecedented toil, worked all night, transporting the gentlemen who, sobered by the imminent destruction of Castle Hagedorn, were now willing to abandon all scruples and fight for their lives. The staunch traditionalists still refused to compromise their honor, but Xanten gave them cheerful assurance: "Remain here, then, prowling the castle like so many furtive rats. Take what comfort you can in the fact that you are being protected; the future holds little else for you."

And many who heard him stalked away in disgust.

Xanten turned to Hagedorn. "What of you? Do you come or do you stay?"

Hagedorn heaved a deep sigh, almost a groan. "Castle Hagedorn is at an end. No matter what the eventuality. I come with you."

The situation had suddenly altered. The Meks, established in a loose ring around Castle Hagedorn, had calculated upon no resistance from the countryside and little from the castle. They had established their barracks and syrup depots with thought only for convenience and none for defense; raiding parties, consequently, were able to approach, inflict damages and withdraw before sustaining serious losses of their own. Those Meks posted along North Ridge were harassed almost continuously, and finally were driven down with many losses. The circle around Castle Hagedorn became a cusp; then two days later, after the destruction of five more syrup depots, the Meks drew back even farther. Throwing up earthworks before the two tunnels leading under the south face of the crag, they established a more or less tenable defensive position, but now instead of beleaguering, they became the beleaguered, even though power-wagons of broken rock still issued from the crag.

Within the area thus defended the Meks concentrated their remaining syrup stocks, tools, weapons, ammunition. The area outside the earthworks was floodlit after dark and guarded by Meks armed with pellet guns, making any frontal assault impractical.

For a day the raiders kept to the shelter of the surrounding orchards, appraising the new situation. Then a new tactic was attempted. Six light carriages were improvised and loaded with bladders of a light inflammable oil, with a fire grenade attached. To each of these carriages ten Birds were harnessed, and at midnight sent aloft, with a man for each carriage. Flying high, the Birds then glided down through the darkness over the Mek position, where the fire bombs were dropped. The area instantly seethed with flame. The syrup depot burned; the power-wagons, awakened by the flames, rolled frantically back and forth, crushing Meks and stores, colliding with each other, adding vastly to the terror of the fire. The Meks who survived took shelter in the tunnels. Certain of the floodlights were extinguished and taking advantage of the confusion, the men attacked the earthworks. After a short, bitter battle, the men killed all the sentinels and took up positions commanding the mouths of the tunnels, which now contained all that remained of the Mek army. It seemed as if the Mek uprising had been put down.

CHAPTER VIII

1

THE FLAMES DIED. The human warriors—three hundred men from the castle, two hundred Expiationists and about three hundred Nomads—gathered about the tunnel mouth and, during the balance of the night, considered methods to deal with the immured Meks. At sunrise, those men of Castle Hagedorn whose children and consorts were yet inside went to bring them forth. With them, upon their return, came a group of castle gentle-

men: among them Beaudry, O.Z. Garr, Isseth, and Aure. They greeted their one-time peers, Hagedorn, Xanten, Claghorn and others, crisply, but with a certain austere detachment which recognized that loss of prestige incurred by those who fought Meks as if they were equals.

"Now what is to happen?" Beaudry inquired of Hagedorn. "The Meks are trapped but you can't bring them forth. Not impossibly they have syrup stored within for the power-wagons; they may well survive for months."

O.Z. Garr, assessing the situation from the standpoint of a military theoretician, came forward with a plan of action. "Fetch down the cannon—or have your underlings do so—and mount them on power-wagons. When the vermin are sufficiently weak, roll the cannon in and wipe out all but a labor force for the castle: we formerly worked four hundred, and this should suffice."

"Ha!" exclaimed Xanten. "It gives me great pleasure to inform you that this will never be. If any Meks survive they will repair the spaceships and instruct us in the maintenance and we will then transport them and Peasants back to their native worlds."

"How then do you expect us to maintain our lives?" demanded Garr coldly.

"You have the syrup generator. Fit yourself with sacs and drink syrup."

Garr tilted back his head, stared coldly down his nose. "This is your voice, yours alone, and your insolent opinion. Others are to be heard from. Hagedorn—you were once a gentleman. Is this also your philosophy, that civilization should wither?"

"It need not wither," said Hagedorn, "provided that all of us—you as well as we—toil for it. There can be no more slaves. I have become convinced of this."

O.Z. Garr turned on his heel, swept back up the avenue into the castle, followed by the most traditional-minded of his comrades. A few moved aside and talked among themselves in low tones, with one or two black looks for Xanten and Hagedorn.

From the ramparts of the castle came a sudden outcry: "The Meks! They are taking the castle! They swarm up the lower passages! Attack, save us!"

The men below stared up in consternation. Even as they looked, the castle portals swung shut.

"How is this possible?" demanded Hagedorn. "I swear all entered the tunnels!"

"It is only too clear," said Xanten bitterly. "While they undermined, they drove a tunnel up to the lower levels!"

Hagedorn started forward as if he would charge up the crag alone, then halted. "We must drive them out. Unthinkable that they pillage our castle!"

"Unfortunately," said Claghorn, "the walls bar us as effectually as they did the Meks."

"We can send up a force by Bird-car! Once we consolidate, we can hunt them down, exterminate them."

Claghorn shook his head. "They can wait on the ramparts and flight-deck and shoot down the Birds as they approach. Even if we secured a foothold there would be great bloodshed: one of us killed for every one of them. And they still outnumber us three or four to one."

Hagedorn groaned. "The thought of them reveling among my possessions, strutting about in my clothes, swilling my essences—it sickens me!"

"Listen!" said Claghorn. From on high they heard the hoarse yells of men, the crackle of energy-cannon. "Some of them, at least, hold out on ramparts!"

Xanten went to a nearby group of Birds who were for once awed and subdued by events. "Lift me up above the castle, out of range of the pellets, but where I can see what the Meks do!"

"Care, take care!" croaked one of the Birds. "Ill things occur at the castle."

"Never mind; convey me up, above the ramparts!"

The Birds lifted him, swung in a great circle around the crag and above the castle, sufficiently distant to be safe from the Mek pellet-guns. Beside those cannon which yet operated stood thirty men and women. Between the great Houses, the Rotunda and the Palace, everywhere the cannon could not be brought to bear, swarmed Meks. The plaza was littered with corpses: gentlemen, ladies and their children—all those who had elected to remain at Castle Hagedorn.

At one of the cannon stood O.Z. Garr. Spying Xanten

he gave a shout of hysterical rage, swung up the cannon, fired a bolt. The Birds, screaming, tried to swerve aside, but the bolt smashed two. Birds, car, Xanten, fell in a great tangle. By some miracle, the four yet alive caught their balance and a hundred feet from the ground, with a frenzied groaning effort, they slowed their fall, steadied, hovered an instant, sank to the ground. Xanten staggered free of the tangle. Men came running. "Are you safe?" called Claghorn.

"Safe, yes. Frightened as well." Xanten took a deep breath, and went to sit on an outcrop of rock.

"What's happening up there?" asked Claghorn.

"All dead," said Xanten, "all but a score. Garr has gone mad. He fired on me."

"Look! Meks on the ramparts!" cried A.L. Morgan.

"There!" cried someone else. "Men! They jump! . . . No, they are flung!"

Some were men, some were Meks whom they had dragged with them; with awful slowness they toppled to their deaths. No more fell. Castle Hagedorn was in the hands of the Meks.

Xanten considered the complex silhouette, at once so familiar and so strange. "They can't hope to hold out. We need only destroy the sun-cells, and they can synthesize no syrup."

"Let us do it now," said Claghorn, "before they think of this and man the cannon! Birds!"

He went off to give the orders, and forty Birds, each clutching two rocks the size of a man's head, flapped up, circled the castle and presently returned to report the sun-cells destroyed.

Xanten said, "All that remains is to seal the tunnel entrances against a sudden eruption, which might catch us off guard—then patience."

"What of the peasants in the stables—and the Phanes?" asked Hagedorn in a forlorn voice.

Xanten gave his head a slow shake. "He who was not an Expiationist before must become one now."

Claghorn muttered, "They can survive two months—no more."

But two months passed, and three months, and four

69

months: then one morning the great portals opened and a haggard Mek stumbled forth. He signaled: "Men: we starve. We have maintained your treasures. Give us our lives or we destroy all before we die."

Claghorn responded: "These are our terms. We give you your lives. You must clean the castle, remove and bury the corpses. You must repair the spaceships and teach us all you know regarding them. We will then transport you to Etamin Nine."

2

Five years later Xanten and Glys Meadowsweet, with their two children, had reason to travel north from their home near Sande River. They took occasion to visit Castle Hagedorn, where now lived only two or three dozen folk, among them Hagedorn.

He had aged, so it seemed to Xanten. His hair was white; his face, once bluff and hearty, had become thin, almost waxen. Xanten could not determine his mood.

They stood in the shade of a walnut tree, with castle and crag looming above them. "This is now a great museum," said Hagedorn. "I am curator, and this will be the function of all the Hagedorns who come after me, for there is incalculable treasure to guard and maintain. Already the feeling of antiquity has come to the castle. The Houses are alive with ghosts. I see them often, especially on the nights of the fetes. . . . Ah, those were the times, were they not, Xanten?"

"Yes, indeed," said Xanten. He touched the heads of his two children. "Still, I have no wish to return to them. We are men now, on our own world, as we never were before."

Hagedorn gave a somewhat regretful assent. He looked up at the vast structure, as if now were the first occasion he had laid eyes on it. "The folk of the future—what will they think of Castle Hagedorn? Its treasures, its books, its tabards?"

"They will come, they will marvel," said Xanten. "Almost as I do today."

"There is much at which to marvel. Will you come within, Xanten? There are still flasks of noble essence laid by."

"Thank you, no," said Xanten. "There is too much to stir old memories. We will go our way, and I think immediately."

Hagedorn nodded sadly. "I understand very well. I myself am often given to reverie these days. Well then, goodbye, and journey home with pleasure."

"We will do so, Hagedorn. Thank you and goodbye."